THEY IMAGINE TEXAS

KEVIN McDERMOTT

THICK
WINTER
PRESS

They Imagine Texas

v3.0

This is a work of fiction. Names, characters, businesses, places, events, locales, and incidents are either the products of the author's imagination or used in a fictitious manner. Any resemblance to actual persons, living or dead, or actual events is purely coincidental.

The opinions expressed in this manuscript are solely the opinions of the author and do not represent the opinions or thoughts of the publisher. The author has represented and warranted full ownership and/or legal right to publish all the materials in this book.

ThickWinter Press

ISBN: 978-0-578-27555-0

PRINTED IN THE UNITED STATES OF AMERICA

They Imagine Texas

Review the past for me, let us argue the matter together; state the case for your innocence.
Isaiah 43:26, NIV

"Texas is, after all, the only place on earth that actually eats its young."
Nancy Griffith

I cannot think we are useless or else Usen would not have created us.
Geronimo, Shaman of the Apache

They Imagine Texas

Review the past for me, let us argue the matter together; state the case for your innocence.
Isaiah 43:26, NIV

"Texas is, after all, the only place on earth that actually eats its young."
Nancy Griffith

I cannot think we are useless or else Usen would not have created us.
Geronimo, Shaman of the Apache

I

Texas Altogether

Perros Salvajes, Tx.

There are many categories of stories. Parable, fairy, holy, love, fable. This story is none of those. As Katherine Moliere might have said, this is a dark story and because of that fascinating—exactly the reason people like hearing what cops have to say.

This story has a beginning but no end.

The Walloon Gardens was a public park in Perros Salvajes. It was a threadbare place, especially for a putative park. There were no gardens there at all, not at any time of the year. To stretch a point one might include a now and then patch of begonias near one of the entrances off Bobby Fuller Boulevard. Every year, before April was even over, the begonias fried in the unmediated heat of West Texas. Then they were composted.

Also near that entrance were two acres of open field unmarked for any sport in particular. There was a public restroom too foul for anyone to use except in desperation, which only made it more noisesome. There was a small playground with a swing and some climbing apparatus.

On a pleasantly chilly morning in early spring Katherine Moliere was on the last leg of a six-mile Sunday run past this unlovely place. Moliere was an intelligent woman—she taught seventh-grade math in a Perros Salvajes middle school—but all the same her surname name was wasted on her; she had no appreciation for satire. She read *The Misanthrope* once at her father's urging. Her opinion was that it tried too hard. She was not the audience for farce.

It was half past eight in the morning, quiet as Sunday can be. Most people in Perros Salvajes were at church or asleep in bed.

Moliere had her hair pulled back as she ran. In any situation Katherine Moliere's hair was exuberant but never more so than when she was exercising. On her father's side Moliere was dark-skinned Haitian, on her mother's side sunburned Irish. This mix in her was handsome in a head-turning way. Moliere had a good face with sharp cheeks. She had a strong, unforgiving nose. Men noticed all this.

At that time Moliere was unattached. Her Sundays were all her own.

Moliere stopped for water at the one fountain in The Walloon Gardens. The fountain was installed beside the playground fence. The water was cold and tasted of dirt—actual dirt—in a way that was not unpleasant at all if you liked life.

Given the day of the week and the time the playground was quiet and nearly empty. There was a woman with hay-colored hair who was reading a picture book to her daughter. There was a man with a little boy. The man was checking his phone. His little boy drank from a sippy cup.

Moliere was bent over the fountain drinking when the man erupted at the boy. With a teacher's instinct she looked up to see how bad it would get.

"Look what you've done!" The man was right away yelling like who cares who hears him. "Again and again and again I tell you not to drink from that stupid cup. For God's sakes you're 11 years old!"

The man's trousers were soaked with milk. For this he gave the boy a whack on the shoulder, hard enough for the kid to fall off the bench and bounce on his bottom. When he landed the kid said nothing. He sat there a moment collecting himself. Or reconciling himself. Moliere the teacher guessed it was the second.

Involuntarily Moliere said "Hey" loud enough that she surprised both herself and the man who struck the little boy. Even the little boy looked struck, in the second sense of the word.

"You've got something to say?" the man asked. "May I help you? You've got a comment?" The front of his pants was milky and wet and it was hard to take this man's anger seriously. He knew it too. Moliere could tell this from the way he summoned affront.

"Don't hit your kid," she said. "He spilled the milk. So what? Are you so injured?"

"My son is none of your business."

"Don't hit him." As a schoolteacher Katherine Moliere liked children though she was not unreasonable about it. Hitting a child was a categorical wrong.

"Fuck you."

"You speak like that in front of children?" As a rule Moliere did not use profanity out loud. In her head though, all the time.

Moliere knew she was raising the stakes with this guy. It was not anger nor even simple indignation, though she felt those things. Moliere just did not like this man, whom she never met until that moment.

Then the man stood up.

The man lifted the latch on the gate to the playground. He came to where Moliere was standing. He was not quite big, probably in his thirties and perhaps getting thicker in his middle because of that. In his wet pants he looked like he had pissed himself.

Moliere was aware of being nearly naked in her white tank top and raspberry-colored running shorts. She thought, If he thinks I'll run then fuck him.

"Why are you trying to start something with me?"

"That's not what I'm doing," said Moliere, though that was exactly what she was doing. "I just want you not to hit your kid."

"If I discipline my son what business is it of yours?"

"If you hit him that's my business."

"And you are who? I know you?"

"No." Moliere felt she commanded him.

"Keep your nose out of what's not your business." The man took half a step. Moliere knew this was a bluff. He expected her to step back. She did not.

"Don't hit your kid," said Moliere. "For anything ever."

"Ma'am, screw you."

"You all right, buddy?" said Moliere in her calm schoolteacher voice.

The boy looked fine, though he was still sitting on the ground. Moliere instantly wished she had not spoken to him. He would be the one to pay the price later, not her. From the resigned look on his face the boy knew this too. Kids in his situation know there will always be more. The boy's face did not impress with its intelligence. Certainly that was no reason to hit him.

"You'd better leave," the man said to Moliere. He took another step. This time it was no bluff. He took Moliere's arm around the elbow and turned her around.

"Go," he said. His voice was quiet, almost friendly, as if Moliere needed counseling.

"Go," he said again, twisting the skin on her upper arm a little more.

The man gave her a bug-eyed stare, which is always more gesture than authentic reaction.

"Go the *fuck* away!" The man bent Moliere's arm back so bad she could not help crying out.

Well before the confrontation in Walloon Park got going the woman inside the playground fence, the one with the hay-colored hair and the daughter, had gone to the far end of the swings and telephoned 911. A pair of officers just ending their shift happened to be passing in their patrol car and took the call. To Moliere it seemed as if the two appeared out of the air like magicians, materializing in the lot beside the playground just in time to see the man bend back her arm.

"What's going on?" said the slightly older cop. He spoke in the most neutral voice a cop can muster, as if he were asking out of genuine curiosity. The cop's name was AJ Munoz; the name badge on his grey blouse said so. AJ was senior enough that he could avoid Sunday shifts if he chose. Owing to tedium in his marriage he preferred overnights.

From the moment of AJ's arrival things went right downhill for the man with the little boy.

The mother of the little girl leapt to her feet and said, "*This* man threatened *this* lady for telling him not to slap *this* child," pointing from one to the next as she spoke.

"Who are you, ma'am?" AJ asked the woman.

AJ continued speaking in the patient way of policemen stepping between disputing parties, like grownups irritated by squabbling children. In other words, he was less interested in justice than in peace. Moliere suspected this was a learned tactic for quieting things down—something taught in the police academy. She never thought to ask Franklin about it until later when it was too late. Franklin was the other cop with AJ Munoz. He was redheaded.

"I am the person who telephoned 911," said the woman on the other side of the playground fence. "My name is Donna Froehlich. And this man is a thug. He hit his little boy, and when this *lady* objected he threatened her. You saw him twisting her arm as you walked up."

"I did see that."

"Well then you saw wrong," said the man. "I was making a point."

"Ask the little boy if he is all right," said Katherine Moliere.

"You all right, pal?" AJ asked the kid on the ground. There was a little annoyance in his voice. Like anyone else AJ did not like to be told how to do his job.

The kid nodded, clocking his father's reaction.

"Come on over here."

The child half rolled over to get on his feet, the way an old man would do it. He looked like a flesh dumpling. Lots of small children are that way but this kid gave the impression of someone who would struggle with his weight all his life.

"What's your name, buddy?

"Eugene."

"Hey, Eugene."

"Hey."

"How old are you?"

"Ten," he said.

"Eleven," said his father.

"Let Eugene tell it, sir. Are you ten years old, Eugene?

"Eleven." Eugene nodded, looking at his father for the OK.

"You sure?"

The boy nodded.

"Your Dad treat you ok, Eugene?"

"OK."

"He ever hit you?"

"I never hit this kid in my life except for a swat once in a while, like everyone."

"I asked Eugene, sir. Does your Dad hit you?"

"No."

"Sure? Roll up your sleeves and show me the big muscles in your arms. Go on."

The little boy did as he was asked and pulled up the sleeves of his pullover.

"OK, no bruises," AJ said to Eugene's father. "I thought maybe twisting arms might be your modus operandi, you know? I would not be surprised if this lady had a good bruise on her arm tomorrow. Do you have a driver's license, sir?"

"Why—was I speeding?"

"I want your identification."

With a show of exasperation the man dug out his wallet and handed over his driver's license. AJ copied the information into his notebook.

"Tibor Rauscha," he said. "Am I pronouncing it correctly?"

"Recognize the name?"

"I do, Mr. Rauscha," said AJ. He observed the other man half smirking at Moliere, almost as if he had said aloud, "See what you got yourself into?"

"You're going to keep pushing this, officer?" said Rauscha.

"Child endangerment is one of those things where we follow the rules to the letter, you know? Otherwise we get headaches."

"'Child endangerment'? Are you out of your mind?"

AJ tore off a carbon of his report from his notepad and handed it to Tibor Rauscha.

"No, I don't think I'm out of my mind. Since you asked. Probably you'll get a call tomorrow since today is Sunday. I don't know from who. For the time being why don't you take Eugene home? Miss," said AJ to Moliere, "may we give you a ride home?"

"I'd rather finish my run. Thank you."

"Would you like to go now, sir?" AJ asked Rauscha.

"I'd like to be left in peace," Rauscha replied. "Why do I need to leave?"

"It settles things, you know? We can tell ourselves we left a pacified scene."

AJ was trying to drop the temperature a little, probably even Tibor Rauscha saw that. He looked to AJ less angry now than humiliated, which AJ was glad about.

The cops waited there until Rauscha walked off with the boy.

Unlike AJ, Moliere did not recognize Tibor Rauscha's name. After five years living in Perros Salvajes she should have. He owned a big house off Nine Mezcaleros Road about a quarter mile from The Walloon Gardens. He was a partner in a Honda dealership on Bobby Fuller Boulevard through which Moliere leased her Civic. The lease had two years still to go.

It is not uncommon for small things to blow up into big ones. Knowing this puts everybody on edge—who can live that way?

For these people at the playground the coincidence of their meeting was the beforehand to the main events of their lives (the livid blonde lady and her daughter excepted). None of them could know that then. Their memories of that day would change in ways specific to each of them, altered by the individual whatnot of experience and the other noises of life.

All the way home Eugene held his father's hand. Stupid that an eleven-year-old boy should be so clingy. A million times his father told him that. Even as a baby Eugene did not snuggle; he *depended* from the neck of whoever held him.

Why were there no birds in this part of Texas? Rauscha asked himself. He was 37 years-old and born in West Texas and it seemed like there were never any birds singing, even in spring. It seemed to him that only in the movies had he ever heard birds sing.

Tibor Rauscha was angry that the jogger woman decided to turn his flare-up into a case for the police. Angry and now preoccupied with it. With the anger. Preoccupied with what this might mean for his involvement with Fanny DaCosta. There could be problems for him now.

Tibor Rauscha was then in transition between Carol, Eugene's mother, and Fanny. Fanny at that time was the sum of Tibor's desire. She was tall for a woman, slender, dark brown, the softest skin he had ever touched. And her hair, her hair, box braids under a bottomless collection of caps that Fanny owned. The first time Fanny removed a cap in Tibor Rauscha's presence his heart nearly stopped; she had already removed everything else she was wearing but seeing those braids falling around Fanny's face was the thing that nearly killed him. It stopped his heart. No joke, he almost died. Some days she wound her braids into a mystic swirl at the back of her head. It moved Rauscha immensely when she did that.

And he loved her nose. Rauscha had a fetish for women with a strong nose. He could not account for it, he told Fanny, but he did. Fanny's nose made his knees weak.

Fanny was smarter than possibly anyone Rauscha ever met. Also, Fanny was a snake, Tibor Rauscha believed it even then. A beautiful snake, right down to the medusa hair. But still a snake, with a snake's capacity to surprise you. Enchant you first though. If Fanny found out about the police report she might shun him.

They never spoke about it but Rauscha supposed Fanny liked children. Generally women did.

Only the pervious week Rauscha met Fanny's mother for the first time. He went with Fanny to tell Mrs. DaCosta that they were engaged.

Before they went to the house in Hay Agua Fanny warned Rauscha that her mother was in some ways a hard person. Judy DaCosta was a proud Black woman and firm in her religious conviction. In no sense was Tibor Rauscha what she had in mind for daughter.

Rauscha spoke to Fanny's mother from his heart, as one will.

"When I look at your daughter I ache," he told Judy. "Not because she is beautiful. Or not just because. When I'm not with Fanny I'm counting the hours until I see her again. Honestly I am. I feel like we won't ever run out of things to say to each other. She has got an open heart, Mrs. DaCosta. She makes we want to have an open heart too."

It was the most stirring string of words Tibor Rauscha ever put together. He meant every one of them. He was proud of himself for that.

Tibor Rauscha could not have known what was to come. Even so, he walked home from Walloon Garden with a sense of unnamed threat to himself, a threat now moving in the world because of Katherine Moliere. He began that night to learn everything he could about her. The first and easiest thing to find out was where she lived.

Four years happened and now it was an October evening, about ten o'clock. There had been an interval of romance for Katherine Moliere. The romance, like her fiancé, was dead. Katherine Moliere was living alone again.

Before bed that night Moliere was locking up her house. In her solitude and her silence Moliere heard her house tick. Click click. Moliere was a middle-school teacher and she got up early. Her dishes were washed and her lunch was made for the next day.

The night ritual of checking the locks tended to bring Moliere's solitude to mind. The same as anyone she grew used to it. There was no choice. But she did not like the solitude of locking up any better than she liked the solitude of sleeping alone. Every night she was bone-tired and eager for sleep; of her current blessings sleep was the prize.

Moliere was not thinking these things in a particular way as she jiggled the front doorknob with a soft shake, just to check. In that instant the door was pushed in.

Moliere leapt back less in fright than in surprise, either way ready to defend herself.

Coming through the door the intruder was already yelling "Do not be afraid! Do not be afraid!"—diction weirdly formal, like that of an annunciating angel.

The hand pushing back against hers was stronger than her own and belonging to a—wow, Moliere observed it right away—beautiful Black woman with braided hair three feet down to her waist and tomato-colored shorts and a yellow polo shirt. In her short stature and her hair and her color scheme the woman was spectacular.

And she was most of the way into Katherine Moliere's house.

"Get the hell out of here!" Moliere heard herself shouting this, heard how afraid she sounded. She was losing against the smaller woman's stronger hands. With one part of her brain Moliere was thinking of what weapon-like thing might be nearby.

"I cannot," said the woman, steadily winning the struggle for the front door. "I *cannot* get the hell out of here. I'm so sorry to be frightening you. But you have to let me in, Katherine."

Katherine?

Unable to hold the door back Moliere backpedaled fast the 15 feet into her kitchen, not for an instant turning her back on the woman. From the drying rack beside the sink Moliere took her breadknife.

Moliere could not help noticing that the woman's mascara was smeared like she had been crying. One cheek was raked by someone's fingernails, presumably not her own. The box braids spilling from under her Rasta cap were gorgeous.

The other woman never moved. In fact she looked puzzled by what Moliere was doing with the big knife.

"I'm not here to hurt you," the woman said. She sounded like her feelings were hurt.

"Get out," Moliere said. But instead of getting out the woman turned and, remembering that it was unbolted, double locked the door through which she had just burst.

"Please calm down, Katherine." Moliere could see the other woman was herself working to calm down. Even in her agitation Moliere observed this.

"Why do you know my name?"

"Because my name is Fanny. My husband's going to be right behind me."

Of course Moliere was speechless.

"He wants to kill me," said the woman. She spoke with spaces between the words, as if Moliere was deficient in mental understanding.

Moliere was not listening. She was all impulse. She held the knife straight out in front of her like a fencer, en garde, aware she probably did not have it in her to stab a person no matter the circumstances, nor any idea how to do it if she did. She put this out of her mind.

"Then phone the police," Moliere shouted, loud as she could in case the neighbors could hear. "Get out of my house!"

"Lot of good that will do either of us, Katherine. You *or* me. And there's no need to shout. I'm only partially deaf. I had scarlet fever once and that did it. But I can hear you fine."

"We're not having a conversation," said Moliere. "You can call the police from that landline over there. If you don't want to use the phone then leave. Either way you're going."

"But my husband's out there. He knows you. I'm not joking about this. Why would I kid you? We don't know even each other. It's my husband who does."

Hearing the woman say she and the husband were acquainted Moliere felt a higher order fear.

"He told me a whole story about you after I found the folder he kept," the woman said.

"Get out."

"He tried to make a big confessional scene so that I'd feel sorry for him. All I told him was, good for you, Katherine, meaning good for *you.* That only made Tibor think we're lesbians together." The beautiful woman never moved when she said these things.

"You've got me confused with someone else."

"To Tibor every woman's a prospective lesbian. He's really alienated."

"I don't know who the hell you are or who the hell you are talking about."

"You know my husband. Tibor Rauscha. You once filed a police report against him for hitting our son in the park. His son."

Moliere retrieved the memory, of course she did, though in the four years since that day she never thought about it except once in a while passing the playground on the edge of The Walloon Gardens, and barely then.

"Back then Tibor wasn't my husband," the woman said. "But he is now." Presumably out of nervousness she tucked her unspooling braids back under her cap.

"Don't tell me who he is. I remember."

"We live on Nine Mezcaleros Road."

"Why does he say I'm a lesbian?" Moliere wondered if her job was now in jeopardy. This was Texas, after all.

"Don't get sidetracked by that, Katherine, or in a million years you'll never understand why I'm here. You may as well ask why he thinks *I'm* a lesbian. I don't know the answer. Tibor has no principles but self-interest and the satisfaction of his psychotic desires. Or however you put it. He is such a moralist—so *he* thinks."

"I'm phoning the police department right now. Don't take another step in my direction." But the other woman was between Moliere and the telephone. Her cell was in her shoulder bag in the office upstairs.

"I won't," said the woman. And calmly too. She put her hands out to indicate peaceful intent.

"Now that I'm safely in your house," the woman said, "I don't need to move at all. If you want to try the police go ahead. But it will just be Kafkaesque for you." The woman spoke in the tone cops use on TV with crazy people.

It was important that Moliere speak. That would demonstrate that she was not intimidated. But Moliere could think of nothing to say.

"Please let me check the locks on your windows," said the woman. "May I do that?" The woman sidestepped toward the front window, her eyes on Moliere for any sudden moves with the bread knife.

"My name is Fanny," she said as she tried the latches on the front windows. Doing that she turned her back to Moliere. It was a gesture of trust. Or some ploy.

"You told me," said Moliere.

"I'm the same age as you. Twenty-eight, am I right? It would frighten you what Tibor has in the folder."

"I don't care." Moliere saw her opportunity and moved to the telephone on the other side of the room. Phone in one hand, knife in the other one, Moliere watched the woman walk from window to window trying all the locks.

"Go ahead and call," said the woman without looking over her shoulder. "It won't do any good except get you frustrated. But go ahead."

Moliere could not work out how to dial the phone without putting down the knife. Before she could solve this problem both women snapped their heads around toward the back of the house. Someone was trying to pull the sliding door open.

"Damn. That's Tibor."

Moliere saw the silhouette of a man out on her back deck. In frustration he was shaking the "French" door hard. He was trying to break its lock. The lock was flimsy and he shook it violently, but it held.

Moliere lowered her knife to her hip and thrust it forward the way gang members do in the movies, ready to fight. Her body was so flooded with adrenaline it made her dizzy.

Had Moliere owned a gun she might have used it then. But having no gun Moliere did a braver thing and went to the French door. With just the double-paned glass between herself and whoever was out there she turned on the light that illuminated the deck. The man out there stepped back, trapped in the light, blinded momentarily, startled like a forest creature.

Without even seeing his face Moliere could feel the man's indignation. His head swiveled around, probably hunting for something he could throw through the door.

"You know I've got all of this on the security camera, don't you?" Moliere shouted. There was no security camera, but the man looked wildly about trying to find one. All her life Moliere had been a good bluffer. She lied easily, even under stress. Situationally it could be a gift.

"Your wife's on the telephone to the police," Moliere said through the glass. She heard her voice coming out of her head, this time sounding more controlled, not frightened at all. "So you should just go. Tibor."

"Don't say his name," the woman behind her said. "He'll get angry."

"And by the way—*Tibor*. I'm not a lesbian."

The two women waited an unknown number of minutes for Tibor Rauscha to try another way in. They waited in quite a serious silence.

Presently they heard Tibor Rauscha's indignant steps splashing through the unraked catalpa leaves on the small lawn of Moliere's house, then the start of his car's engine. He drove away in the angry, over-powered way of cars in the movies. Movies about gang members.

Moliere still did not know why this woman Fanny was in her house. She still had not put down the knife. Her house ticked. Click. Click.

"Why don't you leave now and go somewhere for tonight? Get a hotel room. In the morning you can take steps."

"May I stay here?"

"No you can't stay here! Who the hell are you?"

"My name is Fanny."

"I meant why are you here."

"I am trying to protect us both."

"Don't drag me into your troubles."

"I brought a gift."

Moliere realized that Fanny had been holding a long legal folder in her left hand the entire time. Moliere had not taken this in until Fanny laid the folder on the dining-room table. It was remarkable that this small woman had the strength to push the door in with only one hand.

"That's for you," Fanny said. "May I sit down? After all this excitement I'm a little neurasthenic."

Without waiting for Moliere to reply Fanny sat—collapsed was more like it—in a red couch that divided the living room from the dining room. Her eyes were deep brown and enormous. Her beaded braids fell across her face. Her skin was much better and much darker than Moliere's.

I'm not a lesbian, Moliere reflected, but she is gorgeous.

"I was looking for Tibor's checkbook tonight," Fanny was saying as Moliere flipped through the contents of the folder, knife at the ready should the atmosphere change. "I needed money, don't ask what for. Tibor keeps cash in a box of envelopes inside the desk. He must be the last person in the United States who keeps that much cash around, just wads of twenties from ATMs. I found the folder while I was looking for the money. Sometimes it feels like I have an almost mystic sense of timing."

In the folder Moliere saw her credit report. There was a photo of herself from three years before giving an oversize check to the Perros Salvajes food bank on behalf of the Emma Tenayuca Middle School penny harvest; that was after Franklin died. There were two printouts of news stories about Franklin's death; in the margin of one was written *conflict?* in blue pen. There was even Moliere's most recent teacher evaluation.

Indifferently as she could manage Moliere said, "I'll look at this later."

"Whenever you like," said Fanny. "It's yours now. When I saw 'Moliere' was written on it I thought maybe Tibor had some interest in French theater that I never knew."

It made Moliere's flesh creep that someone was watching her and taking notes, and the whole time she had no idea.

"Tibor knows what you paid for this house and what you still owe on it. He knows you won a teaching award. It's all in there. On the way over I read a lot of it."

"He is stalking me?"

"I don't know if I'd call it stalking," Fanny said. "Keeping tabs. At first it made me wonder if you were a secret girlfriend or something conventional. While I was looking at it Tibor came in and caught me. Instead of getting angry he started explaining. That's when I knew I'd hit something big."

"Tibor's a dark man," Fanny said. "Not in the sense of dark complected like you and me, Katherine, but shadowy, you know? Dark in that sense."

"Now he knows I have this." Moliere was indicating the folder on the table with the tip of her bread knife.

"We chased around the house a little bit when he found me with it. Assuming Eugene heard us I don't know what he thought about *that*."

"Who's Eugene?"

"Tibor's son. He lives with us. I made it out the door fast as I could down the road to Tirso Avenue and called the car that brought me here."

"Why lesbians?"

"Who knows? Why anything with Tibor? Well, I do know why, and it would be that he thinks there are no principles but self-interest. The satisfaction of sexual desires would be for him one example."

"What does that have to do with why someone's a lesbian?"

Fanny shrugged. "Ask him."

"You can't stay here."

"I just want to sit down a little while. My back hurts from being tense. It's like my kidneys are bad all at once. I'm more of a sitting person these days and it's taken a toll on my core." Fanny inhaled deeply and her posture became more upright.

"I'm sorry, no."

"If I could have a glass of wine? Don't get the impression I'm a drinker but between us it gives me a necessary detachment, which right now I need."

"No."

"You're going to call the police?"

"The moment you leave."

"You're wasting your time." Fanny took off her cap and let her braids fall about her shoulders.

"Lady, I need to go work in the morning. Please go."

Fanny sighed. After a moment she smiled in defeat and stood up. She unlocked the door and peeked out into the darkness. In the light of the so-called porch she had a comely profile.

"Hey," Moliere said. "What is your last name? That way I'll know."

"For when the cops ask?"

"Yes."

"Fanny Rauscha is my legal surname. I should never have changed it. If we get to know each other I'll explain why I took Tibor's name. My prediction is I'll be giving it back now."

Fanny left and pulled the door closed behind her. Moliere quickly locked it and threw the dead bolt. This felt somehow rude.

Her house ticked.

Less than five minutes later Moliere heard a car stop outside her house. Then, clear as could be, she heard a voice in the house somewhere say, "Call AJ."

The car from Katherine Moliere's house started by taking Fanny via the most direct route to her home, down Bobby Fuller Boulevard. This two-mile stretch of road was the heart of Perros Salvajes, a bright neon nowhere going in a straight surveyor's line of chain restaurants, gas stations and the Big Horn mall. Half a mile from her house the driver told Fanny he was going to take the back way to Nine Mezcaleros Road.

"The traffic lights at the intersection with Bumpers Road have been out for a month," he said.

"I know," Fanny told him. "Go however you like." Her husband Tibor Rauscha liked to go the side road anyway. In the dark at night he enjoyed the isolation of the two-lane blacktop. In her head Fanny said, "Tibor thinks he is a romantic."

Fanny's driver pulled up two hundred yards from the house at the foot of the long driveway leading to the big house. From there Fanny could see the light was lit in Rauscha's second-floor office.

Tibor Rauscha built this house back when he was still married to Carol. He transplanted a six-deep fringe of mature sugar maple trees to the front edge of the property to hide the house from the road. Except in winter before the leaves fill in you'd never know the house was there. Somehow these maples grew—not beautifully (they looked tormented if you stood close) but they grew. Rauscha irrigated them. If a tree died he sent away to a nursery in Pennsylvania and replaced it.

Rauscha thought he was an arborist.

The top of the drive was a semi-circle described by fountain grass. In the circle was a scale model of the Trevi Fountain. When one sees splashing fountains in that part of Texas they seem wrong somehow.

Why did she say what she did about lesbians? Why did she think it was her role in life to keep the conversation lively?

Watching Fanny sit on the narrow bench that went around the base of the fountain was Eugene. He was looking down at Fanny from the window of his bedroom. She must not want to come inside to him yet, Eugene thought.

Eugene thought of the way walking up the driveway from the road made him feel hidden away from everybody. He liked that. He liked the distant whisper of traffic exactly because it was distant. On summer days the driveway was almost shaded by the weird maple trees. Except for school Eugene never went out anymore.

Up at his open window the night air was agreeably chilly on Eugene's face. From the window he heard the water of the fountain plashing. The wind whispered the tall dry grass planted around the house and the branches of the maples. Didn't Fanny feel the cold in those little red shorts?

Eugene was aroused by the chestnut color of Fanny's skin. But he did not like her. If only Fanny and his father could be made to disappear then life would be better. The whole wide world was weary of Eugene and he knew it. He barely saw his father or Fanny except for when he got hungry and went down to the fridge for something to eat. Fanny said it bothered her that Eugene did not seem to ever want hot food. He could barely be bothered to answer.

"Food is not part of your pathology," she said. "Eat." Eugene ignored her.

Eugene's favorite time of day was when the yellow van to his special school took him away for eight hours. He sometimes thought about taking up a sport that would add two more hours out of the house; funny picturing himself in a team uniform of some sort. Wednesdays he was dropped off at his psychologist. He came home about five in an Uber. Wednesdays were good days. Tomorrow was a Tuesday.

Eugene heard Fanny opening the front door into the foyer of the house on the first floor. Down the hall from his bedroom he heard the talk show his father was watching on the TV in his office. The TV noise was people talking over each other, everyone insisting insisting insisting. Eugene hated that noise.

Fanny and his father were about to converge. His father would have seen Fanny come into the house on the security camera that was on the shelf to the left of his TV. He would have heard the pinging of the motion detector. Most likely he was pretending not to know she was in the house.

Eugene heard Fanny take the opposite staircase, the less direct one that took her past Eugene's bedroom. He went back to his desk and pretended to be at his laptop. His father was not likely to stick his head in to say good night, but Fanny might. Carol, never. It was forever shocking to Eugene that his father and Carol never did better by him. Goldfish got more affection.

Eugene heard Fanny pass by his door and go down the long hall toward the room where his father was.

Eugene heard the wheels of his father's chair squeak and him saying, "Come here, baby."

If only they could be made to disappear.

On the night Fanny broke in at Moliere's house it took 20 minutes before cops appeared. It was a waste of everyone's time, as Fanny predicted.

Moliere watched out her window for the police to show. She expected the wait. Perros Salvajes County was not such a populous place but it was all spread out—taken together about 225 square miles. Apart from the occasional bar fight and family homicide there was little crime in Perros Salvajes, but for the county's underfunded police force covering so much territory was a challenge.

One of the two cops who finally turned up was AJ Munoz, working one of his night shifts. He had his current rookie partner with him, Tonya Hernández, which made her the second woman to visit Moliere's house that night.

AJ and Moliere were something just the short side of friends through their shared acquaintance with Franklin Dell. But they did not see each other much nor even speak, especially given AJ's hours.

"Katherine," said AJ, "I'm glad I got the call. You alright, honey?"

"I had people breaking into my house half an hour ago, AJ."

"They were trying to burglarize?"

"No. One of them was trying to give me something. That folder over there on the table."

"Couldn't they just have mailed it? Forgive me, but I'm not following."

"One was Tibor Rauscha and the other was his wife. She actually managed to get in. She was the one who had the folder."

"Fanny?"

"You know her?"

"Rauscha's a big fish in Perros Salvajes. You *don't* know him?"

"No."

"How can you not?"

"The wife thought I should know him too. I don't."

"Fanny's not the type to break into houses."

"They know *me*, she said. The wife was…"

"Fanny's the second wife."

"She said Rauscha was after her and that she came to warn me."

"If Rauscha was after her why did she come to warn you? I'm still not following."

"Don't grill me, AJ. I couldn't follow it either. She pushed the door in and started warning me about Rauscha and lesbians."

"Why on earth was she warning you about lesbians? Lesbians are perfectly safe. Even these days."

"Not like that. She was warning me that Rauscha thought the wife and I were lesbians. Like in a romance."

"You're not a lesbian, honey. I know these last couple of years have been hard for you…"

"I'm not even talking about that. Look in that folder on the table."

"It says your name."

"Look in it."

AJ did look in it. It was mostly newspaper clips, most of them downloaded. Select Facebook posts, nearly all of them including photographs of Moliere on outings with her students; none were more recent than two years before, about the time Moliere gave up her account. There was a photograph of the Honda Civic in Moliere's driveway. There was a photograph of her house. There was a photocopy of her driver's license.

"I can see why you'd be concerned. Some of this predates Franklin and you."

"Should I be worried, AJ?"

"Not to distraction. Would you like Officer Tanya to stay a few hours? Until the sun comes up? You'd be OK with that, right Tanya?"

Officer Hernández looked like a kid who had not expected to be called on in class; AJ was touched by her shyness but she needed to leave it behind if she was going to grow into the job. This time she rose to the occasion.

"You'd get a night's sleep just having company," said Officer Hernandez.

"No thanks," said Moliere. "I'm not afraid of them coming back. It's the feeling of being watched and I don't know it. Can they just spy on me?"

"Your privacy?"

"Yes. Or something even more than that. I don't know how you name it."

"Show Tanya what's in that folder. I'm going to give Rauscha a call. It's not even midnight."

"What do you want to bet their number's not listed?" Moliere said.

"The wife—Fanny—wrote a note across that folder with a phone number if you want to call. See—she signed it. Take some reassurance from that."

Seven or eight times the phone rang before the voice of a sleepy woman answered. AJ thought the voice was smoky but that was probably just the hour and the being woken up.

"Good evening, ma'am. I apologize for telephoning so late. This is Officer AJ Munoz of the Perros Salvajes PD. If I woke you I'm sorry."

"Is it Eugene?"

"Forgive me?"

"What did you call about? How'd you get my cell number?"

"I'm at the home of Katherine Moliere. She tells me you were here earlier."

"I was."

"With your husband."

"He came later."

"She said you broke into her house."

"It could be read that way."

"How do you read it?"

"I was concerned for her. I meant no harm."

"Why do you need to be concerned?"

"Let me put my husband on."

AJ heard Fanny waking Tibor Rauscha. From what AJ could hear on his end Rauscha was reluctant to rejoin the conscious world. He sounded barely present when he came on the line.

AJ repeated the facts as he knew them and Rauscha said, yes, the folder was his.

"Why would you assemble a folder on Ms. Moliere?"

"It's her credit report."

"Forgive me?"

"She leases her car from my dealership. It's a credit report. Jesus."

"I've never seen a credit report resembles the one I was just looking at."

"I'm idiosyncratic. As a matter of fact I'd like it back."

"I will ask Ms. Moliere if she is amenable. Is this the best number for her to reach you at?"

"This all you want?"

"I'll make my report, as I'm obligated. You'll get a copy. Or you can always download it."

"Report about what?"

"I write the facts down first and then I see how they speak to me. Good night."

When AJ came back Katherine Moliere and Tonya Hernández were at the dining-room table reviewing the folder. They were talking it over, as if it were some kind of dark scrapbook.

"How'd that go?" Moliere said over her shoulder. Her voice sounded less tight, but only slightly.

"It was inconclusive."

"There are things in here I'd rather forget, AJ."
AJ said nothing.
"Here's a picture of me from the newspaper."
"Doing what?"
"Franklin."
"Ah."
"The caption on this one says 'Grief Struck'."

Texas On Its Edge

The odds were good that Moliere and the red-headed policeman would encounter each other again after their first meeting in The Walloon Gardens. Perros Salvajes was a small universe. In a small universe the limited possibilities for things to happen—any things—make coincidence pointless to talk about; probability is more useful to explore.

Not quite three years after her first encounter with Tibor Rauscha in The Walloon Gardens Katherine Moliere was in a bar called Ginny's on Longacre Street in Perros Salvajes. On Fridays teachers from the Emma Tenayuca school sometimes liked to spend an hour or two unwinding there. Cops liked Ginny's, too; the main Perros Salvajes police headquarters was around the corner. They dropped in after their shifts ended. Lots dropped in before their shifts began. One of the latter group was Franklin Dell, who was relatively new on the job and stuck with working nights.

At that time Franklin was distinguished by his solitude. At Ginny's he leaned against the end of the bar at the end nearest the front door. There were other cops in the place, there always were, but Franklin was alone. The night Moliere met him his back was turned to his law-enforcement colleagues and to the two televisions over the bar showing preseason basketball.

Franklin had a solid, strong face but was not by means a heartbreaker. Thought Moliere.

Really, she did not notice him at all. He was tall enough to look over the heads of everyone else out toward the scene on Longacre Street. He looked like he was watching for someone or something out there. Thought Moliere.

When Moliere went to the end of the bar to buy a round that night Franklin removed his attention from the street and gave it all to her.

"Excuse me," he said. "I know you."

"Do you?" Naturally Moliere assumed he was some guy trying to get lucky. She had a rotating collection of what she called her teacher's sweaters and that night she had on the one the catalogue called teal. She knew it made her look good, and she assumed it was the color that attracted this man's eye. She hoped her drinks would come quickly.

"I'm a police officer," Franklin. "We're trained how to remember faces."

"That is a good skill."

"About two years ago you made a complaint about a man smacking his kid in the park—do you remember? I was the officer who took your statement." When he spoke Moliere thought Franklin was laconic in a way that sounded put on, like a movie cowboy in a saloon. But it was not put on. Franklin spoke that way, laconic. He was from El Paso but Midland originally.

"I thought you looked familiar," Moliere said, though really she had not thought that at all. Franklin did not look familiar even with his red hair. "Anything happen to my statement after that?" she asked him. "No one ever called."

"In that kind of a situation nothing hardly ever does. You did a good thing though." When he spoke Moliere looked Franklin over. The same as he was, she was trying to take him in.

"Thanks loads," she told him.

"Every day people hit their kids. Hardly anybody ever calls the cops about it."

"I wonder how the little boy is doing."

"He's probably not so little anymore. And most kids shrug it off. That's one of the things the world's got going for it."

"I'm a schoolteacher. Trust me, most kids don't shrug it off."

"I only meant the guy's probably not a child-beating creep. I can tell when people are nuts. I remember that guy struck me as just petulant."

"Either way, not what anybody wants to see in a parent."

"Most likely it didn't happen again. Because you called him on it. Good work there. Most people would not have said one word."

Moliere's drinks arrived, including the double Dewar's she was looking forward to—her second of the night and her last before she went and got herself something to eat; Moliere knew that if she was not rigid in her rules about drinking she might never leave a bar. What with one thing and another she had the potential to like alcohol that much.

"Gotta go," she said, friendly enough. "Nice seeing you, officer."

Moliere took up the little self-serve salver that was a trademark of Ginny's and turned away with the drinks. Her glass of Scotch looked tremendously inviting sitting on that little tray. Moliere loved Scotch better than any other spirit.

"Yeah," Franklin said, "and I gotta get to work. I should go on a walk to clear my head. Otherwise I get tired. Don't drink and drive, ma'am."

Franklin pushed himself back from the bar. He was a square-headed man with big shoulders. He looked born to be a cop.

After that Moliere did not meet Franklin around the shops and so forth, or walking a beat. Perros Salvajes cops did not walk a beat. For one thing they had a lot of ground to cover. They cruised in cars in pairs. They were one of the feistiest wings of the Texas Municipal Police Association.

At that time Franklin was relatively new on the police force. He got all the crap shifts—nights, weekends, Christmas Day. That was why he worked with AJ Munoz so much. AJ liked the quiet of overnight, liked the shift differential and liked the hours away from his wife. Consequently AJ was a mentor to a string of rookie cops.

Often on a Friday night before Franklin went into work Moliere saw him at Ginny's. Moliere could not imagine going in to work straight from a bar; as a public-school teacher she had never done that even once.

When they saw each other they did not speak. They smiled. Franklin had a nice smile, with some of that cowpoke thing she noticed the first time. It was a genuine smile, and Moliere did not mind smiling back. They were both still young. This smiling at the man she once indexed in her mind as "square head" progressed over the length of six months to nodding.

One evening in mid-May Franklin spoke to Moliere as she was coming back from the ladies room.

"May I be forward with you?" he asked. "May I know your name?"

"It must be in the report that you and your partner wrote in the park."

"That would be the wrong reason for me to ask to review the report. I could face ethics charges."

"It's Katherine."

"Not Kathy?"

"Never."

"Good. My name is Franklin."

"Never Frank?"

"Never."

"Good. Franky?"

"Geeze."

"OK."

"Katherine, may I ask you to a picnic on the Sunday before Memorial Day? I'll be honest with you and admit that I've wanted to ask you out for a while. I believe we would like each other."

"Where'd you get that idea?"

"It came to me." Franklin smiled and she smiled back. "I've been surveilling you and I notice I never see you here with anyone who might fit into the boyfriend category. So I thought I'd take a chance and ask."

Depending on how you were counting at that time Moliere had had nothing that qualified as romance in her life for at least three years. Her last serious boyfriend had been the one she had at the University of New Mexico. He was crazy about New Mexico and thought everyone should want to live there. Moliere thought the exact opposite. Eventually this was clarifying for them both; there were no hard feelings.

Moliere was 26 years old in Texas, and unbothered about it. But the odds on finding a worthwhile man in Perros Salvajes at that age were not so good. Of the women teachers with whom she went to Ginny's on Fridays only one was married; that woman drank even more than Franklin.

"I wasn't aware of being surveilled."

"That's because I'm good at my job," Franklin said. "The hard part is that I don't like picnics. Do you like picnics?"

"I have nothing against them."

"Well, I'm obliged to go. And I'd enjoy myself a lot more if you'd come with me."

For a moment Moliere considered playing hard to get. But it had been a long week and she was tired, and she knew this cop had to get to work. Moliere said yes to the invitation and they went.

Even for west Texas in May the day of the picnic was hot. The park where it was held, la Frontera in the west end of the county, was just as shadeless as most of the surrounding terrain.

By eleven a.m. the shade in that park shrank to nothing. Before the first hot dog was cooked the clutch of cops with whom they sat, gentlemen and ladies both, finished a liter of vodka among them. The vodka and the heat had its effect. By midafternoon two of the men were asleep under the wooden table, one on top of it. They put Moliere in mind of yo-ho pirates on a dead man's chest. Their sober spouses carried on conversation in soft voices. They were used to this scene.

After two hours Franklin made excuses and they left. He took Moliere to lunch because she had not eaten.

"I was afraid you were going to run away," Franklin said over schnitzel at Ginny's.

"I thought about it," she said. Moliere noticed how Franklin's voice had lost the emphasized West Texas drawl he assumed with the other cops. He switched back to being himself. "But you seem nice enough."

"I am nice enough," Franklin said. "I won't ever make you go to one of those things again." It was an odd remark since it presumed that Franklin could make Moliere do anything. And that there would be an again.

"You're nice yourself," Franklin added.

Moliere *was* nice by the common standard, but try telling her that. Since coming to work in Perros Salvajes she had fallen into solitary routines and was developing an idea of herself as misanthropic. This made her feel removed from people and therefore not "nice" in the way that Franklin meant—that is to say, sweet. But she was. Moliere was nice. Though not sweet.

When Moliere was with Franklin her opinion of herself improved, as it will in the first flush of romance. The facts have nothing to do with it. Happiness infected Moliere's self-opinion. In her mirrors she looked prettier.

After the disastrous picnic they went on seeing each other. Owing to Franklin's night shifts this was not convenient. On her side Moliere was pursuing a master's degree in education, which would eventually give her a 10 percent pay bump when she completed it. This difficulty of seeing each other was a plus, really, because it made the romance go slow, and that is always a good thing. If romance takes its time that is better for everyone.

After the debauched picnic Franklin kept his promise. Except for one christening he never again asked Moliere to a policemen's social event. The christening ended similarly to the picnic. But what choice did Franklin have? The little girl was his godchild.

Not counting Ginny's, in the first year of knowing each other Moliere and Franklin went to the one awful picnic, a splashy Texas bar mitzvah, a minor-league baseball game, 47 dinners, 19 Saturday lunches and three movies. It was four months before they spent the night together. After that first year they never spent a night apart until Franklin died. That was two years after they met and nine months after they became engaged.

The foolishness that later developed between Fanny and Moliere would never have occurred if Franklin had been alive. And not just because he might have guided Moliere in the law. Moliere told Franklin everything, and in the telling it would have become obvious that further connection with Fanny was bound to take her nowhere good.

"Franklin was no genius," AJ Munoz once said, "but he had common sense."

Among the ways people get along is by concealing the truth. Dissembling is commonplace. It need not be the same as lying. Everything depends on how it's meant.

For example, concealing the truth from Moliere saved Franklin Dell the awkwardness of explaining why he drank alone. Or why he brought Moliere to a policeman's picnic when all the time he hated picnics. Or why he pretended not to know what happened to Eugene Rauscha, the boy in The Walloon Gardens who was smacked by his father, Tibor Rauscha.

At that time Perros Salvajes county had a population of 6,207. Most of that number was "downtown" close by the commercial strip anchored by Bobby Fuller Boulevard. But even in the unincorporated communities spread over the country everyone had heard the story of Janet Staufer.

Before the crime Janet was known to most people in the square mile around her house by sight if not by name. Thin-faced and curly haired she was a common sight on the large tricycle bike she rode. The bike had a cargo box at the back of it that might be filled with groceries from 7-11 or books from the public library, which were next to each other on Bumpers Road. Nearly every day Janet rode to the library. She took out all the books allowed on her card and the next day brought them back and got more.

Janet could not read. When she was six her brain was injured by her mother. The mother drank. One hungover morning she became enraged at Janet for some reason and banged the little girl's head hard as she could against the kitchen counter. Janet's father, who at that time was beginning the process of divorce (one reason Mrs. Staufer was unhappy though it was pointless to look for causes) saw to it that the mother served jail time. Twelve years later when she was released from women's prison Mrs. Stuffer left Perros Salvajes. No one ever saw her again. She deserved to suffer.

Mr. Staufer and Janet and her two brothers, Gustav and Timmo, went on living in their big house on Nine Mezcaleros Road. Mr. Staufer was moderately wealthy, moderately only in comparison to Tibor Rauscha, who owned the house next door and lived there with his son Eugene. Mr. Staufer founded a contracting firm that built and maintained high-density feedlots; in the maintaining there was serious money. Most weeks he travelled all over Texas and often to Kansas or Oklahoma. When Mr. Staufer was gone his daughter Janet was looked after by Isla Trautwig, a cousin to Mr. Staufer.

On Fridays Mrs. Trautwig made a game of letting Janet bring a simple grocery list to the 7-11 at the intersection of Nine Mezcaleros Road and Bumpers Road. The route was down and back, about a quarter mile each way. Janet waved to anyone she saw and anyone she saw waved back. If she saw Eugene Rauscha she waved. He lived in the big house beside her own. In front of his house there was a beautiful fountain.

Between the two houses was a border of chinquapin oak and juniper planted by Mr. Staufer when Tibor Rauscha began building his house. Rauscha's house resembled a sort of Texas chateau. Mr. Staufer saw what was going up and wanted a screen. On one of the Fridays that he saw Janet go by Eugene called to her through this landscape boundary.

"I have something for you." It was the Easter break from school. All morning Eugene had been breaking sticks in half and piling them up.

Janet was enticed. She came through a natural path in the border between the two houses to see what the boy had to show her. Eugene ran and hid, ran and hid. Later Eugene said, "I wanted her to think we were playing a game. I wanted to make her relaxed."

Eugene hid in the brush behind his house, the place where the desert began. He whistled to let Janet know when she was cold or getting warmer. The whole while he was undressing himself. When Janet found him Eugene popped up and pulled her down by her legs.

Later he said, "I told myself we were making out. Because you make the girl go on the ground."

Barely thinking Eugene pulled off Janet's red shorts and penetrated her. It was the first ejaculation of his life. After that he gathered up his clothes and ran off to his house. He went in through the backdoor that was beyond the pool and the firepit. Inside the big house there was no one. Not his father, not Fanny.

Janet Staufer fell asleep and then after a long while got to her feet and found her way home to her own house. She left the stuff from the 7-11 in the box of the bicycle and went inside to Mrs. Trautwig.

Later Mrs. Trautwig told the police, "All that afternoon she sat and sat and would not say boo." The next morning doing laundry Mrs. Staufer recognized the stains on Janet's underwear and telephoned, first the police and then, after thinking about it, Mr. Staufer.

Mr. Staufer was already on his way home to Perros Salvajes from Desdemona by the time the police appeared. The cops did not wait for him. They took Janet and Mrs. Trautwig for a drive around the girl's familiar paths to see if something sparked. Of course they struck out. Arriving back at the house they observed Janet noticeably agitated when she looked in the direction of the Rauscha house. From there even an amateur would have figured it out.

The two cops went up the same path Janet walked the day before. At the end of it they found one blue sock. The sock went in an evidence bag. One man went to the front of the house and one went to the back. The one at the back was the one who knocked.

Eugene gave them no trouble. He had had a bad night and in a way was glad to see them.

In its cruelty the story was horrible. But it was the sort of horrible that is familiar on the local news. The story had no legs and after a week was forgotten in its details even in Perros Salvajes.

What lasted was the sorting of the consequences for the two families.

In Perros Salvajes Tibor Rauscha was a person with a presence—and not from force of character.

Even on the Texas scale Tibor Rauscha was wealthy. On the Perros Salvajes scale he was stinking rich. By temperament he was a low-profile plutocrat. He did not need to do much to make people feel proud of having met him, or to report that he said thank you for some help they provided. People showed him the deference peasants show the powerful. They admired the smell of money on Rauscha, superstitiously.

Rauscha also had a subtly notorious reputation borrowed from his brother Georg, which added to his appeal; the peasants like the spice of scandal. And Rauscha had one more thing going for him.

Tibor Rauscha's father was a fair-haired man of a German background named Anders. During the Second World War the father's parents came down from Central Texas to take jobs in the Port Arthur refineries. Anders later moved to Houston.

Rauscha's mother, Janey, got to Texas from New Orleans.

She went there direct from Mexico to follow a sailor she knew. But by the time she relocated the sailor had another girl. Janey moved on to Houston; there seemed to be nothing else open to her. In Houston she met Anders, who had taken a job in maintenance at Texas Children's Hospital, which had just opened. They married and had the two boys. Their circumstances were modest. It was plenty for them.

The two boys were light-skinned like the father, Georg more so than Tibor. Janey was glad, knowing a lighter complexion was better for their prospects in Texas. As an adult Tibor Rauscha preferred staying out of the sun; otherwise he got to be what people used to call swarthy.

Ethnic ambiguity was a help to Rauscha and not the trouble it had been to Anders and Janey. West Texas was changing, a little. But Anders and Janey were born too soon.

As with Katherine Moliere no one knew for certain which box to tick for Tibor Rauscha. (Later the irony in this similarity remained unexpressed.) Brown or White? As it suited him Tibor Rauscha could be one or the other. When he started his company, RauschaTech, this chameleon talent extended his brand not just by making the most of minority preferences in lending law but in the way in which it allowed Rauscha to portray himself as a bootstrapping man of color and a country-club Republican at the same time (though Rauscha did not play golf and had voted only four times by the year he turned 35, the same year as Eugene's crime).

One night during the court proceeding Tibor Rauscha said to his wife Fanny, "I feel naked and alone." They had been married one year.

"So your feelings about that girl next door—they are what?" Fanny was never shy about telling Rauscha what she had on her mind. Eugene, Fanny was reminding him, was his child with her predecessor, Carol Peña. If Rauscha felt goaded he knew it was a component of Fanny's spell over him. He would just need to live with it.

"And your son?" Fanny asked. She was pressing an advantage. Now Rauscha was wishing he had kept his naked loneliness to himself.

Eugene confessed to his crime against Janet Staufer. But that was not going to be the end of it.

Rauscha expected a civil suit from the Staufer family. There would have been a dollar figure attached, one that might be negotiated and that in any case was subject to some limit. It was the absence of a limit that unnerved Tibor Rauscha. Janet's father had no interest in a civil suit, no concern for money. He wanted to inflict pain, less on Eugene Rauscha than on Eugene's father. In his heart Rauscha knew he was owed this for his failings as a parent. Just the same he defended himself.

Because dumb was one thing Tibor Rauscha was not.

Though Eugene was a minor Mr. Staufer wanted to go all the way to the end of the line with whatever criminal charge was available. Rauscha and his lawyer could not predict where that might take everybody. The wildness of the emotion that had been let loose was dangerous.

Added to this worry was the judge, William Taylor, who seemed willing to abet Staufer in his passion. ("Abet" was the word Rauscha used in his head. "Abet" conveyed a sense of connivance.)

Taylor was a Black man prominent in Republican circles, which in Perros Salvajes (and Texas generally) were wide and overlapping. Owning some of this ambidextrous quality himself Rauscha hoped to win some of Taylor's sympathy. He even brought Fanny to attend the first two court hearings. It was not subtle and it was not working and anyway Fanny said she would not go anymore.

Owing to delays Eugene's bench trial was into its second month when Rauscha's attorney, Martin Schroeter, implored Judge Taylor that "by the length of this proceeding my client is prevented from beginning the process of healing."

"The court's concern," Taylor replied immediately, "is all with Janet Staufer and not with your client's healing." However, Taylor added, he would consider consigning Eugene to a therapist's care *contingent* on a review of the young man's home environment.

Martin Schroeter heard that and believed his argument had backfired. He expected to be dismissed by Tibor Rauscha. But on the contrary Rauscha saw opportunity; this was because he had the entrepreneurial temperament.

Rauscha's next move was to telephone an acquaintance, Warren Olmec, the police chief of Perros Salvajes.

For the two years before Eugene's rape of Janet Staufer it had been a joke to Tibor Rauscha that his divorce lawyer, Rob "Oscar" Meyer, "won" custody of Rauscha's son Eugene for him. Where was the win in that?

It was Carol who won. She got a house and money and life free of Eugene's presence. The judge in matrimonial court had been a woman—Greta Something—and Tibor Rauscher was counting on feelings of sorority, therefore, to assign custody to the mother. The judge, though, declared that she did not like Carol's mental state.

"Neither do I," Tibor Rauscha told Oscar. "How is that relevant to our cause?"

"The assumption," Oscar replied, "is that people need to be emotionally competent. Otherwise they cannot be nurturing."

"Lots get by good without that."

"Talk to me about this later, Tibor."

Tibor Rauscha asked Chief McOlmec for a favor once before, which was when AJ Munoz had written him up for striking Eugene in the playground, that day when he first met Katherine Moliere. The consideration was granted, and nothing came of AJ's report. When Judge Taylor demanded a home evaluation Rauscha saw his opportunity for a fresh start.

Rauscha, without precisely suborning Chief McOlmec, telephoned him from the house on a Tuesday morning. Rauscha expressed himself regarding the role the Perros Salvajes police should play.

"We have to acknowledge we are known to each other, Warren." Rauscha said this with manly candor. "Take what you know about me for given. But can you use different words?"

"Intensifiers."

"I don't drink, you know, but I would never claim not to drink at all. I seldom drink at home. That's only because I'm never home."

"But you've been observed consuming alcohol elsewhere.

Leaving Eugene in the care of his stepmother." McOlmec was recruited from the detective squad in Henderson, Nevada. He was the first Black man to hold the chief's job in Perros Salvajes.

"We'll leave Fanny out of it."

"I don't know how we do that."

"I'm asking. Fanny does her best with me. Fanny cares for her only mother over in Hay Agua."

"She's frail?"

"You've seen Fanny—she's healthy as a horse."

"I meant 'frail' in the sense of the mother. The sense of the elderly."

"Her mother's 53—younger than you, Warren. But Fanny cares for her in the sense of affection."

"If Judge Taylor construes another meaning," said the chief, "I can't help that."

"I realize."

An hour later the two men had a creative collaboration satisfying to each party's sense of justice. It succeeded in smearing Tibor Rauscha's reputation as a parent but left room in it for refutation should need arise. If anyone had called the pair of them dissemblers they would have been indignant.

All that was needed was a police officer and a social worker to visit Tibor Rauscha's house. They would speak with Eugene, his father and Fanny. It need only be a walk-through. The designated policeman need only sign off on what Chief McOlmec already had in hand.

The designated policeman was Franklin Dell.

There was a year when the voters of Perros Salvajes County voted to slash all forms of county taxes radically. It was part of a movement to starve government, which they thought was a good idea for some reason. The vote produced a number of surprises, including underfunding the policeman's pension fund. There were lawsuits. While the lawsuits were being argued the pension fund was in trouble. The Policemen's Fund was created to fill the gaps while the trouble was worked out. For three years running Tibor Rauscha made a $75,000 contribution to the foundation from the RauschaTech Foundation (which funded nothing else).

The year Franklin Dell was hired was the year the voters of Perros Salvajes County passed their tax-slashing referendum. For two and a half years after that there was not another cop hired in the county. Despite his three years as a policeman Franklin was still regarded as a rookie.

Franklin was beginning to get along in the job. As a regular thing he got fewer bad shifts. He was earning a reputation as a good cop. That would have recommended him to the chief.

McOlmec probably thought giving Franklin the job of evaluating Tibor Rauscha's home was easy duty, a gift considering the friendly understanding at which the chief had arrived with Rauscha already.

Franklin was not averse to easy duty from time to time; he was in a general way a straight arrow but he was not irritating about it. He dimly knew that Rauscha and the chief were cordial. Certainly he knew about Rauscha's support for the police foundation. And as a policeman of three years Franklin Dell also knew that the circumstance of a great many homes in the county might be some category of unappealing. Even bad characters might be doing all they could.

Before going over to the house on Nine Mezcaleros Road Franklin read the document McOlmec put together from the notes of his conversation with Tibor Rauscha. He puzzled over why Rauscha would agree to smear his own self.

Franklin thought, It's like giving away your shadow.

The morning he visited Tibor Rauscha's family Franklin was buzzed in through the front gate of the big house. A thousand times he had passed the place on patrol, usually in the holy middle of the night. He was curious about the sugar maples. Rauscha was a high-profile resident—the only one in Perros Salvajes—and the chief had an unwritten policy of keeping an eye out. Before that morning Franklin never had reason to go up the long driveway.

At the top of the driveway to the house Tibor Rauscha waited for Franklin. There he was on the front step when Franklin pulled in around behind the pretty fountain. He looked older than Franklin expected, it was something about his posture or his hairline. As a policeman Franklin had trained himself to be conscious of these things.

Rauscha greeted Franklin patiently; that was how it felt. They shook hands the way men do and walked into the big house. Franklin was conscious of leaving behind the sunny day.

"Fanny's down the hall," Rauscha told him. "You'll meet her later. She knows you're coming. You're on her calendar."

Rauscha's house appeared to be built largely of marble. Or something manufactured to look like marble. The indoors were cold. It reminded Franklin of his El Paso high school. Although the high school was not cold and always had the sound of banging lockers from somewhere and the noise of voices talking loud enough to be heard. At midday Tibor Rauscha's house was silent.

They went up the cold stone stairs to Eugene's room. At the top they walked down a long gallery to Eugene's bedroom door. Which was closed. So Rauscha rapped on it.

"The man is here I told you about," said Rauscha through the door. Eugene did not answer. After less than half a minute Rauscha let himself in. Franklin saw Eugene close his laptop as the two of them entered the room. The kid turned around over his shoulder like he half expected to be beat. Out beyond his window was the expansive Cihuahuan desert, a portrait of empty in the flat late-morning light.

"This is Officer Dell," said Rauscha. "He only wants to ask some questions about if you're happy."

"How ya doing?" Franklin asked Eugene.

"Fine." Rauscha sat down on the edge of the unmade bed

and tipped an ear.

"Forgive me, sir," said Franklin, "but Eugene and I need to be private." Franklin did not know if that was so or not. He just did not want Rauscha in the room. He made the most of his policeman's uniform.

"Would you mind if I just listen?"

"No, sir. I'm sorry." Franklin smiled and spoke in a light tone, as if everything was just friendliness. When Rauscha left (annoyed) Franklin gave all his attention to the soft adolescent boy at the desk.

"Anything you say to me is between us. Right?"

Eugene nodded.

"You believe that?"

Eugene said nothing.

"Then I guess my first job today is to persuade you. You happy here, bud? Just in general?"

"Sure."

"What do you do that makes you happy?"

Eugene shrugged the 15-year-old's shrug.

"School?"

Nothing.

"I'm asking because I'm always interested in meeting somebody who likes school. I never did. It was alright, you know?, but it wasn't my thing. So I'm interested in people who like it." Franklin meant this as a joke but it did not seem to go down with Eugene.

"You got friends at your school?"

"I don't really like school. I just had to say something."

"Then what do you like?"

"Home. Being home."

"Yeah? What do you like about being home?"

"It's cozy."

Hoping he was not obvious about it Franklin took in the room where he guessed Eugene spent all his time. Every teenager's room is a catastrophe but this was of another order. The Winnie the Pooh rug beside Eugene's bed crunched under Franklin's policeman's shoes.

"Are you going to ask me about the girl next door?"

"No. That's not why I'm here. Like your father said, I'm here to ask if you're happy or not."

"I'm happy."

"You don't seem like it, Eugene. If you don't mind my saying."

"I really am."

"I don't know why."

Franklin's direct approach was not working, obviously.

"Tell me how's your father treat you? OK?"

"Yeah. He's great."

"You do stuff together?"

"He travels a lot for his job. But when he's home he lets me do whatever I want."

Franklin Dell wrote that down.

"When do you see your mother? What's going on there?"

"Usually twice a month. One of them drives me over and I spend the weekend with her."

"You enjoy that? How's that go?"

No answer.

"You don't enjoy anything." Franklin's heart broke for the teenage rapist.

"My mother's weird. All the time she's like she wants to

jump out of her skin. At least she is when I'm around."

"You don't do things with her?"

"If I stay over we never go anyplace. She gets up early but I'm not supposed to talk to her. On Sunday she takes me to her church. Then we go for muffins and the paper. Then she drives me home. Here."

"That doesn't sound like much fun."

"It's not."

"I'm sorry."

"She's alright," Eugene said. "She just feels old I think."

"Is it better with your father?"

"Yeah?"

"It's not a question with a right answer, Eugene."

"Sure."

"He doesn't hit you anymore?"

"What does that mean, 'anymore'?"

"A few years ago when I was still a new cop I took a report that your father hit you."

"I kind of remember. At Walloon Park?"

"Yeah."

"That was one time."

"Sure?"

"Yeah. They leave me alone. It's nice the way it is."

As AJ Munoz would later say, Franklin Dell was no genius but he had common sense. He understood that Eugene was not telling him "I am happy here." Eugene only wished to be left alone.

Franklin closed his notebook and stood up. It was an old policeman's trick AJ taught him.

"OK. I'll leave you alone, Eugene. Oh, one thing I forgot to ask from my list of questions. Your stepmother. You two guys alright?"

"Fanny?"

"You've got another stepmother?"

"Fanny's OK."

"Great."

Franklin got up and shook Eugene's hand. The hand was wet and soft as bread dough.

"Hey," Franklin said as he went to the door, "if you ever want to talk about Janet sometime to someone I can fix you up."

"I'm good."

Franklin closed Eugene's door and went to find Tibor Rauscha.

Rauscha was in his office at the opposite end of the hall. It was 63 paces from Eugene's room. Franklin counted the steps to give his mind something to do besides think about Eugene.

"How was that?" Rauscha asked from behind his desk. Franklin noticed he seemed kind of cheerful in the way he asked.

"He gave me what I needed," Franklin replied. The policeman's instinct was to be evasive. So much the better if that made Rauscha uneasy.

Tibor Rauscha buzzed his wife Fanny. Franklin stood wondering if he would ever want to live in a house so big that intercoms were required.

"You free?" Rauscha said.

As they waited for Fanny to come upstairs Rauscha remarked to Franklin, "Have a seat."

"I'm good," Franklin said the same way Eugene said it.

"He's a funny kid, you know?"

"Lots of people are funny at 15." They both meant funny

peculiar.

"I guess," said Tibor Rauscha. "So you don't think he needs a change of scenery like the judge suggested?"

"Did the judge suggest that?"

"Just that sometimes I worry."

"Baloney," Franklin reflected.

Fanny appeared then. Like everyone who met Fanny for the first time Franklin Dell was struck by her loveliness. That was the word that went off in his head: loveliness. Pendant from her ears and peeking through her braids were sterling silver doves, tiny as could be.

"Thank you for making time for me this morning, Mrs. Rauscha."

"I go by my maiden name," said Fanny.

"Since when?" asked Tibor Rauscha. Franklin took him in.

"I started again."

Fanny did not volunteer her maiden name. Franklin did not perceive any meaning in that. He asked himself if he did and he did not.

"Can we sit and talk somewhere?" Franklin asked Fanny.

"Are you telling me to disappear again?" Rauscha asked.

"It's how we do it." Franklin smiled. Rauscha was being reminded again that right that minute he was not in charge in his own home.

Franklin and Fanny sat out by the blue pool behind the big house. By then the sun was directly overhead. The shimmer on the water was murder on Franklin's pale blue eyes.

"If I put on my moviestar glasses will it bother you?" Franklin asked Fanny. "I promise I'm not trying to look intimidating."

"Do what you need to do," Fanny told him. "You don't look intimidating."

"You're hurting my feelings."

"Is our ice broken?" Fanny asked.

"How would you say Eugene is doing?"

"Now?"

"Ever. Before now. Whenever you like."

"Before," Fanny told Franklin, "Eugene was always quiet. I'm not saying like a disturbed person. He did not manifest that."

"What's your relationship with him? Sometimes I know it's tough being a stepmother." Franklin knew nothing at all about being a stepmother except what he had heard. But he meant to give Fanny an opening.

Fanny took the bait.

"Distant," she said. "That's what I'd say. It is distant."

"I don't follow."

"It's a commonplace. My relationship with Eugene is distant. You asked. Are you thinking it would have made a difference to the way he turned out?"

"I have no idea. Judgments like that I do not make." All day long people make judgments like that. Franklin Dell was no exception.

Fanny played with a turquoise-tinted braid beside her ear. Franklin could see she was thinking him over. He liked having a reason to look at her face.

"I'm someone who prides herself on doing the right thing," said Fanny. "Inside myself I boast about it. Where Eugene is concerned I have to admit that I struggle."

Franklin was trained to stay silent and let the other

person fill awkward pauses. AJ taught him that. That approach would draw more out of Fanny than asking the obvious question, "Struggle with what?"

"Partly you're right," Fanny told him. "Being a stepmother is one of the hurdles. Life is not a cobblestone path anyway, and I understand about children, believe me. But Eugene… I don't know about him. He *radiates*. You think that?"

"Radiates what?"

"Unease. Unhappiness. Spiritual malaise. I'll tell you what else too," Fanny added, "he scares Tibor. I can't talk Tibor out of his convictions about Eugene."

"How much time does he spend with his birth mother?"

"Eugene?"

"Of course."

"It's supposed to be part of every weekend."

"How are you meaning 'supposed to be'?"

"Carol calls up busy a lot. She must think we're blind to her patterns. But we are not."

"Does Mrs. Peña travel for her work?"

"Her name you've got?"

"It's in my paperwork. Yours is not."

"Because I'm stepmother to Eugene."

"For whatever reason."

"Carol doesn't work at all. She did well in the divorce. If you were asking me she should work though. Having something to do she would be happier in her life. Did you meet her too?"

"Someone else is." No one else was.

"After all this how do you think Eugene's going to make out?"

"In his future?"

Franklin nodded.

"The answers are several," Fanny replied. "They always are probably, right? But I'd say not so well, if I'm honest. Everyone can turn their life around—in theory. But how often to you see that in your work?"

"About half the time."

"That often?"

"If I'm guessing."

"Well, I don't think Eugene gets out of his hole he's in."

"He's only a kid," said Franklin Dell.

"But imagine carrying the memory of what he did to the girl next door all through his whole life. No one could put distance between themselves and a thing like that. No one. It will crowd his whole manhood. It would take an awful lot of—I don't even know what it would take. Not even philosophy."

"Help?"

"Touché if that was your intention," Fanny answered. "Tibor's got his hands full. All I was saying is that."

"How has he done managing that situation would you say?"

"This time you mean Tibor?"

"Yes."

"To judge by the result less than adequate. To date. If I'm being direct."

"Do you play a role?"

"Eugene's not my son. I keep peace in the family. If you've ever lived in a family you'd know that's not nothing."

Franklin stood up and thanked Fanny for her time.

"You're going?"

"Yes, ma'am. And thank you very much. If it's alright," Franklin added, "I'll disappear around the side the house to my car. No need disturbing the house any more than I have already."

Fanny shook Franklin's hand without replying. Franklin thought about that as he went around by the Staufer side of the house to his patrol car. He noticed the car had spray all over the driver's side from the splashing fountain. Franklin had a good eye for noticing.

From his upstairs window Tibor Rauscha watched Franklin leaving. He took the steps down three at a time to catch Franklin before he could pull away.

"Are you done? Aren't you talking to me?" Rauscha was smiling as if he were indifferent. But Franklin saw he was out of breath.

"No need, sir. I have the interview you conducted with Chief McOlmec. Goodbye, sir. And thank you."

Rauscha would later claim that this was rudeness.

Rudeness was the least on a list of complaints Tibor Rauscha had about Franklin Dell's visit to Nine Mezcaleros Road that day. Top of the list was that Franklin did not recommend that Eugene be moved into the home of his mother, Carol Peña.

> *"I observed indifference to the boy. From either his father or his father's second wife Eugene is in no physical danger. It is not a good situation. Eugene did not complain of mistreatment in the home."*

This was meant to be a recommendation.

Among Tibor Rauscha's complaints was that Franklin put his assessment on the record, and so bluntly that later there was no room for maneuver. Subsequently a social worker who visited said more or less the same about Eugene and his family.

Tibor Rauscha's fury was obvious in his silence. McOlmec never heard from him man-to-man ever again. Rauscha's annual checks to the police pension funds stopped. There was no tapering off. The checks just stopped. Within the police-force family opinion about Franklin Dell went ice cold.

Franklin was shunned. No one wanted to ride with him. Franklin went back on nights. Once again he was the steady partner of AJ Munoz.

In the family of cops AJ was the peacekeeper; Fanny was right: that is not nothing. A year later it was AJ who insisted that Franklin be invited to the Memorial Day picnic, the one to which Franklin Dell brought Katherine Moliere.

Life is just full of these consequential coincidences.

Texas And Its Customs

Most days Moliere was in school by 7 AM to prepare for the day and to savor the quiet. School began at 8 AM and Moliere liked that time too. She loved the noise of a hallway jammed with children, the moment when their day was all prospect and there was nothing to be afraid of yet.

At lunchtime Moliere did a circuit of her students in the cafeteria. She found their company more entertaining than that of the adults she worked with. The kids were sweet and vied to tell her things; it was a kind of flirting. Anyway the teacher's breakroom was deplorable. It was walled off from the cafeteria with nothing but plywood paneling painted a faux mahogany color. The cafeteria noise was somehow worse inside of this improvised room than out.

At the end of the day Moliere liked the stillness after all the kids were gone and the custodian was buffing the linoleum out in the hall. She worked on her lesson plan for the next day.

After Franklin died Moliere fought off everyone who told her to take a rest from work. She knew she would lose her mind without it. Never mind that teachers and kids all looked her way when she passed. No one knew how to mourn with her properly.

Their awkwardness was only human. Moliere understood.

Now it was the Monday before BooBash, her school's annual Halloween event. Pasted up and down the hallways were posters the kids made advertising BooBash on the following Saturday night. Black-hatted witches, leering pumpkins, sociable ghosts; people need to mock death and pass this need to their kids. It is a healthy thing.

The majority of the teachers at Emma Tenayuca Middle School went to BooBash. Moliere was among the teachers who dressed up. That year she was planning to go as Morticia Addams. She had the black dress and the pancake makeup to make herself look dead.

Moliere was alone in her classroom that Monday afternoon when her phone vibrated. There was a text from Fanny.

Still feel bad about that night I visited you (yes, un-invited!). Would love a chance talk. Do coffee? Ping me back. Please. It may help. F(anny)

Less than a minute later Moliere's phone buzzed again with another text from Fanny.

Sorry to be out of touch. Tibor's blown over it. He has psychotic breaks. Apologies for bothering you (but you still need my help!)

None of the grief and foolishness that followed would have occurred to Moliere if Franklin had still been alive. "I can tell when people are nuts," he told her the first night they met. But Franklin was dead. Moliere texted Fanny

Why do I need your help?

After school Fanny replied to Moliere's text with a phone call. To her later regret Moliere answered. Instantly Fanny was chatting away like an old friend. She asked Moliere to come over to the house on Nine Mezcaleros Road.

"I'm still at work," Moliere told her. "Can we meet another day?"

They met the following Wednesday in the late afternoon at Java Caliente, a coffee place at the further end of Fuller Boulevard. Even against the norm of that insipid strip the café was an anonymous place, almost mystic in its facelessness. It would have made an excellent spot for kidnappers picking up a ransom. At 5.30 in the afternoon hardly anyone was in the place. The light in the sky was beginning to go. It was mid-October.

Moliere and Fanny arrived at the same time; someone watching would have thought it was planned. They walked in together.

"Did anyone follow you?" Fanny asked. She wore a long, belted cardigan that was raspberry colored. She wore leggings that drew attention to her birdlike legs. Those legs looked fragile.

"Why would anyone follow me?"

"You can't ever know. I don't want those rumors about our lesbian love to get around town. I've got family here."

"You're joking."

"Yes, I'm joking. We need to get to know each other better, Katherine." Today Fanny was wearing a knitted red cap to crown her braids; it clashed with the raspberry cardigan but was alright; Moliere was certainty no fashion trendsetter either. She noticed that Fanny's hair was shorter than it was that night she invaded the house. It hung only midway down her back now. Although Moliere was not a lesbian she was still struck by what she could not help calling the prettiness of Fanny's face.

Only one other person was in this place, a not-so-young-anymore blond man with a pink face and dreadlocks tighter than Fanny's.

"Get a load of that guy," said Fanny under her breath. "I should ask him where he goes. What do you do with your hair, Katherine? I like it."

"Never mind about my hair."

"I'm just saying we both have African blood. I know that from reading Tibor's file on you on the way over to your house last week. Your father's Haitian. Under our skins we're sisters."

"Please stop. Why did you want to see me?"

"I think that blond guy is watching us. This time I'm not joking."

Moliere had her coffee light, no sugar. Fanny got a thing with almond-flavored syrup in it that was more milkshake than coffee. They sat as far away from the man with the dreadlocks as they could. They were near the ladies' room and the smell of disinfectant competed with the aroma of coffee.

"Where are you from, Katherine?"

"Why do you ask? Wasn't it in my folder?"

"No. I looked. And I left the folder with you. As you'll recall."

"Then ask your husband."

"Don't be mad. If you like I'll tell you where I grew up."

Fanny sipped her coffee. Moliere could smell its heavy sweetness. A voice from within the kitchen said kind of loudly, "That is not a hat, Erin."

"I grew up in Hay Agua. Have you ever been there?"

"No."

"It's out where the buses don't run."

"People walk?"

"I used an expression. It means it's nowhere."

"I may have driven through it on my way to New Mexico."

"That is more than it deserves. Eleven hundred people, half of them dark like my family and most of them doing OK. These ugly six lanes of traffic," Fanny said, nodding toward Fuller Boulevard, "used to seem so glamorous to me when my mother brought me into town to shop at the mall. When I was a teenager it looked like Times Square—you know, in New York? To me. Being in town used to lift my spirit. Now you drive around here and it's nothing but broken asphalts and whatnot. I went with my mother's church to Port-au-Prince one time," Fanny said more to herself than to Katherine. "Fuller Boulevard looks like the roads there."

Looking through the big plate glass window of Java Caliente Fanny became reflective.

"Something's left me now, Katherine," she said. "There's no joy anymore. There's just Texas." Fanny sat back in her chair and smiled the smile of resignation. "And that is why we are here."

"Why are we talking about this? You said you had something to tell me."

Moliere noticed a coffee-colored hearing aid in Fanny's left ear. Fanny was so beautiful she seemed beyond physical frailty. Discovering that Fanny was hard of hearing made Moliere soften toward her, marginally.

"I do have something to tell you," Fanny said. She set down her tall paper cup on the table portentously.

"Then what is it?"

"Step by step my life has gone screwball."

"What did you want to talk about to me, I meant."

"I am angry at Tibor for being an ass about you."

"That's it?"

"I'm used to being angry at Tibor for being an ass," Fanny said. "But I always get over it. The course of true love. Tell you the truth, Katherine, the other night I was much angrier at you for treating me like a burglar. You probably called the police as soon as I left—'A tiny Black woman broke into my house!' They didn't follow up, did they?"

"Wrong."

"Really? And what did they do for you?"

"Why am I here?"

"I have a way for you to get back at Tibor."

"I don't want to get back at him." This was true but only superficially.

"You do. Look into your heart, Katherine."

"What I don't understand is why he feels a need to get back at me. Even four years ago it was such a small thing. Relatively small. And he's such a big man now. Why would he waste the energy?"

"One reason is that I honestly think Tibor finds *pleasure* in nursing a grudge. It's in his psychology." Fanny tapped her head to indicate *psychology*. "You showed him up," said Fanny. "Men don't like to be shown up. It's their psychology. I repeat."

"If he was going to make trouble for me then why hasn't he?" Moliere did not like to think about what Rauscha's idea of "trouble" for her might look like.

"Tibor has to keep up a façade of law-abiding. He is law abiding, technically, but with him everything is about appearances. That is where he thinks his moral authority resides."

"How long have you known him?"

"Four years. I've been married to him for three. I'm wife number two but I believe I'm about to be terminated."

"What does that mean—'terminated'? Fired?"

"Put away, as the bible says. Or set aside, I forget which. We married after he had his set-to with you. I don't believe there was a connection between the two events, so don't think that."

"Then you didn't have to bring it up."

"The wedding was in my mother's church and all of it. Tibor *meant* it, you know?"

"What does it matter if it was in a church?" Katherine was thinking about her plans with Franklin to be married in the open-air pavilion at a Tres Rocas Park.

"Tibor will tell you he's religious," Fanny replied. "He even built a chapel in that big barn we call home. He paid some guy a fortune to make a mosaic on the wall. The Virgin of Guadalupe. I said, 'Tibor, you're not Catholic.' But he told me that whenever he needed to speak with God he wanted to be able. He is so spiritually mixed up."

"Why do you think you're about to be put away?"

"When you two had your set-to..."

"Please don't call it a set-to. That implies that I was somehow equally the cause."

"At that time Tibor was already separated from the wife. I'm no homewrecker if that is where your thoughts are going."

"My thoughts aren't going anywhere."

"At the time the first wife—her name is Carol, and I'm getting to her—she did not want custody of their son Eugene. Which the court assumed she would want because she's a woman. But times have changed, Katherine. Carol was hoping Tibor would fight for custody. That way when Carol surrendered to what she wanted anyway it would bump up her payday. They were playing chicken with the kid—can you imagine?"

"I don't have to imagine. I'm a public-school teacher."

"But Tibor wouldn't bite. So finally, Carol went to the judge and told him she was emotionally unsuited."

"And Tibor is suited?" Moliere noticed that she had called this man by his first name.

"Not on your life he is suited."

Moliere sipped at her own coffee, which she was pleased to find was pretty good. She was not expecting much from this place. There was a freshness to the coffee's taste that made her think of Christmas morning, good Christmases, the kind she had before Franklin died.

"Tibor ignores Eugene like he's not even there," Fanny was saying. She fondled a braid that escaped from her cap. She played it in her hand as if it were a jewel. "Tibor hardly notices that the kid spends all his time locked in his room upstairs like Mrs. Dalloway."

"Who?"

"From *Jane Eyre*?"

"It doesn't matter. You were talking about the little boy."

"The 'little boy' as you call him is now almost 15 years old. He's a fat little thing, thanks to Tibor. You can see I don't like him any better than his parents do, but let's face facts. He is not my son and he is not my job."

"Points for honesty, anyway."

"Eugene spends all his free time in his room watching porn and playing with himself. I assume. Especially since he raped that poor little retarded girl. You recall that two years ago?"

"I remember it happened," said Moliere. "But I don't associate it with Rauscha."

"That's the way Tibor wanted it. See? That's how he wins." Moliere was thinking Rauscha fascinated Fanny, no matter what she claimed otherwise. Moliere was not so fascinated. Rauscha sounded awful.

"It was all about Tibor, you know?" Fanny was saying. This diatribe was becoming a voyage of discovery for her. "It was all about how Eugene made him look. He tried to pay the girl's father to settle and keep it out of the news. But the father wouldn't take money. Which pissed Tibor off, let me tell you. Excuse my language. Tibor thinks everyone wants money. Tibor probably keeps a folder on that guy too. Tibor's so petulant."

"Didn't anything happen to Eugene?"

"Plan B when Carol wouldn't take him was to make Eugene confess everything and hope people would move on to the next local scandal—which judging from your personal amnesia they did."

"Don't accuse me of amnesia."

"Because of his age Eugene got probation. Tibor also hired that psychologist from the radio show in El Paso—Janice Krug? She told the court that the girl's brain injury acted as protection because it kept her from ruminating on what had happened to her. So that way she wouldn't get depressed about it, so neither should anyone else. Psychology again."

"I don't mean to be rude, Fanny, but can you get to your point and tell me why you asked me here."

"Well, I'll tell you, Katherine. And thank you for calling me 'Fanny'. Tibor and Eugene are supposed to go for monthly visits to a shrink. But the shrink is once again someone Tibor hired himself, so half the time Tibor manages to be out of town for the appointments and she lets him slide. She even comes to dinner sometimes instead of meeting them at her office. She likes coming to the house, apparently. I guess she's got so little of interest in her life; you should see this person. Eugene never comes downstairs when she comes by, and Tibor won't make him. The three of them sit on the stairs until an hour goes by, then the social worker and Tibor have dinner."

"Again, why are you telling me all this?"

"You seem like someone who is interested in children."

"Are you trying to be funny?"

"I need your help, Katherine. I have a plan to bring Eugene home to his mother to live. It's that poor woman's chance at redemption."

"You're speaking gibberish."

"You should see the way she lives, Katherine. Like a discarded person. But Eugene needs a chance, too. I really believe that."

"I don't follow you. You're giving Tibor what he wants. And sending Eugene to the house of a disordered person."

"I said 'discarded'. Anyway, not anymore he doesn't want it. The court won't allow…"

"And what does it have to do with me?"

"After I came home the other night he told me about your fiancée. I didn't know about that. I'm so sorry."

"Stop that." Privately, Moliere believed strongly in revenge if the opportunity presented itself.

"Then call it justice."

"Are you on the level?" "On the level" was a favorite expression of Moliere's father. Moliere always believed it was his first American colloquialism.

"I can't do anything with Eugene, Katherine. And Tibor won't. I told Carol about you, and I told her how you stood up for Eugene that time. Carol said she would take parenting tips from you any day."

"I don't believe you."

"It's true anyhow. I should also tell you that Carol's feelings are easily hurt. Not just by Tibor but by anyone. But

Tibor's a man so the context is different."

"A moment ago you made Eugene's mother sound like a shrew."

"Carol's repented. This is the point I've been making."

"Works out nicely for you."

"Yes, I'd like to see Eugene out of our house. But what *I'd* like doesn't matter. Staying there in that house is killing Eugene. Day after day it's erasing any possibility he has of living any kind of a life. And having Eugene there makes Tibor irascible."

Fanny let that idea hang in the air, the idea that there was redemption available for Eugene after doing something so terrible.

Moliere did not buy it.

"I don't believe your concern for Eugene and my distaste for Rauscha both only just occurred to you."

"The second part did. The first part's been brewing."

"This is nothing to do with me."

"On the way home the other night I thought to myself, Katherine came to Eugene's rescue once before, and now she can rescue him again. It's almost like something in a movie."

"Where's the mother now?"

"Carol still lives in Perros Salvajes County. As part of the divorce she made Tibor buy her a house in the Dry Canyons development. Once you meet her she is honestly not that bad, maybe a little remote."

"You're not making the case."

"In all candor, Katherine, between us I think Carol's afraid Tibor will monkey with the alimony arrangement if she rocks the boat. If you stick up for Eugene that alters the equation."

"I don't see how. What do you mean by 'stuck up'?"

Another pause and another deep look from Fanny's rich brown eyes. They reminded Moliere of horse chestnuts. Moliere was not a lesbian but she thought Fanny had spellbinding eyes.

"I'm aware of how preposterous this is, Katherine. But I don't know where else to get support. If you say no I'm not going to cry about it. But please accompany Eugene and me to Carol's house next Saturday evening. It will buck us all up. Even you—who knows? That last point is the one I've been struggling to make, and I'm just being honest."

"Next Saturday is Halloween."

Fanny smiled. "Are you going trick-or-treating?"

"There's a party at my school. I'm on the list to help out."

Fanny looked at Moliere cockeyed. "Are you kidding me?"

"No, it's part of my job to go." It really was. The Emma Tenayuca school was being starved of budget by the state and the county, and the Halloween event was its biggest fundraiser of the year after the spring carnival. Moliere used to have an image in her head of all the teachers grabbing the kids as they came in through the fire doors and holding them upside down until their pocket money shook out.

Fanny let go of a defeated sigh.

"I'll tell you the truth, Katherine."

"That's a phrase of yours."

"It might be. But my time's up. Tibor's not meant for the day-to-day of marriage. Not that I'm some paragon. But at least I'm around, I'm the willing partner. But I can tell Tibor's made up his mind. That's how I found the folder about you the other night, because I was looking for the name of his lawyer."

"You told me you were looking for his check book."

"For a successful man in this modern day it's surprising how much Tibor keeps on paper. If he ever tries anything big it'll be his undoing."

The next day Tibor Rauscha took a trip.

Fanny was operating under a misconception. Tibor Rauscha was not planning on putting her away. If only she had asked him. He would have wondered where she got any such idea. Comedy relies on misunderstanding to set its plots in motion.

The night they chased around the big house like a couple of cats—the chase that followed Fanny's discovery of the file on Katherine Moliere—Fanny placed the wrong emphasis on her husband's action. She extracted the wrong meaning. Rauscha thought Fanny had wearied of him and was searching his desk to build a picture of his assets. He had been divorced once and he knew how the whole thing worked.

The same as he ever had Rauscha wanted Fanny in ways he owned no words for. He was fearful of speaking all he felt. Sometimes awareness of that fear left him feeling nearly humiliated. Rauscha had that much self-knowledge at least.

After four years together Rauscha still felt the ache that is beyond sexual hunger when he looked at Fanny. He felt the ache he once assumed Carol had destroyed in him. Even after everything fell apart Tibor Rauscha nourished the ache. He needed it.

Tibor Rauscha went to the airport almost once a week but seldom ever went into El Paso proper. He never thought at all about what went on there. The immigrants at the border, day and night, babies crying, parents crying, nonstop misery, volunteers with guns. The years of the pandemic only convinced him that he had been right the whole time about El Paso. When the mayor asked citizens to wear a paper mask Rauscha stayed home, a kind of protest. Seven days a week he got on Fanny's nerves.

"Wear a mask and go out in the world," she said.

"I can't breathe under a mask."

"And I can't imagine if some men got their periods," Fanny replied.

El Paso in the pandemic time got worse and worse. There were pictures on CNN of refrigerator trucks for the overflow of bodies from the hospitals. When Fanny discussed the news at dinner it made Rauscha angry. He said he did not want these events invading his house.

One evening a cop from the El Paso Police Department arrested a Black man watering his own front garden. (The homeowner was wearing a mask, the policeman was not.) That was a one-day story. Another evening a guy shot a midnight burglar in the alley out behind his house. The man went back to bed without calling police, just left the guy lying there for a neighbor to find.

A month after that a high-school girl running from an angry boyfriend tried to hide in the Chihuahuan Desert close to the border. The boyfriend caught her and struck her head with a rock. Male rage unmediated. The girl was killed. All of it was within a ten-mile circle of Rauscha's house.

Rauscha heard these things, he did not hear them. They were nothing to do with him.

For most people the effort of turning their eyes away from the unremitting anguish was exhausting. Not for Rauscha. He had hardly been downtown in nearly 14 years. When 46 people were shot while shopping in a store Rauscha took note—it was hard not to take note—but he knew to keep moving.

What had nearly all Rauscha's interest at that time was a vacant property in Déchets, Louisiana. It was a failed office park, only ten years old. On the day after Fanny met Moliere for coffee Rauscha flew to Houston. From there he was headed to Lake Charles to talk over a purchase price with the current owner. He thought he might like to be a developer. That would be a branching out for him.

According to what he would later tell a political acquaintance, Texas state legislator Andy DiNapoli, Rauscha was in a good mood that day. Driving to El Paso International that morning he got news from his lawyer, DeLorean Mueller, that the Louisiana Department of Environmental Quality was giving RauschaTech a waiver to buy a seven-acre property north and west of Lake Charles. That deal had been ready for nearly a year but was held up by the DEQ. A waiver was needed because the place had been home to a machine shop for 45 years. For most of those years their practice had been to pitch everything from solvents to metallic mercury right out the back door—literally in pails. It was hard on the groundwater. God only knows what it was doing to the crew.

"You called their bluff, Tibor," Andy said. "All that noise about making the property a super-fund site, in which case you'd have walked away—right? Which is what I told the governor's people. He didn't need the headache."

"The land I don't care about so much,"Tibor told him. "I want the empty buildings on top of it. From what DeLorean tells me, the waiver is a promise—a written promise—indemnifying me and my heirs from liability. But I haven't seen it yet."

"Let's hope the next guy keeps the promise," Andy said. "Stay close to me, Tibor."

Rauscha and Andy were partners of a kind. Both kept a specific distance from the other. On Andy's part he was put off by what he imagined was a definite smell of herring in Rauscha's aura. That is not being metaphorical. Herring is what Rauscha smelled like, slightly. Fanny had commented.

"I need to establish who will be my heirs," Rauscha said.

"Your son, yes? And your lawful wedded wife?"

"Fanny, yeah. She has more brains than I ever will. She virtually runs the company now but for deal making."

Andy did not press the point about Eugene. He was aware of Tibor's feelings for his son. They could not even be described as mixed. To a family man like Andy this was a shocking thing. It was also none of his business.

"Maybe before it gets to be too late for Fanny you could have a baby or two more. You'd have more heirs. Cover your bets, you know?"

"That is like buying lottery tickets."

"Children are a gamble, Tibor. No question."

Tibor once told Andy that he wondered if he had forgotten to want sex before he met Fanny. For babies you need sex; this is well established.

"The first year," he told Fanny, "I literally shivered each time I saw her naked. Never have I felt such want in my life. I worry that it might be gone."

"That is just the intimacy. The first year of marriage brings a lot of changes, Tibor. One more thing everybody should know about."

But flying to Lake Charles that Thursday morning Rauscha was in a good mood.

Rauscha happened to know through a new friend on the commerce committee of the Louisiana House of Representatives that the developers of the office park were more eager to get the ghost park off their hands than they might let on. They pretended otherwise when Rauscha met them in Lake Charles, but it seemed they could be moved. The lunch was worth what amounted to a two-day trip.

Before going back to Perros Salvajes Rauscha was flying up for the weekend to a Republican Party conference in Dallas at the Rosewood Mansion.

While Tibor was in Louisiana Fanny was sitting at her desk in her office on the first floor of the house. In the house she never wore the knitted caps under which she tucked her braids when she went out into the world. Her beautiful braids just fell about her face and shoulders.

Fanny had just hung up on a cleaning contractor. It was the one RauschaTech used at its two facilities in northern Indiana. The guy told Fanny that her husband texted him overnight wanting to know how many of his crew were women.

"The short answer is I don't know," the guy told Fanny. He had a not-entirely-American accent she could not place—what would an Albanian sound like? Where is Albania?

"I contract with another businessman," said this guy, "and he finds people. They don't really work for me. He pays them. I just get them work."

"So why don't you ask your contractor?"

"I've got a call in. I'm telephoning *you* because if my guy asks why do you need to know what do I tell him?"

I don't need to know, Fanny thought. And I don't know why Tibor needs to know. What she replied was, "We're doing a general review of our FOIA compliance. Tibor used to be in the cleaning business too. I'm sure you know all about it."

The man on the telephone paused.

"I don't know what that is."

"It's a business thing."

"I'll get a number for you later today or tomorrow. They're almost all women. That much I can say without asking. I send the information to Tibor?"

"Send it to me."

Fanny hung up. Why was Tibor bothering this guy with such a question? How did he even have the phone number for a contractor? What was Tibor up to?

That last question Fanny asked herself a lot lately.

The whole time she knew him Fanny had the feeling Tibor Rauscha was up to something. And this was not always to do with money either. What it was to do with she could not always put her finger on.

Rauscha was on the road until Sunday afternoon. Most weeks he was gone at least two nights. His absence did not make Fanny's heart grow fonder but the breathing room was good for their living together. Until Eugene got home from his special school Fanny could be all alone in the house drinking coffee, microwaving burritos and working.

Fanny's second call was a voicemail to a college kid who did odd jobs for her. She offered him $100 to stand at the foot of the driveway on Saturday night, Halloween, and hand out candy. She did not want children anywhere near the house. It was such a big house set back from the road and away from streetlight that it was easy to imagine kids making up stories about it on Halloween. Fanny did not want that.

On the other side of the closed door behind her was the sound of the cleaning women moving through the house. Vacuuming, mopping, making beds, emptying the family's trash. In between the days when the girls came dishes piled up in the sink once the dishwasher was full. Fanny, Rauscha and Eugene almost never ate at the same time. When they did it was stuff taken out of the freezer—pizzas and other whatnot.

The girls worked for a middle-aged Mexican woman named Mariana. Fanny had forgotten Mariana's surname. Mariana asked $2,200 a month for her girls to come three days a week. Fanny thought that a bargain and she billed it to RauschaTech; the IRS has never called her on it, and if they ever did she would plead ignorance and pay whatever she would have owed in the first place. Once or twice Fanny wondered how the cash was distributed among the four women working for Mariana. Since nobody seemed to be complaining she left it at that.

Fanny liked the sound of the women's conversation as they worked, their Mexican Spanish almost like singing to her uninstructed ears.

Fanny's office was as much of a physical headquarters as RauschaTech had. Notwithstanding the word "tech" in the company's name two thirds of the business was managing a real-estate portfolio—paying the light bill and the other expenses associated with running the properties. Technology support was outsourced to a constellation of contractors across the country. So was payroll, building maintenance and legal counsel (chiefly DeLorean Mueller, who somehow got Rauscha to agree to a retainer *and* billable hours back when. Fanny was wanting to change this. There were plenty of lawyers in this world, she told Tibor. DeLorean should be reminded of that.)

Even before Fanny came along Tibor wanted an enterprise that could be assembled or taken apart with the rise and fall of demand. That is the way Fanny ran things. RauschaTech's total full-time payroll was 43 people, Fanny and Rauscha included.

In their big house Fanny's office was as far from Tibor's as it was possible to be. There was no significance in that, only that Fanny liked the view out the window past the Jerusalem thorn trees Rauscha planted around the far line of the property. The purpose of the trees was to block the view of the solar array he installed out there. (The solar panels were an old technology and contributed almost nothing to powering the house, but they supported RauschaTech's brand as an alternative-energy concern if someone should ever happen to notice them, though they would have to fly over the house to do so.) In mid-winter when the late-day angle of the sun was low the trees glared red in a spectral way. Immediately beyond the trees the desert began. The abrupt transition to empty space played a two-dimensional trick on the eye that Fanny never tired of.

Fanny's eyes lifted up to the desert. It was stony and stark. Here and there was vegetation that made her think of a bald man getting hair plugs and hoping they would propagate. Now that autumn had come some of the cactus nearest the house was turning a subtle yellow out there. The desert looked empty but lots went on. Not long before INS or somebody were out there looking for migrants. Horses, helicopters and drones. Fanny could see them from her house half a mile away. If there were migrants out there no one found them, not as far as she heard.

Why was Tibor phoning that guy in Indiana?

Fanny was not exactly in a reverie but just the same she was irritated when Mariana knocked on the office door.

"Come in."

"Fanny," Mariana said, pronouncing the name "fenny" though she spoke excellent English. "We have our problem."

"What's our problem?"

"Ven equoí," said Mariana in a raised voice. A young woman stepped into the frame of the door. She was dark-skinned, though not the way Fanny was dark-skinned. All the girls looked like Marianna, all on the verge of growing fat like her. This one seemed like she might be about to cry.

"This teta broke your trophy in a million pieces while she was cleaning your bedroom," Mariana said. Fanny saw that the woman behind Mariana was holding the shards of a china cup with a Southern Methodist logo on it; Mariana had made her collect the pieces and bring them to Fanny. Fanny kept the cup beside her bed for pens and stray bits. Or used to keep it. She had no attachment to this thing; she was not sentimental about her four years at SMU. But if it would prove her fealty to Fanny then Mariana was clearly prepared to fire this girl on the spot.

"Accidents happen," Fanny told her. "Please don't worry

about it."

"Pedir disculpas a la señora!" Mariana commanded.

"Pido disculpas. Por favor, perdónne." The girl looked about to come kiss Fanny's hand, and with good reason. Whatever Mariana was paying her was probably supporting several other people. And whatever employer she met next might ask more questions about her immigration status than Mariana. Mariana probably had that woman by the throat.

"It is nothing," Fanny told them both. "Nada. Forget it."

"Tienes suerte esta vez," Mariana told the girl. "Volter altra bajo." The young woman went away relieved. Unless it had all been a con produced by Mariana for some reason that would play out later. Which Fanny thought was a possibility.

Mariana lingered in the doorway.

"Something else?" Fanny asked her.

"When we took the sheets off your son's bed," said Mariana, "we found they were cut up in strips. Like ribbons. Should we wash them anyway?"

"Yes." Fanny flinched at the suggestion that Eugene was her son; what a misconception. Had she been paying the cleaning women directly Fanny would have offered a pay differential for cleaning Eugene's room.

"They look like they were taken with a knife."

"Wash them anyway and put them back on his bed. Thanks."

Fanny had meant to sound abrupt. She wished to be left alone. She was never more than polite to Mariana anyway, and just the same Mariana liked her.

Maybe that was only in comparison to how much Mariana *dis*liked Tibor Rauscha. Fanny could tell she did, even if she could not have said why. If Fanny had a theory about this it was that Rauscha and Mariana shared Mexican roots, although he was only half Mexican on his mother's side. But since he had gotten so much wealthier he was in Mariana's eyes a jumped-up anglo.

Say this much for Rauscha: He knew what he had in Fanny.

RauschaTech hired Fanny for her first full-time job when she was a brand-new computer-sciences major out of SMU. It was not Tibor who hired her but the search firm RauschaTech employed to contract technical support. RauschaTech was just beginning to grow a national profile at the time, even if owing to the force of history its center of gravity remained West Texas.

Fanny stayed with that job long after she should have left it. A teenager with sufficient geekiness could have done what she did. The only reason she stayed was her attachment to Perros Salvajes, or more precisely to the fact that her mother Judy lived on the edge of the county. That was the main thing.

When at long last Fanny was given something interesting to do it was to manage a forklift upgrade of the servers at the McAllen facility. They were replacing old Oracle servers, roughly half an acre of SPARC T3-1s. Fanny's job was to manage the porting of client data to the new servers. One day she happened to ask the facilities manager what was happening to the old machines.

"Nothing's happening to them," he said. "We pay Mexicans to take out the hard drives and shoot them with a nail gun. They think it's hilarious. Don't worry, dear. The client data is safe, if that's worrying you."

That was not what worried Fanny. She personally wiped every hard drive herself before pronouncing a machine dead.

Fanny was no crusader but it pissed her off that all the nastiness built into those old servers—lead, bromine, PVC, lithium, *arsenic* for God's sake—was percolating from some dump somewhere into the shallow Ogallala Aquifer. Out of an abundance of youth she FedExed a three-page letter to the house on the Nine Mezcaleros Road where Rauscha was still sharing a bed with Carol. (Fanny would later insist on a new bed.)

Rauscha's first reaction to Fanny's letter was that she was shaking him down. He was mistaken.

"She is in earnest for some reason, Tibor," DeLorean told him. "I talked to her and I asked."

"Do we need to?" Rauscha asked.

"Yes, or technically."

Rauscha, still suspecting a con, gave in. He even had the smart idea of issuing a press release about how RauschaTech contracted with a Mexican "extraction recycler" to recover the hazardous materials in the old servers. God knows what they did with the materials that were "recovered". Doing what the law required the company to do anyhow added to RauschaTech's green reputation. It was like the solar panels on the roofs of the company's server farms. A gesture.

Just to be on the safe side DeLorean suggested to Rauscha that the company also hire Fanny fulltime.

"That way she's compromised," DeLorean explained.

Not three months later Rauscha visited McAllen for a photo op with the new servers arrayed behind him. That was the first time he laid eyes on Fanny. She noted the surprise in his face. Rauscha already knew she was a girl. But a small, beautiful girl no one thought to mention.

Tibor Rauscha's heart knew much delight.

Things progressed. It took two years but they progressed. The pursuit had to be all on Rauscha's side; as Fanny later told Moliere, she was no home wrecker. Before Fanny would agree to be all on board she wanted the divorce from Carol final. She was not negotiating. (If she had been negotiating this would have been the right way to go about it.)

That was three years ago. Carol was out, Fanny was in. And for the time being Fanny ran RauschaTech.

From the beginning Fanny was conscious that Rauscha's associates took in the fact of her—Black, talkative, young, beautiful, then back to Black again. These associates believed they knew what Rauscha saw in her. They were wrong, and Fanny made them know it. She had an engineer's temperament, and every word she said was exclusive of anything that was not solution-related. This is a style that can rub some people the wrong way. Being female and Black at the same time did not help.

Fanny liked this.

Married to Rauscha Fanny did not work for free. RauschaTech paid her $240,000 a year to be a senior partner (which made a total of two senior partners). In addition, she was paid 10 percent of the company's pre-tax earnings. Fanny got a lawyer of her own to work out that deal with DeLorean Mueller. Rauscha was surprised by this but Fanny knew he liked her for it. In a low-overhead business with revenue of $30 million or better, depending on the year, Fanny did not need to stay married to Tibor for material reasons.

After what happened between them the night she found the Moliere file Fanny was not altogether sure she wanted to stay married to Rauscha for any reasons. But another part of her was curious to see what he was going to do. She enjoyed the suspense.

Fanny recalled when she had no trouble at all saying she loved Tibor Rauscha. It was the clarity of his values; that's what it was. He was a middling-looking man, and in the beginning he was enough in awe of Fanny that he was careful with her, which could be called tender. He flattered Fanny in his attention to her. She knew he was a man who focused on only the several things he thought important. Which could be said to resemble virtue.

Fanny was not oblivious to the fact that decent people would have found it odd to call the limited list of things Rauscha wanted "values". All that had mattered at the time she married him was that on his list was (A) herself; and (B) the opportunity he gave her at RauschaTech. There are other definitions of love but those were in the ballpark.

All her life Fanny was waiting for a man like Tibor Rauscha. Because all her life Fanny knew when people looked at her they saw a short Black woman. She went around thinking this, that the world could not get past her gender and her skin color. Her German-Mexican boyfriend did not seem to notice.

In Fanny's high school the Black kids and White kids had lived in tribes. Fanny could not remember one who ever crossed over, not even one. This was not from racial antipathy (though some of the white kids came from whole families mean as snakes). That part of West Texas attracted numbers of retired military, and that trumped demographic differences most of the time. It was like they all knew a secret handshake unavailable to civilians. But Hay Agua had roots as a Texas freedmen's colony (est. 1871) and 150 years later Black people were still the majority. In their loving embrace Fanny felt so sometimes smothered she could not wait to get out.

At SMU it was better. Fanny made white friends but they and she were perpetually conscious of possibly putting their foot wrong. Self-consciousness was there all the time; it made Fanny's college dating life uncommonly earnest. People cannot live like that, on edge all the time. It is unsustainable.

Around Rauscha Fanny felt she could breathe *out* for the first time in her life. Rauscha had a fetish for her nose, not her skin color; he was always going on about her nose. So with him everything felt optimal. Times when Fanny's mother used to visit the pair of them used to giggle in the dark like teenagers about the noise they made. It was the closest Fanny ever came to romance.

No more. Fanny came to see that she was maybe not so young for much longer and that unless something mortal happened to Tibor Rauscha they were going to be together a long time.

Fanny's phone pinged. There was a text from Katherine Moliere.

Help Saturday night I can. At the party until at least 9. Let me know where.

Now Fanny was looking forward to Halloween for the change it might bring.

Texas Trick or Treat

BooBash at the Emma Tenayuca school was the same every year. Haunted house, paper skeletons, fanged bats, blood everywhere. Everybody down to the toddlers in their zombie costumers was in a giddy mood. All the kids gorged on candy. They were drunk on beet sugar. The winner of the costume competition was a student with a chainsaw through his head. It was as if hell had emptied. The kids loved it.

Moliere moved through the chaos dressed as Morticia Addams in a black gown she found at Salvation Army, the skirt down to the floor and her arms in elbow-length black gloves. Her face was made up to look deathly white. She moved through the chaos of the school hallways feeling sort of stately, like the peacefully dead must feel.

Before she met Franklin Moliere did not used to feel single at these things; after he was gone single was all she felt. This was why she felt her body relax when she saw her best friend on the faculty, Allen Luu, who was managing the bedlam at the bouncy house. A *haunted* bouncy house.

Allen had a turban on his head and was handsome as could be. There was a time when Moliere thought Allen had a crush on her. It was just his friendliness.

Allen's fiancé was collecting tickets. The fiancée (whose name Moliere resisted learning (psychology, Fanny would have said but which happened to be Julie) wore some mediaeval looking gown in turquoise with a pretty fringe on it and beads on the bodice. It was not the most unTexas thing imaginable.

"Who are you two supposed to be?" Moliere asked.

"Othello and Desdemona. The kids don't get it, I don't think."

"The allusion is a little advanced for them," Moliere told him. "Also you don't look like a moor." Allen was Vietnamese, maybe the only Vietnamese for 1,500 miles until you got to Galveston, Moliere thought, though she was wrong about that. In a turban Allen looked good.

"I've got a pillow in the car that completes the effect," he said.

"It's brocaded," Julie the fiancée added. The fiancée wore a stomacher that Moliere guessed she made herself because it was also brocaded. Clever with her hands apparently.

"All the kids are giggling at the idea that Mr. Luu brought his girlfriend," Julie said. Somehow Julie was reproving Allen but Moliere could not put her finger on it.

Moliere met Julie twice before. She knew Julie was an adjunct in the English department at UT El Paso (hence the Shakespeare stuff). Without quite putting it this way to herself, Moliere knew Julie was educated above her station. Someday she would bring trouble to Allen.

"Sweet" is what Moliere said about the brocaded pillow.

"We are going to a party after this," Allen said. "Why don't you come with?" Julie the fiancée beamed. Moliere knew Julie was hoping the invitation would be declined.

After Franklin died Allen was kind to Moliere, like everyone else at school. But unlike everyone else he continued keeping his eye on her. Moliere misunderstood Allen's concern as a romantic interest. She was almost disappointed when he turned out to be merely a nice guy.

"I've got a kind of date later," said Moliere to the party invitation. The fiancée's shoulders relaxed.

"Good," said Allen, looking pleased to think Moliere had a fella to take her out for Halloween.

"Not that kind of date. Don't get your hopes up, Othello."

Allen grinned nicely. Then he turned to the fiancé and said, "Oh fay, it waxes late."

"That is from *Romeo and Juliet*, Allen." Moliere actively disliked Julie the fiancé. If Allen was thinking of inviting Moliere to the wedding she hoped he would not. Probably Julie the fiancé did too.

The chair of the BooBash committee was Donna Froehlich. Froehlich was the woman with hay-colored hair who called the police that Sunday morning four years before, that first time Moliere encountered Tibor Rauscha. Ever since that day she had seen herself as Moliere's ally. Moliere never believed she needed an ally.

The toddler that Froehlich was pushing on a swing that Sunday when small things blew up into big ones was now a third grader. She was among the most unpleasant children Moliere could imagine, more smart than intelligent, which obviously is not nothing. It was not enough for the mother, who had the girl tested for the district's gifted-and-talented program every spring without success. Moliere thought the only thing that would ever define that girl's life was being mean, mean in a way that was temperamental and out of which she would not grow.

Moliere had playground duty one afternoon when the Froehlich girl walked up to an older boy and called him fat in front of his friends—just for nothing. Moliere saw it all and sent the little girl—Jasmine, that was her name—to the guidance counsellor. Moliere knew the girl felt delighted by the score she made. Tonight she was dressed as Snow White.

"Katherine," said Mrs. Froehlich. She must have had a first name but, as with Allen's fiancée, Moliere resisted learning it. "You're working the haunted house for an hour?"

"I'm headed there now." Froehlich, Moliere knew, was disappointed that they were not better friends. Also that she was going to keep at it anyway. Donna Froehlich was all presumption.

"Keep an eye on the eighth-grade boys," Froehlich told Moliere. "They're getting handsy with the girls once they're in the dark." Froehlich was growing hippier by the month.

"I'll club them," Moliere said of the eighth graders, but Mrs. Froehlich barely smiled. There did not seem to be a Mr. Froehlich in the picture, but Moliere had never had the daughter in any of her classes. Thank God.

Moliere worked her hour at the haunted house, glaring at the eighth-grade boys to let them know she was on to them. At 8.30 she left to meet Fanny. It was only then when she realized she had no change of clothes. She would have to go and meet Eugene's mother in her Morticia costume.

After nine o'clock the trick-or-treaters in the streets were generally the older kids. Knowing middle-schoolers as she did Moliere suspected all of them of something as she drove to her rendezvous with Fanny. She observed what appeared to be a fashion for dressing like a jaded divorcée among the girls, all hoop earrings and heavy blue mascara. She laughed at her own disapproval.

Moliere remembered Franklin hating Halloween with all its stupid mischief and unwatched kids. To a degree he would never admit Franklin aligned himself with the bitter Christians in Perros Salvajes who saw Halloween as consorting with the devil. What good could ever come from that?

Under a street lamp Fanny waited in solitude. Moliere did not know her because she had cut her hair again. Now it was nearly shoulder length. It changed her profile. Only her dark skin in that pale-faced neighborhood gave her away.

Moliere pulled up and powered down her window.

"Are we walking?"

"God no," Fanny said. "It's seven miles. We'll take my car."

"What do you mean? Where's Eugene's mother?"

"Carol got some cold feet about leaving the house. She is a recluse. You know how they get after a time."

"A recluse is the woman secretly longing to be a mother again?"

"We'll have to bring Eugene to her," Fanny said. As if in reply. "I'm parked up there." She pointed at the corner.

Moliere was conscious of two things. One, dread. Two, the chill of the October night, which even in West Texas can require warm clothing. She had only Morticia's Black lace gloves on her hands and her finger bones ached.

Fanny's car was parked at the dark end of the street beneath where the lights had run out. Moliere cried out—really, cried out—when she opened the passenger door and saw that in the back seat were two large White men.

Moliere knew then that she was about to be murdered. She would be found dead the next day in the desert dressed like Morticia Addams. What would people make of that?

"These are little Janet's brothers, Gustav and Timmo. Naturally they want to help. Personally I think they're entitled."

"This is a kidnapping. Of me and then Dino."

"Eugene. And Katherine, don't be silly—how can you say that? You *agreed* to join us. Why would I have to kidnap you?"

"You didn't say anything about this."

Gustav or Timmo said from within the car, "Don't be like that." They did not seem nice.

Moliere saw her moment. She turned and ran as fast she could in her black high-button shoes. Fanny got into the car and caught up before Moliere was more than half way down the street.

Fanny yelled through the open window on the driver's side as the car rolled along beside Moliere.

"We're only going to pick up Eugene," she shouted. "But only if he wants to come with us. If he does not then we've got Gustav and Timmo to help. Please don't be a dope."

Even running at top speed Moliere could not outdistance the car, what with the shoes. She scouted for a patch of brush into which she could disappear. Or a busy street with Halloween urchins down which she could turn. But somehow now they were all gone.

"Get in the car, Katherine."

Moliere kept running, sure an idea would come to her if she just kept moving. When Fanny slowed for a moment Moliere pulled ahead. Then the car wheels screeched and Fanny's car was up the road fifty yards in front of her. One of the brothers leapt out and stood in Moliere's way. She turned and headed the opposite direction toward her own car. The silhouette of the other brother was waiting that way.

Moliere was defeated. She surrendered.

What time had it become?

First brother held open the car door. You'd think he was a valet at someplace swank.

Moliere got in. Sitting in the front seat she felt like crying but she did not. She would not.

"Geeze, Katherine," Fanny told her. "My goodness."

"I'll find a way to punish you for this, Fanny. Swear to God I will."

Fanny locked down the doors of the car with a finalizing thump.

"Punish me tomorrow."

Demonstrating an indifference to stop signs that Moliere hoped would attract the notice of some cop—she imagined AJ Munoz coming to her rescue—Fanny drove to the far side of Perros Salvajes and the house in which she lived with Tibor Rauscha and his son Eugene.

Fanny drove with absorption in her driving, like someone as cold-blooded in her intention as a killer from the movies.

They turned into the long driveway of the big house. As they did the gates in the low wall swung open. The college boy Fanny had hired to hand out candy at the bottom of the driveway had closed shop and gone home. Fanny never slowed down.

Here and there down the long driveway the lenses of security cameras hung in the transplanted maple trees. It did not take a practiced eye to find them; they reflected the car's lights like the nighttime eyes of animals. The whole world knew who lived behind the screen of trees on Nine Mezcaleros Road. Naturally Rauscha protected himself from intruders.

The big house at the end of the drive was illuminated like a catering hall.

"What a place," said one of the brothers, who only lived next door. "What's it like to live here, Fanny?"

"Cumbersome."

Fanny parked at the top of the driveway and said to Moliere, "Ring the bell and go get Eugene." She spoke quietly but hardly in a whisper. Fanny did not worry about being heard. It was her house, for one thing.

"Why am I the one to get him?" said Moliere.

"Because Eugene won't come out for me, Katherine. Duh. He hates me. That is just logic."

"You think your husband's just going to let me in so that I can drag out his son?"

"Tibor's away. He went to Dallas for some political get-together. He's gone till tomorrow night."

"Then why's your house all lit up?"

"God only knows. Really, God only knows."

Moliere got out of the car with the intention of scouting around for a way to escape. She saw none.

Hoping the whole time something would suggest itself Moliere stepped up on the front porch of the house and went to the door. The wind whispered the maple tree branches in the ominous way of every film ever made about Halloween night.

"Go on," said Fanny through the open window. "The keypad is that thing to your left. The code is 7bigboy. Tibor named it for his penis. All lower case."

From within the house—right above her head, she thought—Moliere heard music playing, faint but music no doubt about it. Nothing with a big beat like what she would expect from a 15-year-old boy but melodic, dreamy like a love song. Someone singing.

Above the door was the blue-black lens of still another camera. Moliere looked straight at it, wanting her face to be seen. She mouthed "help".

Moliere entered the code on the keypad. From somewhere inside the house she heard a robotic voice speak. When no one came to the door she was relieved. Maybe Fanny would have to call off the kidnapping and Moliere could go home.

"No one's answering," she told Fanny from the porch.

"He's home. Eugene doesn't do polite things like open the front door. He's passive aggressive."

"I'm supposed to just walk in?"

"Yes. It's my house. If cops were to show up now you can say I gave permission."

Moliere walked in. The interior was blazing with light from sconces; the house had overcommitted itself to sconces. In this brightness Moliere squinted. She was standing in an entrance hall that would probably be described as "grand" when the house was sold one day. It was not grand, it was just empty space.

The white walls were bare of decoration. The floors were of a blue-veined marble that went as far as Moliere could see into the adjoining rooms. The dreamy music she heard outside was coming from the floor above. Now that she could hear more clearly she recognized the music was some sort of female voice cooing over a piano.

Instead of going up the stairs toward the source of the music Moliere went to the big dining room, knowing the kitchen would connect directly to it. She was glad to find the kitchen in darkness. She would open the kitchen door and run as far and fast as she could.

Unlocking the door she was startled to see one of the brothers standing under the single porch light looking straight in at her. It was number two brother, the smaller blonde one.

"I wanted a cigarette," she said through the closed door.

"You don't smoke."

"You don't know that."

"Just get the fuckin kid."

This brother opened the unlocked door. He was not much taller than Moliere but he was 100 pounds heavier—not muscular but heavier. Just by moving in her direction he crowded her back into the kitchen. He turned Moliere around with force, then shoved her ahead of him back into the dining room and toward the staircase in the entrance hall.

"Who the hell do you think you are?" Moliere said loudly, hoping someone would hear her.

"I think I are big enough to hurt you if you don't do what you promised. That is who I think I are."

Moliere measured the value of provoking this one. She would accept being hurt if she were confident of some rescue. But this was not a public place, and no one would come to her rescue. Franklin was dead.

"Go up the stairs, Katherine."

"I'll be looking for another way out when I do."

"The fuck you will."

"You'll see if I'm bluffing." She was though. Bluffing.

Moliere climbed the marble staircase to the top floor, making her footsteps heavy as she could.

The sound of music came closer. It was not a woman's singing after all but some boy band. She recognized the tune as one with a hook that her kids at school sang obsessively.

"Open your heart / close your eyes / Let whatever comes / Come"

What the hell did that mean?

The singing came from a room at the opposite end of a gallery that began at the top of the stairway and ran maybe 60 feet long to the opposite landing. Eugene had to be in the room with the music coming out of it.

The runner down the gallery was Persian-inspired. It was dirty and threadbare. Down the length of the long peach-painted wall were framed prints—Frederic Remington on one side, Audubon on the other. Just the sort of prints wealthy people with no actual interest in pictures would hang on their walls.

Moliere passed a large wood-paneled room that must have been a kind of office for Fanny or Tibor. There was an ugly mahogany desk in there with a mess of papers on top and a printer behind it.

At the end of the hall Moliere looked in on Eugene. His bedroom door was wide open. He sat at a red schoolboy desk looking at porn on his laptop. The music Moliere heard was playing over the video he was watching, the volume way up. Eugene was masturbating, his eyes locked on the screen.

With a weird politeness Moliere knocked.

Eugene leapt to his feet, pulling his pants together as he did.

"What the fuck!" he said. Moliere felt so awfully tired.

"You've got nothing to worry about but you need to come with me, Dino." Moliere made herself say this with some energy. Moliere hated making the kid feel frightened. She pitied him. Simply standing there she knew everything that his life would be.

"I'm a friend of your mother's, and she needs to see you. Fanny's going to take us there." Moliere almost laughed to imagine how she must have looked in her Halloween costume. Like some sick killer, undoubtedly.

"Fuck you. Fanny hates me. And my mother doesn't care enough about me to feel one way or another. If you want to steal from my father, go right ahead. Just leave me alone."

"Do I look like I can hurt you?" Buckling his belt as he talked Eugene looked like anyone could hurt him. He was dough-faced and soft—the end-state of a human boy who ate bad food and seldom rose from a chair. He was allowed to exist as an aggregation of protoplasm in an upstairs bedroom, and everyone thought that enough.

Second brother came up behind Moliere. Without hearing him she knew it from the way Eugene's eyes widened.

"Please get in the fuckin car, kid."

Eugene was speechless with fright. Meanwhile the sex video behind continued to play. There was a woman with smeared mascara.

First brother came into the room. What would they do if Eugene would not come along? Carry him down the stairs and toss him in the trunk of the car the way kidnappers are expected to do? Impossible to imagine Eugene putting up a fight. From the look in his eyes he would sooner die of fear.

"These are friends of your step-mother," said Moliere.

"No they're not. They live next door."

"We're the brothers of the girl you raped. You might remember us from court." Eugene's face went whiter than it already was. From not leaving the house Eugene was very white to begin with.

"The judge said she consented."

"A brain-damaged girl can't consent. Your father bought the fucking verdict."

"Ruling."

"Come on," said second brother, firmly. He certainly did not sound like the good cop, if that was even the idea.

"Please don't hurt me." Now Eugene started to cry. The scene was preposterous.

"Did my little sister cry like that?" said the first brother, taunting him.

"*Shut up*!" said Moliere. "Look, Dino, no one's going to hurt you."

"My name is Eugene. You want someone else."

"If you don't get your fat ass down the stairs I might hurt you," said second brother. "We're not fucking around."

"Shut up!" Moliere shouted. "Come with us. We're going to visit your mother. You'll be back in an hour unless you decide to stay with her."

Eugene was not falling for it. Going down the stairs he was shaking so much that Moliere worried he might wet himself. Which, she considered, might have been one way of ending this thing. But he made it to the door without losing control.

"You first," said one of the brothers, the fair-haired one. He meant Moliere.

"Why?"

"Because you're already on the tape. Duh."

Moliere stepped through the front door and out on the porch. Fanny still waited at the top of the driveway.

"Hi, Eugene," Fanny called from behind the wheel of the car.

The wind still blew like a Hollywood Halloween. The year was shifting from West Texas autumn into West Texas winter. Even in the circumstances Moliere could not help reflecting that there was no pleasant melancholy in the arrival of winter as there was in the arrival of autumn. There was only dread, the extinguishing of light and the expectation of worse to come until spring returned, God willing.

"Stop," said fair-haired brother. "Look to your right. See the cloth on the white chair? Find the roll of duct tape under it and tape the cloth over the camera."

"I can't reach that high."

"Stand on the goddam chair. Jesus, you're bad as him."

Moliere, ridiculous in her costume, stood on the chair and taped the cloth over the camera lens. In the act of stepping down from the chair she had the inspiration to flee into the desert behind the house. She yanked off the cloth and ran, betting that she would be filmed until she disappeared around the side of the porch.

Moliere took to her heels.

In the light from the house Moliere found what seemed to be a path through some brush and maybe beyond to the desert. Bumpers Road was half a mile from there. She could see automobile headlights and she ran in that direction. But after 50 feet or so the path simply ended in some dense brush. Moliere was nowhere.

Moliere ratted her way in the bushes and squatted there hoping she would be unfound. She did not hear anyone following, so that was promising. Maybe they would forget her now they had Eugene. As soon as she heard Fanny drive away Moliere was going straight to the cops.

"Don't fuck around anymore, Katherine. Get up."

It was blond brother looking down at her, the shorter one who could not speak so well. The word "gunsel" from the old detective novels came into Moliere's mind.

This brother's name was Timmo.

They drove to Carol's house stuffed into Fanny's red Tesla, Fanny and Katherine up front, Eugene in the backseat between the two brothers. In the electric car the air grew stale.

Fanny was plainly more relaxed now that she had Eugene in her net. She played the radio. She favored easy-listening music with lots of strings and love songs with disturbingly craven lyrics if anyone ever bothered to think about them.

"I'll do anything / I'm begging you / Please don't leave"

It was off-putting.

Fanny seemed to like every tune the radio played, stepping up the volume with each new one until Moliere finally could not bear the noise.

"Love is in the air, in the thunder of the sea," Fanny sang. *"Love is in the air, la da da da da da dee.* I remember my mother singing along to this one as she drove me to kindergarten one morning. It was a specific day. Love was as far away as could be from my Mom's air," Fanny laughed, "but she was belting this song out like she was in church. I'm not saying *she* was preposterous."

None of the others answered, none of them laughed.

Eugene knew he would remember the old song too whenever he thought about this night. For a long time it had made him nearly sick to realize there were things a person could never forget, things that would pile up in the head that he would have to endure alone until, relieved, he entered the grave.

Eugene was afraid of the two men on either side of him in the back seat. They smelled of sweat and worse they smelled of the hate they had for him. Their sister had something of the same smell about her. Eugene could not help remembering a smell. That smell was one more other thing he was never going to be able to forget.

Eugene did not think the girl's brothers were going to hurt him, not physically. Unless they were lying about going to Mom's house. If it turned out Fanny was driving into the desert instead then Eugene would know that he was dead, dead with that stupid song still playing in his head.

Can I die from madness, Eugene wondered, can being crazy kill you just by itself? Like a heart attack? Right that moment Eugene was hoping this was possible. He wanted no more life.

Fanny, he was sure, just wanted to annoy Dad, that is all this was. She did not expect to get away with this whatever it was. Eugene had the insight.

The not-bad-looking woman in the front seat next to her—"Katherine" Fanny had called her—what was she?—Mexican? no, the hair was wrong—obviously she did not want to be here either. Much as he hated Fanny Eugene did not think she would take them out to the desert and shoot them in the brains. But he could still see clearly what that would be like. Fanny standing and watching.

In Eugene's vision of being murdered Fanny was wearing a long coat like a cowboy's duster. She would probably be talking. To the last minute of his life Eugene would have to listen to her yapping. Then the woman in the front seat would try running away again, and they would shoot twice and miss her before she went down on the third shot.

The two guys guarding him right now—the goons, they would be called—would dig a hole. But they would be in a panic and not dig deep enough, and wolves or whatever is out there would dig up Eugene and the woman and chew on their flesh. Then the cops out searching for them would find their chewed-up corpses because they noticed vultures circling. Maybe they would think Eugene was the teenage lover of the woman in the front seat, which would be cool. For the world to remember him like that would feel like vindication, though just what it would vindicate Eugene did not know how to ask himself.

The cops would find something—a shell casing, a thread, blood under somebody's fingernail—and they would trace it back to the brothers. Of course, the cops would reason, of course. Because of what Eugene did to their sister, the thing for which he would die unforgiven in the desert. The brothers would be the natural suspects. Then they would finger Fanny to avoid Huntsville.

Eugene liked that expression for it, "finger".

The drive to Carol's house took just under 30 minutes. Eugene's mother, Carol Peña, lived on the opposite side of Perros Salvajes, just beyond where the density of tract housing was greatest and where the houses got bigger as the land got cheaper.

Eugene was mentally removed from the trip, lost in his fantasy of being murdered in the desert. It was one way of removing himself from the circumstance, from the reality of the stuffy car and the stinking men either side of him. Eugene was far from everything. Far from God, from hunger, from the loneliness with which he was so familiar that he did not even think to name it.

Eugene had only ever been to his mother's house four dozen times in his whole 15 years. He could not have located it on a map. But he knew the house. It had a barnlike shape—a saltbox more appropriate to New England than the West Texas desert but when did that ever matter? It had two floors and five bedrooms for some reason.

Carol lived there alone. She had barely furnished it, and in every season Eugene found it cold—not metaphorically, though that too, but literally cold. Except in the dead of summer it got cold at night in this part of Texas. And still Carol would not heat the place.

Fanny parked in the wide driveway of the house beside a Chevy SUV.

"Stick with us, Katherine," she said to Moliere. "We won't need long."

In the front room of the house someone flicked the curtain back and looked out before dropping it back. Carol, obviously. Fanny waved hello to the curtained window.

The five of them went up the walk to the front door. Eugene observed how that woman Katherine was still checking around the surroundings for a place to run, no matter what Fanny said. She would not get far, Eugene thought. The chaparral terminated out here; the builder had cut it back to make room for the house. Katherine would need to run a quarter mile before she found anything like a tree to hide behind. Why was she dressed that way? She looked like an idiot, dressing up. Eugene forgot that it was Halloween. Halloween was just another night.

Fanny rang the bell. Before they heard Carol's footsteps coming to the door the five of them waited a solid awkward minute.

For some reason Carol Peña was blonde now. Eugene knew she was 43 but she could have passed for a well-preserved 60; her face was just that tired. Carol was not chic, and she was not so beautiful anymore. She came to the door in a pre-faded hooded sweatshirt, worn against the cold inside her house. Carol had a probably still useful prettiness, though what she might ever use it for Eugene had no idea. He almost never saw his mother. He knew almost nothing about whatever life she led. She never talked to him.

"Yes?" Carol said, hardly glancing at Eugene let alone greeting him. She was addressing Fanny. Eugene could see her being as brave as she could be facing up to the five of them at her front door.

"We have brought you Eugene," said Fanny—cheerfully, like she was surprising Carol for her birthday. "He would like a talk with you."

"I would not," said Eugene.

"Eugene *needs* to talk you, Carol," Fanny said, dropping her voice into a more serious register. It was like she was resilient.

"I *don't.*"

"May we come in?"

"No," said Carol. She had bowls of Halloween candy by the front door just in case trick or treaters came. Hard to imagine kids would come looking for candy in this desolate neighborhood on the edge of the desert.

"Carol, it's important."

"Tell me here, Fanny."

Eugene smirked. Fanny assumed Mom would lie down for her. Fanny never expected resistance; that was her credo or something.

"Your boy needs a parent, Carol," Fanny began. "His father ignores him. We know that. Certainly I'm not his mother. We know that. If I'd ever had an interest in children I'd have had some of my own. But I did not because I don't. Just the same I *feel* for Eugene, Carol. Living with us is not doing him any good. You see these two men behind me? They are the brothers of the retarded girl Eugene raped."

"I did not rape anybody."

"She is not retarded," said the tall one. "She is brain damaged from an accident."

"These men beside me need to know someone has taken Eugene in hand, Carol. His character is still not fully formed. Take your son into your home, Carol. God wants you to do that."

Now it was Carol who smirked.

"Who are you?" Carol asked Moliere.

"I was compelled to come along." Eugene thought Moliere sounded like a woman testifying in a court.

"This is Katherine Moliere," said Fanny. "As far as I'm aware she is the only person who's ever stuck up for Eugene in his life. You probably don't remember her. Let Tibor tell you about her sometime."

"You told me I was expected!" said Moliere

"I wanted you here as a kind of prop, Katherine. A moral prop." Fanny never took her eyes off Carol. "I hope to remind Carol before we are done that Eugene is a child who deserves love from someone. That someone should be you, Carol. Admit to yourself that you miss him. He is a diseased child. You are his cure."

Eugene was curious to hear what his mother would say to that. In his whole life he never imagined someone missing him. He overlooked the portion about being diseased.

"My life is arranged," Carol told Fanny. "It doesn't include Eugene. Don't mess me up." At least she turned to her son. Carol said, "It's better for you." Carol spoke in a small voice that even at 15 Eugene was convinced she put on for the effect it had on men.

"Oof," Fanny said. "Carol, you're cold. How do you think you make Eugene feel?"

Eugene did not think anything his mother said could make him feel anything at all—not sad, not happy, nothing. To admit this was his sole strength.

Eugene knew not to consider Mom too much. Even now, trying to stand up to Fanny, she crouched in the doorway of her own home like some animal ready to bolt, afraid of begin eaten. He saw the picture of him she kept on a table near the door. It was taken when he was still little kid, the closest he had ever been to adorable. And still Eugene knew he could live, he could die, it was all the same to her. For that matter it was all the same to Eugene. He looked forward to being asleep in bed later.

"You won't even fight me, will you, Carol?" Fanny said.

"No, except to say I wish you would not use my name so often. Please go away." And Carol closed the door.

"I guess that is that," Fanny said aloud. She stood on the doorstep in quiet reflection.

"You said you told her about me," said Katherine Moliere, "that she wanted to meet me."

"She was not at her best."

The brothers studied Fanny like troops awaiting their next command. Fanny was out of ideas for the night. She turned and walked back to the car.

"Can I ride in the front going home?" said blonde brother. "With the fat kid in the backseat it's cramped."

"No," Fanny said.

Fanny drove Moliere back to the quiet street where her car was parked. It had toilet paper hanging from the roof and shaving cream on the back window. Happy Halloween.

"Do you mind if I put you out here, Katherine?" she said. "I'm bushed. I'm just bushed."

"Let me speak to Eugene—alone," Moliere said.

In the front seat of the car Fanny looked hard into Katherine's face, and then back at Eugene sitting between Timmo and Gustav.

"At least you learned his name. Are you up to something, Katherine?"

"Yeah."

Moliere and Eugene got out and walked a little way down the street.

"How are you?" Moliere asked him.

"Ok."

"I'm not. This was some stuff tonight."

Eugene knew she was conning him. He said nothing.

"I still don't know what Fanny thought she was trying to do."

What did she want him to say? Was one of the brothers going to appear over her shoulder again? How did she know

Fanny? She was sort of pretty. This woman had passionate hair, like she could barely hold it down. He was changing his opinion about her hair.

"I'm sorry for the way you live, Eugene," Moliere told him. "I'm sorry for what they're making out of you."

"What are you talking about?"

"I can't do much about it. But if you ever just want to talk you can find my eMail on the Emma Tenayuca school website. OK?"

"Just leave me alone. I want to go home."

"Solitude makes people crazy, Eugene."

"I'm fucked and you know it. I was born fucked." Eugene liked how tough that sounded.

"If you only live inside your head you'll never get healthy. It's a long life and you're not done."

Moliere appeared to be about to offer her hand and then appeared to think better of it.

Fanny was turning the car around behind them, washing them both in the harsh white light of the car's high beams; they both look burned in that light. When she braked—hard—Eugene noted the skulls of both brothers in the backseat snap back hard like bobbleheads. Funny.

"Come on, Eugene," called Fanny from behind the wheel of the car. "Get in. This evening has been a waste of everyone's time and I want to go to bed. Good night, Katherine. Get home safe."

"Remember what I said," Moliere said in a low voice to Eugene. And she walked off down her street.

"What'd she want?" Fanny asked Eugene when he got in the car.

"Nothing."

"She didn't want nothing. She invited you to walk up the street with her just to say nothing? People don't do that."

"Fanny, I don't need to say shit to you."

Fanny had not the interest to pursue it further; Eugene could tell. She cared nothing about him. That extended to whatever he might plot with Moliere. In any case, what exactly would they plot about? Fanny was not dumb. But her lack of interest made him brave; Eugene could say what he liked.

Timmo asked if he could sit where Moliere had sat up front beside Fanny.

"Where she sat is still warm," he said as he settled in.

Half the way home to the house on Nine Mezcaleros Road Timmo said he was hungry and could they stop.

"Do we have to?" Fanny told him. "I'm really beat."

"Just a burger," said Timmo.

"I'm hungry too," Eugene said.

All this had happened and it was still barely eleven-thirty.

Texas Unforgiven

Carol stood watching from behind her curtain 15 minutes or more. Even after Fanny backed out of the driveway and drove off with Eugene and those other people Carol stood and watched. She wanted to be sure they were really gone.

Carol was not ready for bed. Carol was never ready for bed. Lots of nights she stayed awake until the light was in the sky again.

Carol double-checked the locks on the doors and windows of her house. She poured herself some vodka and cranberry juice over ice. Every night she drank this. In the mirror over the bar there was a tired-looking blonde mimicking her every move.

The woman in the mirror looked like she had had a shock. Her eyes were pink; they popped a little. There was a raw quality to her skin, as if her face had been rubbed hard with a cloth. Carol knew how to fix that up with powder and mascara so that her skin would shine and her eyes would pop but in the right way. But around the house Carol wore no makeup. She lived alone—who would look?

Once Carol wore makeup all the time. Fixing her face was what she did after brushing her teeth in the morning. She expected to be observed. Then one day Carol grew weary of it. She would have no more of making herself attractive—for what? To catch the interest of some man?

Carol was the oldest person she knew. She was still trim with small hips but the rest of whatever it was that used to make men look at her was slipped away. Even when she was 19—about the time she met Georg and Tibor Rauscha—Carol had a strong intuition that she was in her zone of maximal beauty. Carol did not understand how she acquired this gift of beauty, but she knew she had it. And that it would not last.

When Carol was 15 her pastor told her how during services he listened for her voice in the choir—"like sky-blue velvet," he called it. Even at 15 Carol knew Rev. Lear was listening to something other than her hymn singing; her voice was not so sensational. Still, she went to work on her vocal quality for the rewards that it might bring.

Young men did not used to steal glances at Carol Peña; they stared. But Georg Rauscha also talked. Georg had nerve. He was handsome enough, but better than that he was like the Hollywood version of a man, or Carol's version anyway: coarse then sweet, this rough thing then that soft thing.

Carol did not delude herself that Georg was a nice man. He said "fuck" all the time like someone with Tourette's. He smelled of tobacco. Sundays he slept late and mocked Carol for going to church. His friends from childhood were juvenile and around too much. He had the food habits of a 15-year-old. He stiffed waiters and mocked the infirm. He was a thief.

But Georg was loyal as a savage to her. The idea of cheating on Carol might occur to Georg—he was a man, after all—but he never would. And when Georg's business with his brother Tibor went down the drain because of Georg's shenanigans he was also loyal to Tibor. Georg could have made his sentence lighter by taking Tibor down with him. He did not.

In her memory of marriage she recalled Georg as unethical but constant. Between these traits there was no contradiction within the content of her memory.

Before he turned 21 Georg Rauscha had a degree of wealth almost unheard of in Perros Salvajes, certainly compared to other young men. In that respect he was a good catch. Carol's marriage to Georg was not a transaction, or no more a transaction than any other marriage. Carol loved the idea of being married to someone like him.

For a while Carol and Georg had fun, spending money like there was always more coming. Because there was. Carol lived in a far nicer house than either of her sisters. She had a passport and went to Europe once and Mexico four times. Every year they leased new cars. They joined a wine club. Carol's only job was to look after their possessions and acquire more. If that sounds boring, it was not; it was luxe. Carol had all she wanted.

Having nothing else in mind for his life Tibor Rauscha followed his brother to Perros Salvajes from Houston and joined him in the cleaning business. At their peak the Rauscha brothers had more than a dozen clients, good customers, for their office-cleaning company. Georg set it up so that customers automatically debited their checking accounts each month. Nearly from the beginning he was withdrawing what he called "surcharges" at first and then called "tips". Giving himself a "tip" of, say, $119 a month (always an odd amount and so less noticeable). He made sure it was a small enough amount that a client paying $4,500 a month would barely pay attention. He was right. For a while Georg knew the pure joy of something for nothing. The mistake was that Georg tipped himself the same amount every month.

Tibor Rauscha had never actively agreed to the scheme. But he accepted his cut. In those days he felt Georg was smarter about everything but about money especially. It required no decision to simply let the money come.

It took three years but eventually one client's accountant spotted the fraud. Then it seemed everyone woke up at once to the way they were being scammed. To Tibor Rauscha the stirring among the customers was like a murmuration of starlings he once saw over the Chocolate Bayou rice canal near his Aunt Gretal's house in Brazoria county.

When it turned out Georg and Tibor Rauscha had tipped themselves almost $75,000 the size of it surprised both of them.

Georg was not so smart that he avoided sixteen months in jail. (The judge in Perros Salvajes county court had her eye on a congressional seat. Given that goal it was a good idea to be seen as tough on white-collar crime, so bad timing for Georg.) To his credit Georg took all the responsibility, letting the world think he had robbed his own brother. His brother Tibor let the world think as it liked.

Every single Saturday Carol drove to El Paso to visit Georg in the Rogelio Sanchez state pen. The rest of the week she looked after Tibor, the admiring younger brother working to salvage the business and, when salvaging finally failed, trying to begin something new. Without Georg in his world Tibor was lost.

Carol knew Tibor Rauscha was smitten with her. She was still more or less in her zone of maximal beauty in those days, though she was beginning to shade its bright edge. When she was in the office with Tibor she often glanced up and caught him sneaking a look at her. She would smile when she caught him at it, to put him at ease. She treated Tibor like the bashful little brother he was. This idea of herself—faithful wife and protective sister-in-law—gave Carol a confidence, a sense of herself as capable, she never knew before or had even pretended.

On Sundays when she took Tibor to church with her she felt exactly like a big sister would, Tibor beside her in the pew.

Meanwhile Georg's time in jail was ruining him.

Carol could not miss the signs. Just the same she was unprepared for the day about a year into his sentence when Georg said he had spoken to his defense attorney back in Perros Salvajes about getting a divorce. He was not gentle about it.

"Don't even argue, Carol," he told her, "because the mind's made up. Bad enough all my money went for lawyers. I don't want to give up the rest of whatever's left just to keep paying your bills."

"That's your idea of marriage? You don't think I'm in this for the long haul? For forever?"

"Fuck, Carol, nothing's forever. Even you don't believe that."

"I do."

"For Christ's sake, we're 23 years old. You think you're going to be it for me the whole rest of my life—really? And that I'm going to be it for you? Christ."

"Georg, you're pretending. This is not who you are. When you love it's for keeps."

"You watch too much TV."

"In your head you think you're giving me a release from you or something. You don't have to do that."

"I'm releasing *me* from *you*."

Any doubt about Georg's sincerity was erased by the package of documents Carol received later in the week from Georg's lawyers. They proposed an equal split of property—the equity they had in the house and half the $20,000 the couple still had left in cash. It was not nothing but it was not much. That was when Tibor took Carol in.

Back then Carol was still more a girl then a full-grown woman. She wore her hair in a corona of black curls around her pretty face, all wild. Wonderful. Before that time Tibor never had romantic designs on Carol that he was aware of. Having a sad, pretty woman in the house created opportunity for those designs to get started.

Tibor Rauscha was good to Carol. He gave her whatever she needed at a time when he had not much of it himself. He gave her the bedroom in his apartment while he slept on the couch. This lasted about a month until once again Tibor was sleeping in his own bed. When Carol told Georg that she and Tibor had fallen in love Georg said, "You're both fucked in the head."

"The laugh will be on you, Georg."

"Not hardly."

In those days Carol's father, Petey Peña, worked construction. Petey was kept busy taking down the prefabricated buildings that sprouted all over west Texas in the 1980s, most of them housing the countless machine shops that serviced the oil fields. When the Texas economy went to pieces in the oil slump of the 1990s those little companies went to pieces with it, leaving empty buildings behind. By 2000 a good number of those buildings still had not found new businesses to occupy them.

Petey happened to mention to Rauscha once that lots of the owners could not even afford to tear the buildings down. With the economy bad they could not be sold. In 2011 Tibor bought one for a dollar and a negotiated deal on its unpaid property taxes. He purchased 23 Sun servers on eBay and contracted with a data-services business to provide customer-service and tech support. RauschaTech opened for business.

We are more than a server farm! That was RauschaTech's slogan from the beginning. RauschaTech was nothing *but* a server farm.

That first facility Rauscha bought had solar panels hammered into its roof by the previous owner. They were never plugged into the power grid. They were just up there on the roof. Tibor connected them but the panels did not provide remotely enough electricity for all the servers running inside the building. Tibor did not care about this. He promoted RauschaTech as a green business. For $375 he got an art student at El Paso Community College to design a logo for the company. It was mostly the solar panels and the sun smiling down.

This was all Tibor Rauscha's idea. Carol saw imagination in him that was suddenly abundant once he was no longer in Georg's shadow.

In its second year RauschaTech bought another abandoned machine shop in northern Michigan, then another in Nebraska.

Server farms were a cheap business to enter and the overhead was minimal. RauschaTech contracted for everything it needed. Rauscha just bought the vacant properties for housing it all. That was the business.

After a while Rauscha owned so much of the market that he could undercut anyone on price. At that time labor was so cheap that it was nearly free. He concentrated his growth strategy in fire-at-will states. Later that changed.

Tibor Rauscha had never had the experience of a woman concerned for him, and he was honestly grateful. Before everything went wrong he loved Carol as much as he loved his brother Georg. At that time.

Meanwhile jail made Georg unhappy in ways he would never get over. The change was not even all that gradual. Well before he divorced Carol Georg decided his life was done with, beyond repair, beyond God's grace.

On the day of Georg's release his brother Tibor offered to arrange a car to bring him home from Rogelio Sanchez to Perros Salvajes. Georg turned him down. He declined to come back to Perros Salvajes at all. He moved into a motel in Horizon City for perhaps a month. Eventually he got a place in Fabens, where the Church of God in Christ arranged a job for him driving for a beer-and-soda distributor.

After Georg was settled there a few weeks his brother Tibor went over to see him on a Saturday. They met for lunch at a Hawaiian barbecue place. It took some convincing getting Georg to go.

Georg came in wearing a dirty red tee-shirt, camouflage pants and a trucker cap—the full redneck uniform. In the old days he wore clean vanilla-flavored khakis every day with a rotating collection of pastel polo shirts. Now he looked like a loser going nowhere, which he was.

"How are you, buddy?" Tibor Rauscha asked his brother.

"Delighted to be here." Georg's face was not just unshaven but dirty.

That was as rich as the conversation got. At home that night Rauscha told Carol that it was among the most awkward meals he ever ate, and with his own brother of all people.

"I think neither of us can adjust to the change in our status," he told Carol. "Me doing alright. Him not. You know?"

Rauscha offered to cover his brother's rent for as long as he needed help. Georg said no emphatically. But in time he took the money, an arrangement that lasted five months. That was when Georg's housing situation changed.

Say this for Georg: One thing prison did not change in him was that he remained a one-woman-at-a-time man.

Georg's job in Fabens came with a daughter belonging to the man who owned the distributorship. The daughter's name was Norma Solalinde. Norma's father Dominic was not pleased at all about this romance. But Norma lived on her own with a daughter she had in a previous relationship with a man whom Dominic also did not like; *culeros* was Dominic's word for his daughter's taste in men. Georg repeated it to his brother Tibor when he told him about Norma, like it was a big joke.

"Maybe you watch out for that guy," Rauscha warned Georg about the father. It was not the father who needed watching. It was Norma. She was the one who got Georg.

Norma was willful, that was only the word for her. Willful. *Voluntarioso.* If Georg wanted her, his brother thought, let him have her. Whichever way the romance with Norma played out, any sort of obligation to Georg could transfer at least partly to the Solalinde family. That would have been fine with Tibor Rauscha, whose family feeling was then at a low ebb.

After moving in with Norma Georg came home every evening like the most married man in the world. And still Norma never trusted him.

"Mi ladrón," she would tell him sweetly.

There was one summer day in his first year of freedom when Georg went to a christening—of all things—in El Paso. The father of the baby was a guy Georg met in facility, Robert Smith, a good name for a forger, which is what he was and why they sent him to jail.

Georg and Robert were the sort of white-collar criminals who were surprised to find themselves in prison; if ever they thought about their sins they did not conceive them to be on a scale grand enough for jail. The two friends stuck close to each other while they were inside. After their release they remained friends. Having Georg present for the christening was Robert's way of saying "See—I'm making it."

Georg told Norma that he would be staying the night in El Paso.

"There's a party at the house," he told her, "and I'd like to be able to drink. Robert asked me." And still Norma called his cell at half past four in the morning and demanded that he come home. She had not slept. She told him she was having some emotions.

"Get in your fucking car and get home right now," she explained.

Georg was too sleepy to consider the pros and cons of ignoring Norma's demand, and he agreed to come home. Leaving a note for Robert

—Norma called. She cannot help loving me. Maybe the next kid called to Jesus will be mine!—

Georg left the house and started for Fabens.

At that hour on a Sunday morning Georg was one of the few people out on the road. The sun was only just creeping up. At his exit off I-10 another motorist was pulled over on the shoulder replacing a driver's-side tire. The man stepped back to admire his work and Georg, his eyes half closing with sleep and squinting into the rising sun anyway, did not see the guy until he was 30 feet away.

Georg's reaction time was good but not enough. He was still doing 50 when the car hit the man. He had never hit anything with a car before but Georg knew from the sick sound of it the guy was dead.

Georg's instant thought was that he was going back to jail. He did not want that.

Georg hit the accelerator and took off in the direction of Norma's apartment. He never made it. A woman in a car behind him, observing a trucker pulling over to see about the murdered motorist, followed Georg and watched him park beside the McDonald's on Camp Road to think things over. She phoned the police and seven minutes later cops surrounded Georg's car. He gave the police no fuss. Start to finish the whole event lasted 20 minutes.

Georg confessed unreservedly to manslaughter, leaving the scene of an accident and unlawful flight. He told his brother Tibor that he did not want a lawyer. Georg wanted to be punished. His remorse was so obvious to the judge that he was allowed out to await sentencing. Norma would not have him back, though. Instead Georg rented a room all by himself at the Best Western in Clint.

Then one day Georg was gone from the Best Western—no note, no phone call to anyone, nothing. He still had keys to Norma's car, which he stole out of her driveway. He took it to the border crossing at Fort Hancock and parked it there. CCTV showed him walking into Mexico. And then walking back into the United States about an hour and a half later after he got himself some lunch. Georg was a poor criminal; he had no gift for it. He should never have gone in that direction.

Carol drove with Tibor Rauscha to the sentencing at the courthouse in El Paso. She went not for Georg, whom she pitied but nevertheless despised. She went to court for Tibor, who was naturally upset.

Georg's face when he was sentenced to 15 years was vacant of any feeling. Not sorrow, not fear, nothing.

The bailiff cuffed Georg and led him to prison. Now

they would all be old when Georg got out, and already Carol was pregnant with Eugene.

They never heard from Georg after he went away. Georg asked Tibor not to visit, and so Tibor did not. Tibor was seldom home anyway; even Carol felt like she hardly saw him. He was buying empty warehouses and machine shops in any part of the country with a troubled local economy. He had a nose for these situations.

Tibor Rauscha and Carol got wealthy fast, wealthier than anything Carol would have known with Georg. Within five years Tibor went from facing prosecution for embezzlement from his mop-and-bucket business to owning a technology company worth $300 million. She never forgot the morning their personal assets passed the $100 million number. The markets were open in New York and they were both naked, hitting refresh on their Fidelity accounts over and over until the magic number was passed.

One year they rented a vacant funeral home that had gone out of business for a Halloween party, using the stainless-steel embalming table for the bar. It was quite a life. Carol's father Petey, who co-signed the loan to buy the original facility in near El Paso, was made a small partner in RauschaTech and retired to Puerto Vallarta, where he smoked Cuban cigars and drank Johnnie Walker whiskey all day.

These events changed how people thought of Tibor in Perros Salvajes, and by association how they thought of Carol. Carol loved every minute. She had nothing to do but decorate the house and get pregnant with Eugene. Having a baby seemed like the next thing to do.

That was when the animal joy of being in bed with Tibor Rauscha began to leak away.

It is terrible to say but Carol and Tibor Rauscha never liked baby Eugene. He did not do anything. Not just when he was an infant because none of them do, but when he became a toddler. Eugene was slow to toilet train, slow to talk, slow to catch on to the things to which they expected he would catch on. Eugene needed both of them every minute. Carol and Tibor were sorry they had him.

There, it is said.

No more than she foresaw her divorce from Georg did Carol see Fanny coming. Later, when she met Fanny for the first time at Eugene's probation hearing, Carol was surprised by this beautiful Black woman for whom Tibor had left her. Carol had been anticipating a babe, a scheming blonde babe. She could not imagine that Fanny might have wanted Tibor. Carol may have been an attractive woman but the first thing about romance she did not understand.

Before going to bed Carol on Halloween night Carol called Tibor Rauscha's cell-phone to tell him that Fanny had been to her house with Eugene and several people she did not know.

The next day when Tibor Rauscha got his ex-wife's voicemail he was less angry than bewildered. Or so he said on the telephone to Fanny. She told him Carol had misunderstood.

"Carol hates it when anyone speaks from the heart," Fanny explained.

Rauscha liked Fanny better when she was blunt, blunt just like himself. He liked to give her credit for honesty.

Texas state senator Andy DiNapoli spent half that day in Dallas with Tibor Rauscha. They both attended a meeting of the state Republican party at Rosewood Mansion for an "issues retreat". Tibor Rauscha was not a registered Republican nor a registered anything else. Andy knew he went to Republican events as a matter of business obligation; Rauscha would visit the Democrats too if he thought that would ever get him somewhere in Texas, which it would not.

In Dallas politicians made speeches about things Tibor Rauscha seldom thought about—Israel, abortion, guns, God,

Washington, Muslims, immigration, Texas football. If no one stopped him they would go on about abortion and football and Israel for days.

(Rauscha did not own a gun; he told Andy that he had ordered his Range Rover with the gun-cabinet option but kept it empty. Another time he mentioned forty-five years ago his mother walked into Texas from Mexico, so that made him descended from at least one immigrant. Rauscha supposed nobody should do that now. But when people argued about the subject he found his attention soon exhausted. In Rauscha's eyes these were someone else's troubles.)

At issues retreats Andy DiNapoli was the only person Rauscha talked to. At these things the men were less than smart (that included Andy) and the women were smart but would not talk to Rauscha. They eyed him liked they were on to him, he thought—about *what* even he could not say. Certainly he felt it.

Rauscha, like the other non-politicians at the retreats, understood that his role was to listen to the speeches and write checks of at least four figures, if not on the spot then later. Not in so many words but the checks were conditioned on getting what the check writer needed.

Andy understood the terms of the transaction too. In Tibor Rauscha's case he wanted water approvals (and exceptions) for work on Lobos Aullando, his town-house development north of Galveston. Lobos Aullando was in Andy's legislative district.

Lately life had gotten more interesting for them both. Now Andy was asking Tibor for more than the customary

$2,000 he usually handed out to these characters. Andy DiNapoli had come down with a case of ambition.

Every four years Andy was reelected with ease. But a court-ordered redistricting the year before moved the lines of his district, putting Andy into competition with another Republican, Louie Hensarling. Andy and Louie both agreed it was a dirty deal.

"We are babes in the woods about politics, Andy," Louie told him. Andy was not so sure that Louie was as innocent as he pretended.

But.

Ed Schroeder, the Congressman for that part of the state, personally erratic but somehow long-serving, decided he was done with politics, done with life, really, if pressed. Andy wanted Schroeder's seat in the House. Andy wanted to go to Washington. Andy wanted to be a congressman. Andy wanted Rauscha's money.

Texas, including Andy's part of it, came out of the 2008 financial crisis as well as any place. Real estate was not too much off its highs of 15 years before. But there was one patch of overreach 80 miles from the Gulf Coast, and Andy represented it in his state senate district. It was a town that used to be called Trippingdale; a California developer renamed it Lobos Aullando because it sounded more indigenous and because in the developer's mind the old name had associations with narcotics.

Tibor Rauscha was sitting up late one night in a Galveston hotel room unable to fall asleep when a story about the place came up on the local TV news. Rauscha had feelings for Galveston and the whole of Brazoria County. His father had people there; some years in summer his parents sent him with Georg to stay near the Gulf with his cousins. Later when Rauscha met Andy he made sure to say that he was not watching TV news from any interest in current events; it was out of nostalgia.

In its original sense of a broken longing nostalgia was the thing Tibor Rauscha was feeling. The marriage to Carol was losing altitude at about that time, and he was recently smitten with Fanny. He was feeling the stress of his situation. He was glad for opportunities to travel and to leave Carol—and Eugene—for a while. Tibor Rauscha was never a reader so TV was all he had for quieting his mind. Try to imagine that.

Lobos Aullando was a golf-and-condo development that had unexpectedly lost its principal backer. The half-built houses were standing untouched except by a "collaborative" of Panhandle graffiti artists who were squatting and making some statement or other. The taps that fed the lake were turned off. The carp that the builder of the development had stocked in the lake he built lay dead and stinking in the mud.

Water wasn't abundant in that part of Texas—water was not abundant anywhere in Texas—but there was certainly water in the Gulf of Mexico. Lobos Aullando was premised on a desalination scheme that would pipe water from the Gulf and process the salt out of it as it made its way beyond Galveston to sprinkle the fairways and refresh Dead Fish Lake (that was one idea they had for calling it. For the amusement.). The plan had been to make the pipeline pay for itself by allowing towns along the way to buy fresh water out of it, all they wanted. "A sustainable Eden" the original developer called it.

This big vision had two problems. The first was that the desalination technology did not work at the volumes needed. The second was the developer's partner. He was a Saudi who got called home a month ahead of a Justice Department report connecting him to money flowing to a terrorist organization in Hungary—"a different sort of pipeline" the TV reporter could not resist saying in her TV reporter's voice.

The other local angle for the news station was that the Saudi borrowed the jet of a Midland oilman—Johnny "Amazing" Grace—and used it to fly home to Riyadh ahead of the FBI.

"Dumb prick," Rauscha said to Andy that first time they met. "Johnny and I invested together a few years ago and it worked out OK. Well, fuck him, that's over."

"I would not ever count Johnny out, Tibor," Andy told him. "You have to bury an oilman with a stake through his heart or they just keep coming back. We like life." Originally Andy was from Connecticut. He grew to love Texas lore.

Naturally after the Saudi financing collapsed the localities were having second thoughts about Lobos Aullando. No taxpayer money was spent and still everyone involved looked stupid. And possibly anti-American into the bargain.

The earth under the development was subsiding because the builder insisted on pumping water out of the ground to irrigate the golf course even before anyone had played a round; he wanted a mature-looking layout on the day the place opened. Through two straight years of drought he carried on; it was hard not to be impressed with his tenacity. But now some houses sold as lakefront were no longer that.

Meanwhile the people who bought in the first phase of houses lived in fear that if the water ever came back they would be in a flood zone. It was a perfect headache.

Tibor Rauscha twitched at the opportunity; he said as much to Andy. He was already in the business of negotiating for distressed property. This was the same thing, wasn't it?

Through a mutual acquaintance in Austin Rauscha arranged a call with Andy. He made it clear in that first call that he wanted no part of any golf course. The one at Lobos Aullando was not even half finished anyway.

"There's too much boom and bust in golf," he told Andy. "I don't know why people keep building those things. You can't make a living."

All Rauscha wanted to own was the right to subdivide the land and put up more townhouses. For that to make any sense he needed good water. He could buy whatever construction expertise was required to finish building the place. And Andy DiNapoli. Rauscha would buy Andy DiNapoli.

Well guess again, Tibor Rauscha.

About conservation districts and ground water Andy DiNapoli understood nothing. He cared less than nothing. But in the classic fashion Andy fixed things up for Rauscha.

First there was gentle pressure on the local governments with zoning authority at Lobos Aullando. Andy told them a story of jobs, tax revenue, fresh fish for gorgeous water fowl to eat.

Less gently Andy warned that somebody like Tibor Rauscha could sue and sue "until the county buckles under the burden of legal fees. I'm telling you," as Andy told one district manager, "if you don't give Rauscha his water this district has issued its last permit." Andy styled himself a rascal who got things done.

When Andy moved to Texas from Connecticut 20 years before he was a Roman Catholic in the insurance business. In Texas Andy was born again as a whiskey-drinking Baptist by the grace of the boss he worked for. Andy's wife and three daughters had little interest in any of it and were signed up members of their local parish, St. Marguerite D'Youville.

Also by the grace of the boss he worked for Andy was a wealthy man, like Tibor Rauscha. He was a partner in Platz Heidrich, an oilfield services company that had been his insurance client. He could therefore afford to serve the people of his district on a salary of $7,200 a year. There he worked to block legislation in any way antagonistic to the future of oil and gas.

Tibor Rauscha was not one of these people who spent much time reflecting on being Texan. Andy was such a person because he was a convert; res ipsa loquitur. He wore a black straw cowboy hat (wrong, Rauscha knew) with a business suit and bloused his pants into his boots. (His old Baptist boss did it so Andy did it too. Imprinting.) Andy's accent was born again like him. It now had a twang more common to Rauscha's part of the state than to Galveston. Once he had that perfected more or less Andy was ready to run for office.

On the last day of the issues retreat Andy told Tibor Rauscha of his plan to run for Congress and go to Washington.

Like a shy person who's managed to make a friend Andy attached himself to Rauscha at the farewell cocktail party Sunday afternoon.

The night before there had been Halloween-themed fun and games, and Rauscha went to be bed early. The Sunday cocktail party also had a Halloween theme including a drink made to look like candy corn using orange juice, vodka and condensed milk. How could people want such a thing? Andy sipped at one and set it aside.

"Glad I tried it anyway," he said to the middle-aged woman keeping bar.

Andy smiled broadly with Rauscha for all the smart-phone snapshots. Rauscha understood that it was good for Andy to be seen beside him at this thing. Rauscha was a wealthy entrepreneur with Hispanic allusions.

In the moments when they were left alone Andy went on talking about his campaign for Congress. He said to Rauscha he was working out his platform.

"There's a Christian dimension to the issues you and I care about," Andy said. "I'm not afraid to say it."

"When you took my campaign donations you did it because you're a Christian?"

"It was never about the money, Tibor. I was glad to partner with you on behalf of the people in my district. They profited."

"It wasn't about the money?"

"I did it because getting you what you need is good for the people who voted for me."

"So it was about the money."

"Carful, Tibor, or I'll forget we're amigos."

Andy was teasing.

"My whole argument is that the punishing taxes on hard-working people like you who've succeeded is contrary to God's will—something like coveting thy neighbor's goods, you know? Isn't it? Why should some of us own all the costs and own all the risk but then if things praise God work out be asked to share all the benefit? When I put America first in my foreign policy...."

"You've already got a foreign policy, Andy?"

"Nuts to you, Tibor. I know you're joking me." That day Andy wore custom boots and a brown wool suit. Rauscha, whenever he traveled, took care to look like he had just come from New York and his Italian tailor. He believed this costume gave him leverage over the cowboys, and he was right.

"When I put America first in my thinking," Andy was telling Rauscha, "it's because jumping around the world trying to put out fires *other people* start is contrary to common sense *and* to what I read in my Bible. Both. When I stand up in the legislature in Austin to speak for beleaguered middle-class families—which I happen to know we both believe in, though you might be a divorced man—it's because I believe in a Christ-centered household. I read my Bible, Tibor, as I know you do."

"That is why I'm a happy guy."

"And I read my Constitution. They are not in conflict. They are in conversation."

"Where do you get this stuff?"

"I really think there's a reason why God put all these political thoughts in my head."

"God or Scotch?"

"God *and* Scotch," Andy answered with a chuckle. He accepted Rauscha's jab good naturedly; he was obliged to. "I don't drink," he said, "just when I'm talking. I've got the thin skin, which is rough on a public servant. The Scotch helps with that. But that doesn't make me wrong, Tibor. I know you know this. You can do anything you want to me. I'm willing to be persecuted." Andy took another sip.

"If you run for Congress," Rauscha told him, "things like water permits are going to be someone else's problem."

"That is not true, Tibor. I'm not an idiot."

"Idiots get elected all the time. Someone ought to worry about that, but not me." Rauscha also reminded Andy that he lived in a different Congressional district, one with a congresswoman who generally thought the way he did. Rauscha had been to her house twice, once in the old days with Carol and once with Fanny since.

"If I lose in the primary," Andy replied, "which by the way I *won't* lose, I'll be back in Austin just the same. And you'll continue needing good old Andy's influence with the conservation district." Not in so many words but Andy was telling Rauscha that he would remember who supported him.

Rauscha looked at Andy quite some time. And then he nodded.

Andy insisted on driving Rauscha to the airport later that evening. On the way Rauscha mentioned that he was being pestered for a donation from the Shriners Children's Hospital in Galveston.

"Did they get my name from you?"

"Probably not directly."

"They should back off. Tell them to."

"We don't speak."

"They're asking me for cash outright. I don't want to do it and won't do it with my own money. It pisses me off, people always wanting something."

An orange Volkswagen drew up on Andy's left side and accelerated past him with an irritating buzz.

"Eat 'em up, Otto," muttered Tibor Rauscher. "Fucking Germans." Rauscha and Andy were a mile from the airport.

"Don't make jokes, Tibor. Aren't you German yourself? Rauscha?"

"You're wondering?"

"Anyhow, I have Germans in my district and they vote. Not as a bloc but they vote."

That Sunday night Tibor Ruscha flew into El Paso International on the last flight from Dallas. His plane landed late, about eleven o'clock, and from there it was a 90-minute drive to Perros Salvajes.

Rauscha never minded the long drive to and from the airport to Perros Salvajes. Nearly every week he did it at least once. The Range Rover was comfortable, and more and more in his life Tibor Rauscha liked being comfortable. And alone. He was turning 40 the next spring, and maybe in a few years he would not like solitude so much. That was among the things he thought about when he drove.

Sometimes he rolled the windows down and slowed the car a little just to sniff the night air. Doing this made him feel almost poetic in his heart.

That night Rauscha's head was not crowded with philosophical reflection. He was thinking about going home to Fanny. He hoped she would be awake.

He turned off for Perros Salvajes onto Highway 19. One hundred yards on he hit a pothole big enough to swallow a baby.

Tibor Rauscha was home again.

Texas in the Headlines

In the last month of the three years they were together Moliere mentioned to Franklin that she would like to have a look at a deciduous tree.

This was in October. At that time of year in West Texas there was little of autumn in the postcard convention of blazing leafy trees. Sometimes after an autumn rain colorful blossoms popped out on cactus and the other desert whatnot, which was pretty. But Moliere was used to what the desert did.

That year she and Franklin went camping at Lost Maples on Columbus Day weekend. Because of the holiday Moliere had the Monday off from school. And for once Franklin did not pull a holiday shift. On the Friday they drove as far as a Best Western in Junction. It had a crunchy carpet and a sticky bathroom floor. They were so glad to be off the road that they did not care about the housekeeping.

They had sex, they fell asleep. That was that.

Saturday morning Franklin and Moliere woke early and left for the park. They claimed their campsite and without pitching their tent left immediately for the trailhead. The weather was good and they spent the afternoon walking. Under the color-drained canopy shading the trail the day was cool. Not so particolored as Moliere hoped but nice, all the same.

About one o'clock they stopped and ate sandwiches bought the day before from a fancy deli in Perros Salvajes. They sat on a rock ledge looking west. Through holes in the shifting clouds overhead shafts of light darted like theater beamlights, first here and then some other place. Franklin called them "Jesus lights." The effect was touching.

Between bites the subject of wedding planning came up; it was getting tiresome to talk about and Franklin asked if they could not just elope.

"Fine with me," Moliere told him. "We'll tell everyone I'm knocked up."

"That would be mean to Léon." Moliere's sister Patrice eloped because she was knocked up. Léon had been worried sick about her, although not because of the being knocked up. It was because Patrice had separately told Moliere and Léon that the baby's father—a blond senior airman at Kirtland Air Base named Duval—had hit her.

"How can you keep going out with him?" Moliere had asked her sister when she heard.

"Because I love him," Patrice answered.

Katherine Moliere was 15 at that time but she knew self-deception when she met it. Explaining it was still beyond her. She was horrified at her sister's trap. So was Léon. And this was before the baby came. When Léon found out about Duval he implored Patrice to come back and live with him and her mother, Maureen, who was still alive then.

"If he comes around I'll kill him," Léon promised Patrice. "I'll quit my job and every day go to work with you." By nature Léon was a peaceful man but he meant every word.

By then Patrice had moved Duval into the house she was sharing with two roommates. She refused to come back home. And so Léon went around to her house on a weekend when he knew Duval would be there. He pounded on the door until the sleepy-eyed Duval opened up.

"Is my Patrice here?" he demanded in as even a tone as he could manage.

"You know she's at work, Mr. Moliere. You need something?" Duval's yellow hair was an affront even to the fair-minded Léon.

"I wanted to be sure she was out. Listen to me, Duval. Patrice won't report you for what you did..."

"What'd I do?"

"...but I sent a registered letter to the police. They know about you now. I've started your file. If I can find out who your superior is at Kirtland I will write to him too."

"I'm exasperated to hear that, Mr. Moliere. We argued. That is the only thing that happened. Patrice said she forgave me."

When Patrice found out that Léon had come around to the house she was furious.

"How dare you jeopardize my relationship," she told him. Not told but wept.

"But he hit you."

"Duval can be sweet."

When Moliere told him this last part of the story Franklin remarked, "That's always the MO with these guys. I see men like that at least three times a night on my shift—boyfriends, husbands. They hit a woman then ask her for sympathy. They don't ever improve. They are a waste of space."

"You cops are hardened," Moliere said.

"It's nothing to do with hardened. I've got inside knowledge of men."

Franklin did not want Duval at the wedding. He met him just once at a dismal Thanksgiving with Moliere's family in Albuquerque and it was all he could do not to spit. When it came time to leave for Perros Salvajes Duval embraced Franklin in a brotherly hug; Duval wanted to be the sort of man who hugged, Franklin could see. It was repellent, odious, obvious.

"I understand your argument," said Moliere, "but since that one time I don't think there's been a problem."

"You think Patrice would tell you if there had been?"

"I keep thinking the guest list should be longer," Moliere was telling Franklin, and she was not changing the subject. "I thought I was popular."

"No one knows more people than 53. You have all these people on Instagram and you think you know them. For a party fifty-three is a lot of popularity."

"I have lived in Perros Salvajes six years and there's no one I call a best friend."

"Me?"

"Someone I don't sleep with. If you should fall off that cliff over there I'd have no one I really like talking to."

Franklin looked at the cliff.

"Cops are insured, aren't they?" Moliere asked him, observing how he studied the drop. She already knew Franklin was insured. When they bought their house the previous year the bank required life insurance as a condition of their mortgage.

"You'll have to make it look like an accident."

From their perch on a rock the long autumn sunlight shone across Sabinal Canyon. The melancholy of the light ached their hearts. They savored the stream of solitude. It was a hot day though.

"You want some sunblock for your forehead," Moliere said. "If you don't your skin will burn and your police hat will hurt when you put it on." Franklin's skin had no pigment at all. Two hours of walking on that overcast October day gave his face a tomato shade. Moliere thought it must be painful to have skin pale as Franklin's.

"Are you saying our racial difference has come between us?" Franklin said. "Has it finally happened?" Like Moliere Franklin was Irish on his mother's side. His other side was some Norwegian. Franklin was white as any Texan could be without passing out.

"Don't joke about that too much," said Moliere.

"It's hard knowing how much is too much."

"Just don't be my Uncle Brian."

"Who's your Uncle Brian?"

"My mother's brother. When she and my father got engaged he was the first one my mother and father told. They thought because he was young Brian would be on their side. First thing he said was the babies would look funny. Big joke. Did I come out funny to you?"

"No. And I've seen you naked."

"Once he realized they were serious Uncle Brian wouldn't leave Mom alone about my father. Brian was worse than her parents. They weren't thrilled, I'm not saying that, but they liked my father so they got used to the idea of a Black man for a son-in-law."

"How does anyone not like Léon?"

"When I was a kid Uncle Brian teased me about my hair so much one time I ran away crying. I was probably 13. My mother said that until he met Duval that was the only time she ever saw Dad ever really explode, because of me. 'You don't know the Irish,' Dad told me,'" putting on her father's rumbling Haitian voice, "'yo panse twòp nan tèt yo!'"

"What does that mean?"

"It's not complementary. The punch line was that Brian swore he was only joking, you know how people say that so they can get away with murder. After that my mother wouldn't have Brian in the house. Brian didn't care. He didn't want any forgiveness."

"She cut off her own brother? Good for her."

"She cut him out of her heart. Then Brian died. The problem took care of itself."

About four that afternoon they came off the trail. The sun slipped away. The air grew chill.

It took Moliere only a few minutes to get the tent up; she was the camper, not Franklin. He was a city boy. In the way of gear he owned nothing; for this trip he needed to buy the first sleeping bag of his life. More than once since she moved to New Mexico Moliere had noted how the people in Texas led mainly indoor lives. For all they were moved by their incantations to the wide-open spaces the wild west was a place most Texans seldom visited in person.

"About our state," Franklin agreed, "we are all hat and no cattle."

Moliere emptied the duffel bag in which she kept all her teachers' sweaters and put all their food in it. She sent Franklin to acquire a load of firewood from a sullen-looking man in a red cap waiting in his truck next to the campground gate. The man was sunburned like Franklin. He was not chatty like Franklin.

The campground had showers, cellphone reception and an ice machine. It was what Moliere disdainfully called "car camping." Other than for sleeping outside on the ground it was almost like the Best Western.

Moliere and Franklin drank Scotch with the dinner they cooked—steaks, grilled peppers and half-cooked potatoes they buried in the campfire. Once the sun went down they drank some more and watched the fire go out. They were at 2,500 feet and when full darkness descended the air grew cold, almost winter-night cold. Moliere showed Franklin how to zip their bags together.

The night was seriously dark to the unaccustomed eyes of city people. In the serious dark Moliere and Franklin made love in the cold and afterward laughed at how frozen they were.

"I can barely see you in this dark, Katherine," Franklin said.

"You need something?"

"My hands have eyes. I swear to God, Katherine, they talk to me. They tell me you're beautiful."

"Your hands should shut up and rub the warmth back into me. That's their job."

The two of them fell asleep. And that was that.

The plan for the next day was to go and see the Frio River Bat Cave. But at seven a.m. Franklin was awakened by the ringing of his phone. His ringtone was the emperor's theme from Star Wars. Moliere had been after him to change it for a year, it was that annoying.

The caller was the duty sergeant in Perros Salvajes, Bobby Alessandro, asking Franklin to come in. A new guy scheduled to take the Sunday overnight had shingles and could not work. They needed Franklin to cover for him.

"I heard shingles are painful," Franklin said.

"You can get a shot for it."

"I was going to go see the cave with the bats."

"If it's a consolation," Alessandro told Franklin, "you'll be on with your old buddy AJ. He's been mentoring the kid this week so he's on the duty roster already."

Moliere was disappointed, of course, but she knew things like this were the lot of a cop's girlfriend. Additionally she was hungover a little from the night before and OK with missing the bats. (She did not say the second thing. It was better to earn credit for seeming forbearing. In any human relationship that is as good as money in the bank.)

With 12 hours before Franklin had to be home to Perros Salvajes they took their time about breakfast. Moliere scrambled eggs over the fire. The fire made her hair smell like wood smoke. Wood smoke is aromatic at first and then becomes tiresome.

After breakfast Moliere went and showered. There were other ladies there, pleasant people, talkative. They showered under the big blue October sky, all the ladies naked in their many shapes and skin tones and ages. The morning air was so cold it made them laugh under the water, Moliere too.

Moliere was back 30 minutes later. Her natural curls were sprung the way they always were when they were wet and before she put goop on her head. Moliere was not smelling like smoke. Now she was fragrant with soap and shampoo.

When he saw her Franklin said, "You ought to wear your hair like that all the time. It kills me."

"It's too much work when it's this way."

"It brings out the Léon in you."

Loads of times Franklin told her something similar. Often in bed he traced with his fingertip the freckles dotting the bridge of Moliere's nose and spilling across her beige skin like the stars in a dark-cloud constellation. Franklin said this, that Moliere's freckles were like a constellation.

"I love your skin," he would tell her. Once he traced the freckles on her back with a ballpoint. He told her they made the w-shape of Cassiopeia. Moliere took his word for it. She could not see back there, and Franklin was not the sort of person to pretend knowledge of a thing.

Perhaps it was the disappointment of needing to leave early, or the mild hangover she had or that she was getting her period. Maybe it was remembering Uncle Brian. Or maybe it was just a motiveless malignity, which happens. Whatever it was Moliere decided to be irked at what Franklin said about the Léon in her.

"Are you uncomfortable that I'm not all white, Franklin?"

"Pardon?"

"I'm teasing."

That was all of it, the whole exchange. But Moliere was doing something other than teasing; Franklin could tell. At this distance there's no way to say now what the other thing was. If you asked her even today Moliere could not tell you.

"What's the matter, Katherine?" The sky above them was black and blue with dense air coming. Rain for later.

"Nothing's the matter." Which every single time means the opposite.

They packed up the campsite in silence, more or less. Moliere broke the zipper on what had been her teachers' sweaters bag. Moliere drove them home. Once they stopped for gasoline, once for sandwiches.

"You mind that I have to get back for tonight?" Franklin asked her.

"No." Moliere gave him three hours of this. All the way home to Perros Salvajes she nursed her irritation just to keep it going. She was locked in her sullen silence. She wanted to break out but could not. The devil had got in her. He would not free her tongue.

With so little conversation coming his way Franklin let himself nap for the last hour of the drive. Franklin used to be a world-class napper; he just closed his eyes and it happened for as long as the napping opportunity presented itself. Nothing ever seemed to interfere with his ability to sleep, which only annoyed Moliere. He was putting something in the tank for his over-night. Franklin slept with his head against the chilly window glass of the passenger door and fogged it up. As it waited for rain to fall the world outside was grey.

When they arrived at their house in Perros Salvajes it was about six o'clock. The afternoon was ended and at that time of year night was already coming. The rain had settled in for the evening.

Franklin asked Moliere if she would like to have dinner at Ginny's. No, she would not.

"Just a drink? I'm not on until ten o'clock."

"You drink too much. How do you show up at work with liquor on your breath?"

Finally Moliere had landed one. It showed on Franklin's face. He stopped being patient.

"Pearls in your oysters, Katherine," he said as he left the house. No kiss, no squeeze. "See you in the morning." Franklin left the house and drove to work.

And that was that.

AJ Munoz was no happier being on for a Columbus Day night shift than Franklin was. The chilly rain coming down did not help. The pair of them bitched companionably and expected a quiet time of it.

About eleven-thirty, not two hours into their tour, AJ and Franklin got a domestic dispute at the Los Nopales trailer park. That was nearly out of the county altogether and very close to being not their problem. The 911 caller was from a neighbor of the shouting couple, the Chanterelles.

"Oh good," said AJ recognizing the name. "Mr. Guns." They headed without special urgency for the trailer park. Couples shouting at each other was not ordinarily much of anything besides discouraging. Dollars to donuts when they arrived the wife says everything's fine, sorry to bother you, officer. Beat the hell out of a woman, threaten her, and she cannot stand to see the bastard in trouble. And now their guy is *really* pissed off.

"Mr. Guns?"

"He is a second-amendment nut. He thinks the government is coming for everyone's arsenal."

"Make our job easier if they did." AJ said later that he noticed Franklin being a little acerbic that night—that was AJ's word for it, "acerbic".

"You know this guy?" Franklin asked.

"He has this website called 'Mr. Guns'. I made his acquaintance last summer. He told me he hadn't worked in three years. He blamed the government."

"State or local?"

"Just government."

"How does anyone not work for three years? Just the boredom of it must be awful."

"The website gives him something to do with his time, I suppose."

"How often do you talk to him?"

"I did not say we talked. The one and only time I met this guy was at the Bighorn Mall in Concolor. It's the weekend before school started in August, and the mall was packed. And here's this guy stalking around with a Bushmaster slung over his shoulder."

"Honest to God? What the hell for?"

"To make his point about guns. That is why I'm trying to explain, Franklin."

"What *was* his point?"

"I shouldn't say it was a Bushmaster. That's more than I can attest to. Some variety of long gun."

"What's he look like? Is he known?"

"'Is he known'? What the hell is that?"

"Would I *know* him?"

"He's scrawny in a way that made him look squirrely. Like someone who itches." The heavens opened and Franklin turned the wipers up higher. "Anyway, he goes into a shoe store, right? To browse, he tells the manager. 'You don't need to be armed for browsing here, sir' says the manager," AJ said, putting on a prissy store-manager voice. "Which I think was brave of the guy but which only sets off Chanterelle about his rights. Which is I guess what he wanted. So now the manager's worried something's going to start. He calls us. Barbara Rossiter was my partner then—remember Barbara?"

"Sure."

"We get there. If it was a Black dude they would have called in a SWAT team by then and Chanterelle would be lying on the floor dead. Instead he gets the two of us."

"Animal control."

"Barbara and me were very mellow but basically like the store manager we were curious to know why Chanterelle needs an elephant gun to go the mall. And when we ask him he starts a lecture about the state of Texas open-carry law which frankly I've never understood in all its details, between us."

"Me neither. Between us."

"He says to Barbara and me, 'I am educating people today about their right to defend themselves in daily American life blah blah blah.' Like he is Mad Max."

"In that movie."

"Barbara steps out and radios whoever the duty captain was that day. He can't help her with the law either. He wants to call the DA to get an opinion but it's a Saturday so all Barbara and I are left with is our natural charm."

"How'd that work out?"

"Got him to back down and leave the store. Marched

out still carrying the gun over his shoulder. Probably playing soldier in his head."

"You're an excellent cop, AJ. Guy could have lost his marbles on you."

"Barbara was the excellent cop that day. She has the good-cop thing down cold, you know? Calmed every situation right down just being there."

"That was the end of it?"

"We walked out with him and he's suddenly our best friend. He respects law enforcement, he says. Somehow he ended up telling me he used to work as a stitcher at the Buddy factory before they took the manufacturing to Mexico."

"Not a lot of call anymore for boot stitchers in this country."

"You think there would be call. People *wear* cowboy boots."

"Too expensive making them in Texas," Franklin observed, "paying people what they need to live. Buddy can make them for less in Mexico and people will still buy them. What is Chanterelle—French?"

"With the *elle* on the end I'd guess, yeah. But he is from here."

"Guns are an expensive interest for a man with no income."

"Mrs. Chanterelle works retail."

"That's where the big money is."

AJ laughed.

"I can't wait to meet them," Franklin added. "The husband sounds like an idealist."

"That was Franklin," AJ told Moliere later. "He always had an insight." After he died Franklin would always exist in an ideal state for AJ and Moliere. That was unfair to his memory because it robbed him of his other human parts.

The rain stopped. There was no moon.

All the lights of the trailer park appeared to be on when Franklin and AJ rolled up. Big stadium lights up on poles lit the dirt lanes between the white trailers. Lamplight from within the trailers added to the illumination—how did the people living in that place sleep nights? Wide puddles between the trailers reflected the light.

It was not hard for AJ and Franklin to find the double-wide where the Chanterelles lived. It was down a lane called Dominick Place between an even row of trailers.

For the middle of October it was a warm night. To let breezes in the Chanterelles' windows were up. That way everyone heard them yelling. A crowd of a dozen or more, children included, was collected out in front of the trailer. For the neighbors this performance of raw emotion was like hearing opera on their radio.

Their voices rose and then fell in something like harmony. The other one would back up and try to score a point, then simultaneously they both erupted again. Franklin and AJ had heard this duet lots of times. Lots of times it was way worse than the performance the Chanterelles put on that night.

Franklin put one foot on the step-up and rapped with his knuckles on the metal-clad door. No one answered and he rapped again, harder so the Chanterelles could not pretend they did not hear him.

From within the trailer a man's voice was heard saying "Oh *fuck* you whoever it is" as Mrs. Chanterelle opened the door. Before Franklin could identify himself as a police officer she was shoved aside by her husband. He fired once directly into Franklin's chest. He killed him.

AJ said afterward that he remembered being distantly fascinated at how the gun's muzzle flash set fire to Franklin's blue blouse for just a Moment. Some part of him hoped the flame might cauterize the wound.

"My whole life I wanted…," said Chanterelle. He did not finish the sentence, stopped maybe because the solemnness of murder, penetrated even his pickled brain. But saying that he turned the rifle on AJ and pulled the trigger three times. Somehow he missed. Not "somehow"; Chanterelle had been drinking Jack Daniels all night and was blind drunk, after all.

The noise was deafening. Inside the noise AJ was wondering if he was dead with Franklin.

As people always do, AJ said everything seemed to happen in slow motion. He even remarked the sound of a stray bullet pinging another trailer and worried for its occupants.

"Did you ever die in a dream?" AJ asked Moliere later. "This was like that. I was thinking, If I am having this thought then I must still be alive."

There was screaming behind AJ. There was himself lifting his service weapon from its holster and flicking off the safety with his thumb in the same motion. There was Chanterelle's thin face colored from the bourbon he had been pounding all evening. There was the barrel of Chanterelle's rifle hot on the skin of AJ's hand as he pushed it aside.

AJ shot him in his middle. Chanterelle looked startled. Mrs. Chanterelle fled out the back door of the trailer—there was no other word for the way she took off, said AJ—*fled* for what she must have assumed was her life.

AJ turned his back on Chanterelle and bent over Franklin. He checked the pulse in his partner's neck. There was none. Franklin's mouth was open in an O-shape, like a singer holding a note. Thirty seconds before he was alive; then he was completely dead. And that was that.

His hand still on Franklin's neck for the comfort AJ turned to look at Chanterelle lying on his back. Blood puddled on his torso in a shiny muck. Chanterelle was moaning in tremendous pain from the wound in his left side. Amazingly his drunken eyes were open and staring at AJ. Chanterelle tried to raise a hand. There's something he needs, AJ reflected.

"I'm gonna watch you bleed to death," said AJ.

But that was not what AJ did. The way he told it to Moliere, "in the next moment I felt God at my shoulder—really, Katherine, truly God. He was telling me that all life is precious to Him, that no matter what this man had done to Franklin I had a holy obligation to save him if I could. It took everything in me to move away from Franklin and help Chanterelle. I prayed in my heart, Lord, keep me close. If I ever get to heaven it will only be because I did that."

At 2 AM that night the county executive of Perros Salvajes, Rhonda Cruz, telephoned Moliere from the

Perros Salvajes County Hospital to tell her Franklin was dead. Chanterelle was upstairs in the same hospital. Chanterelle pulled through. He remains among the living, minus his spleen and two ribs.

Assigned to a no-hope lawyer named Steven Charles—a man so forgettable that the news accounts called him just "public defender"—Chanterelle offered a plea of diminished capacity. His offer was turned down by the prosecutor's office. Accepting his reality Chanterelle conceded first-degree murder, hoping for life instead of death.

The court asked Moliere, as Franklin's fiancé, to make a victim-impact statement, but she wanted none of that.

"What do they *think* the impact is?" she asked the district attorney.

Instead, Chanterelle told the court he was remorseful in a brief speech public defender wrote for him. "I was only joking," he added on his own. The judge heard him out and one month later had him brought back to court and sentenced him to death.

"Death is the obvious choice," said the judge.

When Chanterelle heard the judge's sentence he turned to Steven Charles and told him, "I hoped for better." They were standing at the defense table as Chanterelle was buckled into irons.

"It didn't help you killed a fuckin cop," public defender replied.

"In for a dime, in for a dollar," Chanterelle told him. They shook hands. Neither realized that the microphone at the table was live and amplifying their exchange to the courtroom generally. For a day or two the state of Texas was incensed. Then Texas went on to the next thing.

Chanterelle still sits in Huntsville, filing appeals, still promoting the diminished-capacity angle. It's not going to work, and he will be executed eventually. Mrs. Chanterelle divorced him quick as she could and moved up to Oklahoma. She can survive her old life if she can just keep looking forward.

About Chanterelle Moliere barely thought—no hate for him, no rage, nothing, as if he were only fate's agent, nobody to her. But regret regret rose up around Moliere's ears for the way she behaved toward Franklin on the last day he was alive.

The musty sheets on the bed they had not made on the day they left for Lost Maples lay in a tangle for days. They left the bed unmade when they drove off. Moliere's theory was that if they came home from the weekend to an unmade bed they would be compelled to wash the sheets, like it or not. Domestic calculation like that now belonged to history.

On each of the three nights after Franklin was murdered Moliere burrowed herself into the musty sheets to roll in his scent the way a dog might do. Her need was that primitive.

There was confusion about cemetery arrangements. Moliere had met Franklin's family only a handful time in the several years they were together. They seemed to like her well enough but still saw her as "the girlfriend". She was not consulted on a burial place for Franklin.

Franklin's sister Molly phoned two days after the shooting to tell Moliere the family had decided on Green River Cemetery—which was a long way east of both El Paso and Perros Salvajes, half the way to Louisiana. Moliere was not offended because she did not care. She stayed in bed for three days. On the third day Léon and Patrice came from Las Cruces and drove her to the funeral.

Cops came from as far as Seattle and Boston to Franklin's funeral; it is a tradition among cops to do that for their dead. By the cops (if not by Franklin's family) Moliere was cast in the part of the widow at this event. That was how it felt to her: like she was cast in a part; *someone* had to perform the role of widow in this ritual. Moliere was expected to behave with quiet grief, and she did.

AJ was there but he was given no part to play. Moliere asked that he sit next to her. Léon and Patrice were on her other side. Her eyes focused on the little blue policeman's Stetson that separated Franklin's birth and death dates on his headstone. It even had a tiny gilt badge on the crest. Instead of seeming pious it looked adorable. Molly's idea.

A photograph taken by the *El Paso Times* that day shows Moliere looking stunned as a policeman in white kid gloves whom she never before met came and offered her "the condolences of the entire department". In the instant the picture was made Moliere was thinking this was an offensively empty thing to say. This thought, however, showed on her face as stoicism.

The photograph ran with the caption "Grief struck" under it. "Wonder struck" would have been as apt.

Moliere only wanted to be through to the other side of the ceremonials. She wanted to be left alone with a sucking wound that the word "grief" did not begin to cover.

Moliere stared at the box with Franklin in it. After he was dead no one asked if Moliere wanted to see his body; if they had she would have said no. It would be two years before Moliere visited Franklin's grave. It troubles some people to visit graves. For one thing they find themselves thinking of the ghoulishness happening in the box under their feet. This was not the case with Moliere. Thinking about Franklin in the box did not make him any *more* dead.

What haunted Moliere's heart was the image of Franklin's back before it was blown apart, his broad shoulders as he left the house for work for what she did not know was the last time. This—the back of him, the walking away—became the entire content of Moliere's memory of Franklin's final night on earth.

II

Texas Pierces the Astral Plane

Two weeks after the Halloween kidnapping Moliere was alone in her house on a grey and sullen Sunday.

The night before Moliere sat up watching an old movie on television—a technicolor thing from the 1950s about a plucky unwed mother abandoned by a useless but irresistible young man, who remains in the picture for reasons that are not clear. All the young movie stars acted up a storm over everything; that movie must have made millions. While watching it Moliere finished a bottle of wine. Now it was the morning and her head hurt and her mouth was lined with boiled wool.

Headachy, Moliere listened to her house tick. It was cold in her house. That was not helping her mood. Her house was often cold; it had thin exterior Texas walls. Winter—wet, light-deprived winter—was a thing waiting outside her house that morning.

Dread—dread, the real thing, dread the way the word is used in the Bible—dread came over Moliere. It was like a cold patch in a lake, pulling her down.

For a while when she was maybe 14 Moliere's father Léon had her seeing a child psychologist in Las Cruces about her cold patches. Moliere was in the thick of puberty then and her mother had died the year before. Léon worried that his daughter's trenches of silence were in some way related to these two events. The doctor to whom Léon sent his daughter did not think so. After a year of Saturday mornings with Moliere the shrink told Léon that his daughter was simply prone to reflection.

"But Katherine seems *too* thoughtful at times," Léon said.

"So let her be a philosopher," the shrink told him. Léon did not think too much of that guy.

The cold patch in Moliere's lake was there all the time. More than once she talked to Franklin about it. If his death figured into this at all it was because, when he was alive, Moliere was too busy with him to allow every dark feeling into her head. After Franklin was killed she recalled this as his gift to her.

Obviously an exception was the last day of their time together.

Not quite two years on from Franklin's death the cold ticking house with its thin Texas walls was no longer full of his smell, a smell Moliere always thought was a cross between bread and unwashed hair; she loved that smell. For the first two months after Franklin died his things kept his smell alive in the house—his shirts in the bedroom closet with his scent on them, for instance—until the afternoon Moliere willed herself to take them all and bring them to the God's Good Grace mission at the far end of Fuller Boulevard.

Except that Moliere needed somewhere to sit she would also have disposed of the four red chairs Franklin persuaded her to buy for the kitchen table. She never liked those chairs for their color. Or the red couch he persuaded her to buy.

For those first two months after Franklin's murder Moliere saw no one and declined all invitations. She went nowhere for Thanksgiving, nowhere for Christmas. Except to the grocery store she barely went out of the house at all. She hated the possibility of meeting someone she knew and having to say how she was doing. But every few days she went through a liter of scotch and then she would need to go to buy more.

For a while Moliere was drinking a little when she came in from school in the afternoons. She saw where that was headed and this at least she stopped. She began running again instead. Running was an imitation of her old life. It helped a little in returning her to the world.

Had she returned to work the day after Franklin's funeral Moliere would have found her way back to life faster. That is what AJ Munoz did, and it was good for him.

Instead Moliere took a leave of absence from her teaching job until January, after the Christmas break. When she returned she found she welcomed the distraction of the world's continued turning. Still, for a long time she was sick with the recognition that she would never be given a chance to erase the petulance of her last day with Franklin.

In that first year Moliere saw a therapist once a week to talk about this. Health insurance barely covered any of it.

"What do you think Franklin would tell you if you could say all this to him?" her shrink asked one day.

Moliere did not even have to think about what would Franklin would tell her. "He wouldn't tell me anything," she said. "He would laugh at me."

"Well, there you go," said the therapist. "This doesn't have to go on being raw, Katherine. You can grieve. But you can live again too. Don't keep calling back the past. It's like willing the return of a toothache. People cannot live like that."

"I don't want that."

"Which?"

"I *want* to call back the past. I want the past to come back. I want the pain."

Moliere kept alive her grief because it fed the memory of Franklin. Every anecdote she recalled turned on some grain of ingratitude in her. She would not forgive herself.

Moliere thought a great deal about the meaning of forgiveness at this time, beginning with herself. She meditated on the power of forgiveness, its limit, its sources. Moliere could have opened a Forgiveness University and taught no other subject.

Forgiveness University might offer a Masters degree in the limits of contrition. Self-guided study for the raddled self: the core of the curriculum would be this conundrum. The examination questions put to the student would be: (1) Describe the condition of your remorse; and (2) What is self-love? The candidate's essay would be graded pass/fail.

For nearly two years, almost from the moment she was awakened by the two a.m. phone call from Rhonda Cruz,

Moliere had a domestic scene playing on continuous loop in her head. In it she entered her ticking house and walked in on Franklin at the stove cooking for her. Franklin liked rice for the comfort in it. Rice always featured it in the meals he made her. In the scene that Moliere imagined she dressed Franklin in his red Texas Rangers sweatshirt and a pair of tired jeans she used to be after him to replace.

"I'm sorry for yesterday, Franklin."

"It was nothing." They had sex, they fell asleep, the rice burned. And that was that. She never had to think again about the day before.

One day when she told the therapist about her scenario he told her, "You make yourself prey to your thoughts, Katherine."

"You'd have no customers if people did not do that."

"It's good you can make jokes. It's evidence of mental health." Moliere liked this therapist and was concerned to think she might be regarded as a difficult client.

The phrase the therapist used—"prey to yourself"—was something Moliere had heard a thousand times, but this time the time the image struck home. The picture of herself cowering *from* herself—what would Franklin make of that? It would only diminish her attractiveness.

That moment was not the end of Moliere's grief; nothing will be, even now. But it is correct to say that it was the moment when she began to pick up her head again, at least a little bit.

All that aside, it was not coincidence that Moliere began to feel her way clear only after the Christmas break when she returned to school. She needed to work. Work was the beginning of feeling her way back, or at least to her accommodation of life without Franklin in it.

Four years later in the weeks after trick-or-treat with Fanny she drew on this education in respect to Eugene Rauscha.

About eleven o'clock on the hungover Sunday morning Moliere willed herself out of the house and went running, thinking this might help shake off the bad feeling of hungover Sunday solitude. It did not.

Moliere ran with no path in mind. By some homing instinct she headed for Emma Tenayuca elementary, thinking she would turn there and run back home. The distance was five miles round trip. Several times she was surprised to discover that she had stopped running and was walking, so distracted was she.

On the return leg of her run Moliere passed people leaving the Presbyterian church. Moliere stood and watched from across the street. Part of her wondered if maybe she would do better with religion. Faith of the kind they had in the Presbyterian church was not a subject Moliere knew about. Her father and mother said hardly a word about it growing up, for or against that she remembered. Her sister Patrice told people she was saved now, but Moliere believed this was more to do with spending a couple of hours on her own on Sunday mornings; *that* was her salvation. Franklin once said he believed in a passive way—"It's the only logical thing," he said in connection with the death of his one uncle. At the time Moliere did not think to ask why he should believe this.

Moliere's faith was in the right here, the right now. That was her theology. She had no long-term perspective on pain, or on happiness, except in her knowledge that even with very good luck most of us get plenty of both.

Looking over at the Presbyterians Moliere reflected, I could do with some rigor.

On the steps of the church the Presbyterians stood and visited with one another. Sunday did not seem to be bothering them. The pastor was out there in his blue vestments giving them each a hug and shaking hands. His shiny bald head nodded benignly in every direction.

Those are the whitest people in Perros Salvajes, Moliere thought. See how they smile. Probably all talking about Jesus. Anyone could walk up to them and they would be just fine.

And here Moliere saw Janet Staufer come out of church with an older man who Moliere correctly guessed was Janet's father.

Janet was the girl Eugene Rauscha raped, no matter how the judge ruled it. Janet was not a girl, in fact, but woman. She was easily 25, older even. She held to her father's wrist with both hands as they stepped out on to the shallow pronaos in front of the church and into the day. Janet looked not fearful, not happy, not watchful. She had no expression. Moliere had never seen this in anyone, man or woman.

Janet's father was different. As he stepped into the day with his daughter his instinct was to look at the sky, checking up there for more rain.

In class the next day Moliere kept losing her place. She was teaching the kids about math integers by using the example of golf, a game she had a hard time understanding. She did not play golf and never in her life knew anyone who did. Half her students did not get the point she was trying to make. Nothing else they did in life prepared them for the idea that accumulating the fewest points wins.

That afternoon when Moliere checked her school eMail there was a note from Eugene Rauscha.

Could call you up? OK if you don't want.

Moliere felt a shiver of repulsion at the thought of him and of the evening they spent with Fanny two weeks before. No matter that she well remembered inviting him to write if he ever needed.

Moliere searched her head for a word meaning foolishly compassionate. She picked "sucker".

Moliere replied to Eugene that he should send her his telephone number and she would telephone him that evening at 8.30. She phoned him from one of her red chairs. First she poured a drink.

"Hello, Eugene. How are you?"

"Fine."

"I was so happy to get your eMail this afternoon."

"I sent it last night."

"In a way I was just thinking of you."

"What were you thinking? Just so you know, I'm underage."

"What can I do for you?" Instead of another sexual remark Eugene replied at once that his therapist had fired him the week before.

"How do you mean, 'fired'? They don't do that. I see a therapist myself."

"This one did. She told my father I did not want to get well. What's your therapist's name?"

"Do you think she was right?"

"I don't know what the hell she even means."

"What'd did your parents say?"

"Nothing."

"They must have said something."

"They don't say *anything*. They want me to go away, that is all they want. They want me not to have hurt that girl. Seeing a therapist was my punishment for what I did. The judge that sentenced me said I had to go."

"I'm still surprised a therapist could fire a patient."

"Client. I could tell from the first day she hated the sight of me."

"So how are you feeling?"

"That is something the therapist would say."

"I'm not your therapist. I'm only asking." Moliere's impatience revealed itself a little in the tone of her voice, which was tight.

Eugene sighed hard. Even over the phone Moliere could hear how his whole body gave itself to that sigh.

"I feel like I'm going to hell for what I did."

"You don't mean that."

"I do. I mean it. I'm sure I'm going to hell."

"You mean you're upset and you feel awful? Or actually?"

"Actually."

"Put it out of your mind. There is no hell."

"There is. It's the only logical thing."

"Why? You believe in God?"

"No. I just believe in hell."

"You can get better. You should not hate yourself. You're a kid, and you've got such a long way to go. I know it doesn't feel like that now."

"No one will ever forgive me what I did."

"Or you won't forgive yourself. Is that it?"

"What does that even mean?"

"It means you know you fucked up in a major way and hurt someone. Real bad. But it would be a sin to write off the rest of your life because of one really bad mistake."

"No."

"No what?"

"No, I can't forgive myself. She is the only one who can forgive me."

"Who's she?"

"The girl."

"Janet Staufer?"

"You know her?"

"No."

"You taught her in school? How do you know her name?"

"I watch the news, like everyone else."

Moliere immediately knew she had said the wrong thing. Eugene went silent. She was afraid for a moment that he had hung up.

"Eugene?"

"What?"

"Because of her injury Janet can't say she forgives you."

"I know."

"You can't ask for that. You'll hurt yourself wanting that."

Made by nature of repulsive materials Eugene was slavering for compassion. Moliere was moved by this.

"What are you doing next Sunday morning?" she said, surprising herself. "I have an idea."

"What idea?"

"I'll take you to church."

"I'm not praying to fucking God."

"I don't care if you do or not. When I see you I'll explain. Say you'll come."

"Not too early. I work late."

I can imagine, Moliere thought.

"I'll pick you up at the bottom of your driveway at 8.30 Sunday morning. Try not to wake up your parents. I don't want to have to deal with them. Dress a little nice."

That next Sunday was warm for November, like a day in early spring. It cheered people up even if winter with its short, dark days was coming. Usually on Sunday mornings it was right over the roof of church. That Sunday morning the sun was not. It floated over the trees on the southern side of the church, right straight above the donut place. The light was different too.

Janet noticed that up in the sky the sun was in a different place.

Janet and Dad were usually among the first people to arrive for church—"to be sure we get our favorite seat," Dad always said. Janet sat next to Dad in the first pew. She did not like having people in front of her at church. If she could not see what was going on up at the altar she got restless; worse, she got annoyed and fussed, and that made Dad a little mad.

Before the service began Janet would swivel in every direction to watch the people arrive. It was exciting. Many of the people would smile at her and say good morning, Janet;

she knew their faces. They wore all different clothes and different shoes. It made Janet happy seeing all the kinds.

Church was warm. Janet liked the smells of the people and the candles and the waxed floors.

Piano music began. Janet swung around in her pew to watch the people on the side of the altar start singing in their red robes. They held up their hymn books as if they were holding birds in their hands and wanted to show everyone. Janet understood that the lady who played the piano told the singers what to do by waving her hands. It was fun knowing an instant before the choir did how they were going to sing next.

Looking over her shoulder toward the rear of the sanctuary Janet saw the boy.

The boy emerged from the white light filling the frame of the double door at the back of the church. He was looking for a place to sit, Janet knew it. A curly-haired lady touched the boy's elbow and pointed where. They looked like shadows moving.

Janet's heart stopped from fright. She said, "Dad, Dad. The boy is here." She began to cry, but not too loud; she did not want people to know. But she made Dad turn around. She pointed. Dad saw the boy at the back of church, and he nodded. His face pinched.

"You are with me Janet," said Dad right into her ear. "Nothing can hurt you as long as you are with me. Did you know that?"

Dad hugged Janet close with one heavy arm. That felt good. She felt protected. But she still felt worried. She had to say yes.

Everyone stood and the choir began to sing a different song from the first one. The song said *All I have needed Thy hand hath provided.* Janet understood this meant the beginning of church. Music made Janet happy and this was music she knew well. Knowing it well was what made Janet feel safe. And then happy because she loved hearing the dark sound of Dad's voice when he sang. She liked the coffee smell of his breath, intimate as Sundays. She lost herself in all this and forgot about the boy at the back of church.

A woman and then a man read from the big red book on the high table—"the lantern," Dad called it. The woman and the man read different from the way people usually talk.

Then the choir sang again.

Pastor John Moore waited on his big chair for the singing to end. His head rested on his hand like he was sleepy. His head was skin on the top and reflected the light shining down from the ceiling. His shiny head was like the bulb in a lamp.

When he stood up Pastor John Moore was tall, big. He moved to the pull-pit slowly, like a sad man. Then when he started talking he put on a smile like something funny just happened to him. He did this every week. Janet squinted to see.

"Welcome on this beautiful autumn morning that the Lord has given us," Pastor John Moore began in a loud but not scary voice.

"Ah men," said someone, and then more people repeated "ah men".

"What a day you've picked to come to church," said Pastor John Moore. "This time of year the days are growing shorter, and really we ought to give thanks today by going outside to feel the autumn sun on our faces, to store it all up for the coming winter. So this morning I'll make it brief—never a bad thing in a sermon anyway."

Pastor John Moore looked down at his papers. He rocked once on the heels of his shiny black shoes before he began.

"As you know," he said, "today is my last Sunday here at St. Andrew's. We are a small congregation and the reason for my leaving cannot help being well known. I don't mind you knowing, please don't feel awkward about it. Among a pastor's most important jobs is adding new members to the congregation—'growing the market,' as my son says. Don't hate me, he's a banker."

The people laughed a little. Janet knew that John Moore had told a joke.

"In the last six years," he said, sounding tired, "our numbers have not grown but shrunk. And the congregation has voted not to renew my contract. The parish business committee has certified the vote. You may be surprised to hear that I don't blame the people who voted against continuing my role as pastor. I understand that it is part of my job."

Pastor John Moore laughed lightly but this time no one else did. There was worry in the air all around the church. Janet could smell it. The smell was like metal shavings at Dad's work bench when he used the big sharp drill punch.

"I want you to understand how much I've enjoyed knowing all of you," said Pastor John Moore. "I mean that sincerely. Since the vote my friends have been sounding me out on my feelings about leaving—in a well-meaning way, I know they weren't prospecting for gossip. My friends are concerned to discover whether I feel some bitterness about how the contract vote turned out. The answer is none, I feel none. My mother lost her husband to a war, a child to an illness and finally her lifelong job to a young man willing to work for less than she was getting. And yet she was the one who told me 'Don't eat bitterness, John. It will end up eating you.' My mother was right."

Church was so silent that Janet wondered if Pastor John Moore was mad and if the people were being yelled at. Sometimes her father yelled at her brothers. John Moore spoke so quietly, which a lot of the time is the way people speak when they're mad. That was how Dad yelled at Janet's brothers.

"We come to church to hear the word of God," he said. "For another half hour or more I still get paid to preach the word in here. And so I would like to take as my text today—the last one I will ever preach upon to you—from Galatians 5. Do you know it? I think of it as the one about liberty, and so now that I'm at liberty it feels appropriate."

Again John Moore waited for a little laugh from the people. None came.

"'For, brethren,'" he began, his voice a little louder than before, "'ye have been called unto liberty; only use not liberty for an occasion to the flesh, but by love serve one another. For all the law is fulfilled in one word, even in this; Thou shalt love thy neighbor as thyself. But if ye bite and devour one another, take heed that ye be not consumed one of another."

In the raised volume of his voice Janet could tell Pastor John Moore enjoyed saying the words. He let the words ring in the church until their sound decayed. Janet still had half a feeling that all the people were being yelled at.

"Bitterness is a biting and devouring of the self—'so that ye cannot do the things that ye would,' as Paul says in his letter. When we forget to love one another, Paul tells us, bitterness moves in on our lives and makes itself at home. Paul then gets really specific about the harms inflicted when we forget to love. You'd better hide the children for this list. Adultery, fornication, uncleanness, lasciviousness, idolatry, witchcraft, hatred, *variance*, emulations, wrath, strife, seditions, heresies, envyings—I like that one: 'envyings'—*murders*, drunkenness, reveling, and—this one's my favorite—'such like'. Paul reminds us that as an encouragement to love one another God offers more than threats. The fruit of the spirit, he says, is love, joy, peace, longsuffering, gentleness, goodness, faith, meekness, temperance. And 'against such,' says Paul, 'there is no law.'"

Pastor John Moore looked out over all of them and smiled.

"My interest in selling you that message of hope was why I took this job," he said. "And now it's my parting gift to you, free of charge. Go and love one another. That is all. God bless you. Drive safe. Ah men."

As he always did after speaking Pastor John Moore went and sat down for a moment. Again he looked to Janet like someone wanting a nap. But then he roused himself, and when Pastor John Moore stood everyone else did too.

There was more singing that the choir led. Then Pastor John Moore prayed over the wine and the bread that had no taste. They passed around the little clear plastic cups of the wine. Dad toasted Janet. He lifted the little cup with the red wine and said, "To my wonderful girl" the way he did every Sunday. Then the church sang more.

Pastor John Moore gave the benediction and there was more singing.

The best part for Janet was the end when everyone walked down the center aisle of the church while the choir sang them out the doors. Everyone was always smiling when service ended. Janet liked that so much. She wished every day was Sunday. When she was full of church it made her feel like water flowing.

Pastor John Moore stood just inside church framed in the sunshiny doorway shaking hands and saying a brief word to each of the people. Dad said to him, "Best of luck to you, John. It's a shame what's happened."

"Maybe I'm not so sure," Pastor John Moore but he said "thank you" to Dad. He shook Janet's hand. The flesh of his hand was warm and big.

"God bless you, Janet," he said. "I promise to remember you always. Whenever you look up at a cloud or see a big rainbow you can know I'm thinking about you. OK?"

Janet did not answer. She knew Dad would take her for donuts at the place next door to church. Every single Sunday they went. For the treat. Her mouth watered without her even knowing.

All this distracted Janet's thoughts away from the boy. When she came out into the sun holding Dad's hand it was with a start that she saw the boy again, waiting with the curly-haired lady at the bottom of the church steps almost in the street. She could tell they were waiting for Dad and for her.

The curly-haired woman touched the boy's arm to make him stay where he was. She came over to Janet and Dad, and she spoke to Dad. Janet held Dad's heavy arm with both her hands and put herself at an angle to the lady. The lady's crazy hair frightened her.

"May I speak to you for a moment, sir?" she said.

"No, you may not. Not if it's about him. Please let us get by."

"He would like to ask your daughter's forgiveness."

"For what that young man did there is no forgiveness."

"You just came out of church. There's forgiveness for all of us. I'm not trying to be funny."

"God offers forgiveness. I'm not God. I'm Janet's father. She is all my concern in this world. God can take care of everything else, including me. And I'm not trying to be funny either. Let us by, please."

"But you're a Christian."

"I'm not that kind of Christian."

"Eugene is eaten up with grief."

"My daughter was eaten up with fear after she was raped. My brave daughter, who made her way in this world against odds that *thank* God you can't imagine. What he did to her ripped her up inside—physically ripped her up. And he left her pregnant. My girl had to have an abortion, did you know that?"

Janet was not understanding all that Dad was saying, but she heard the shaking in his voice. She *saw* the shaking in the features of his face. She knew he was angry and something else she did not have a name for. That was why he dropped the volume of his voice. Not because the people were turning to look at him but because of the thing she did not have a name for. She worried that it might explode him.

"I didn't know that," said the curly-hair. "I can't imagine the burden on your family."

"'Burden'? It has nothing to do with burden. My daughter was raped and made pregnant against her will. She *has* a will, you know, in case you wondered. The cruelty in your friend there was that he couldn't imagine what she could want. Or he didn't care because he was stronger than she is. Let him go to hell."

Dad spoke fast but he spoke quietly. He did not want anyone to hear the feeling in his voice. It was private. He used that word with Janet: "private". Janet knew she was being protected.

"His life is already hell," said curly hair.

"It pleases me to hear that. Honestly, it pleases me. But if there's any kindness in *you*, ma'am, then you will help Janet forget him. Which she has been doing pretty well until just this morning."

The boy stood between Janet and Dad and the donut shop. The boy looked down at the ground. Dad walked around the lady with the crazy hair without saying goodbye. They stepped well around the boy the way a person steps well around dog poo.

Janet held Dad's arm with both hands. Dad let out a long breath the way Janet did herself when she was puffed from running in the yard. She was thinking about the kind of donuts that had honey on them and she was noticing her body relax. She let out a long breath just like Dad would do.

Dad said, "Don't look back, baby. Just keep on walking."

Eugene watched Janet and her father walk off toward the donut place. The sun glared whitely.

"I'm sorry," Moliere said.

"What were you expecting?" Eugene replied. "I got it coming." Moliere couldn't argue.

Eugene said nothing else in the car going home. From time to time he felt an irresistible need to breathe in deep but otherwise was without visible emotion; his emotions had all checked out. He craved donuts.

Eugene pressed the dongle on his key chain to open the gates to the long drive to the house up to the house from Nine Mezcaleros Road. Moliere did not know about the two speed bumps in the driveway and hit the first one hard, jolting herself annoyingly. She pulled in behind Rauscha's second car, a Range Rover that raised the earth's temperature half a degree every time he drove it.

"I'm sorry this morning didn't work out, Eugene," said Moliere. "But you'll figure out another way forward. Nothing's ever over until life is over."

"Stop," Eugene said flatly, and he got out. "I don't fucking care. I really don't. Thank you anyway for trying. I like your hair."

Eugene got out and went straight for the big house. He entered the code into the keypad beside the door and found it would not open. They changed the code again without telling him, again.

Fanny was pulling in right behind Moliere as Eugene rang the bell. She stopped her car six inches from Moliere's back bumper, boxing her in. Once again Eugene witnessed Moliere being kidnapped by Fanny. He watched to see what happened.

Fanny got out from behind the wheel of the Tesla she drove to the kidnapping. She held up a big white paper bag, big enough to need both hands.

"Kaiser rolls," Fanny said. "I got a dozen. They were warm when I bought them. Why were you out with Eugene? You are the most unpredictable woman."

"I took him to church."

"Are you joking?"

"I took him to church."

"Well good gracious," said Fanny. "Come in and have one of these here rolls." Fanny had cut her hair shorter than it was on Halloween night and she had tipped it blonde. It was threaded with clear glass beads. Thanks to those beads the effect of the sun on her head was one of saintliness.

"I need to leave."

"Come have one of these rolls."

Moliere was captured again. She followed behind Fanny up the steps to where Eugene was still standing, observing the two of them.

"I reset the password if you're wondering," Fanny said over her shoulder as she tapped they keypad. "Seemed like the sensible thing. Out early this morning, Eugene?"

Tibor Rauscha was in the outdoor kitchen at the back of the house, the one beside the pool none of them swam in. Rauscha was grilling pork roast on the smoke stove. Lately he had taken to thinking of himself as a chef. He would cook things. The other night Eugene heard him telling Fanny that he had ordered a smoker.

"Hey, it's the kidnapping gang," Rauscha said. There was a thin bandage taped to his cheek. On the table near him there was a bowl of blueberries. The berries were so fat that Eugene knew they would have little flavor, with none of the slight tartness he liked in berries.

"Did you all come to surrender to me?" Tibor Rauscha asked.

"Funny, Dad," said Eugene.

"How did you get out this morning?"

"Door. I opened it and just walked through."

"Don't be fresh, Eugene. Where'd you go?"

"On a date with her," pointing to the Moliere.

"Did you get lucky?" Eugene and his father both snickered at the idea of ever getting lucky, in any sense including the obscene.

"Stop it, Tibor," Fanny said.

"Join me over here at the fire pit. Want some pork?"

Eugene did not know anything about barbecue but the meat looked overdone. The animal fat shimmering all over it made his stomach turn, given the early hour especially.

Instead of volleying back over the net to his father Eugene surprised everyone by beginning to cry. He pushed past Moliere and disappeared up the steps to his room.

"Christ," said Tibor Ruscha. "That kid. Sometimes I'm afraid of him, honest I am." Eugene heard his father say it.

The only advantage of being Eugene was that he could simply exit a scene and no one tried to stop him. No one expected him to do a thing. That way it was more convenient for everybody.

Upstairs Eugene fell back on his unmade bed. When the Mexican women came during the week they made his bed. Apart from those days it was always a pile of blankets and sheets. Tibor and Fanny never said a word about it.

One night a few weeks ago Eugene took both the bed sheets and stretched them between two corners of his desk and the end of his bed. He did this a few times before. He liked to imagine himself in a knife fight and the sheets were men closing in. He danced, it felt like dancing, as if he were surrounded, slashing with the pocket knife he took from Tibor's desk. He tore the sheets open with the knife, stabbing and liking the sound of the ripping. He liked the feeling of moving.

When his bed was made by the Mexicans after the knife fight he expected the sheets to be replaced but they never were. That was his big fuck-you from the Mexicans. And he could not tell anyone.

Well played, señoritas.

Next to Eugene's bed was a powder-blue end table. He

had the table since infancy. It was small, furniture for a baby's room. Carol bought it before the divorce. It was so familiar that Eugene did not recognize how childish it was. Without even needing to lift his head he fished in the little drawer for the plastic bag he had stuffed there last summer. It was from the Gran Oso store near his school. He had been saving it.

Eugene shook the bag out and pulled it down over his head. Sunday morning sunlight came at him through the windows. It was bright enough to let Eugene see through the bag. From within the bag he could see the picture of the happy bear printed on the bag, only in reverse.

Every time he exhaled the bag lifted from his face and let in air. He could still breathe. But Eugene was accustomed to frustration. And this would be the last time he would ever need to be patient.

Eugene removed the bag from his head. He crossed the room to the desk where he did homework and otherwise watched porn. Somewhere in the desk there had to be a rubber band. The one he found was good and thick—exactly what he needed—and it was green like he imagined a jungle was green.

Eugene lay down on the bed and tried again. It took work pulling the tight rubber band down over the bag as far as his throat. The bag tore a little on the top but this time the seal mostly held.

Quickly the oxygen was gone from inside the bag. It took much less than a minute, he guessed. But he was not counting the seconds. He was fighting through the animal panic at being unable to breathe, controlling his reflex to gasp. The best way of fighting the temptation to live, Eugene decided, was to try falling asleep. He closed his eyes and asked his desperate heart to please calm down for just a little while.

It crossed Eugene's mind to wonder where he might be when he woke up. Nowhere, he expected. He had no preference anyhow. No hope, no interest at all really, one way or the other. He did not wish to die. He wished not to be. He wished his life to stop.

Eugene dreamed of travelling on a train. He was a child again—just a little more than a baby. He was riding the train alone. Eugene was not scared to be alone. Just the same he thought it was irresponsible of someone to let a baby child ride a train alone.

The train stopped a lot, and at each station the car Eugene rode in became more crowded. Little Eugene was squeezed against a window by a big red-faced man next to him. The man wore an overcoat and all by himself heated the air in the train car.

Eugene felt claustrophobia gathering on him, a feeling that he could not move even if he wanted to. Little Eugene made himself brave by forcing his attention on the scene outside the window—the empty landscape of southern New Mexico he used to stare at going back and forth to that place in Las Cruces where they sent him. St. Dymphna's, crucifixes everywhere. He used to pass the time spent traveling to that place imagining that one day he would move to that landscape—away from what he had done, away from his father, from Carol, just away.

Eugene used to daydream of the house he would build

in the desert, imagined it in detail; the daydreaming calmed him. The design of Eugene's house changed from time to time but some things always stayed the same. The outside of the house would be yellow to look pretty against the sere landscape. The inside would all be on one floor. When he walked into it there would be a step-down into a big living room with an orange couch. There would be no windows looking out on the road. But at the back of the house he would put in a great big walls of glass so that he could sit still and look west across the emptiness.

Maybe the train is taking me to my house, Eugene wondered in his dream. Finally.

A murmur rose up inside the train car. Out the window the little boy saw a thunderstorm boiling up over the horizon. It was coming for them all. The air was getting heavier by the minute. The lights inside the train were dimming. People were scared.

Eugene watched himself watch the people. As much as he was afraid he was excited just as much. He felt the ache that he had lived with all his life dissolve.

This moment was a joy to him.

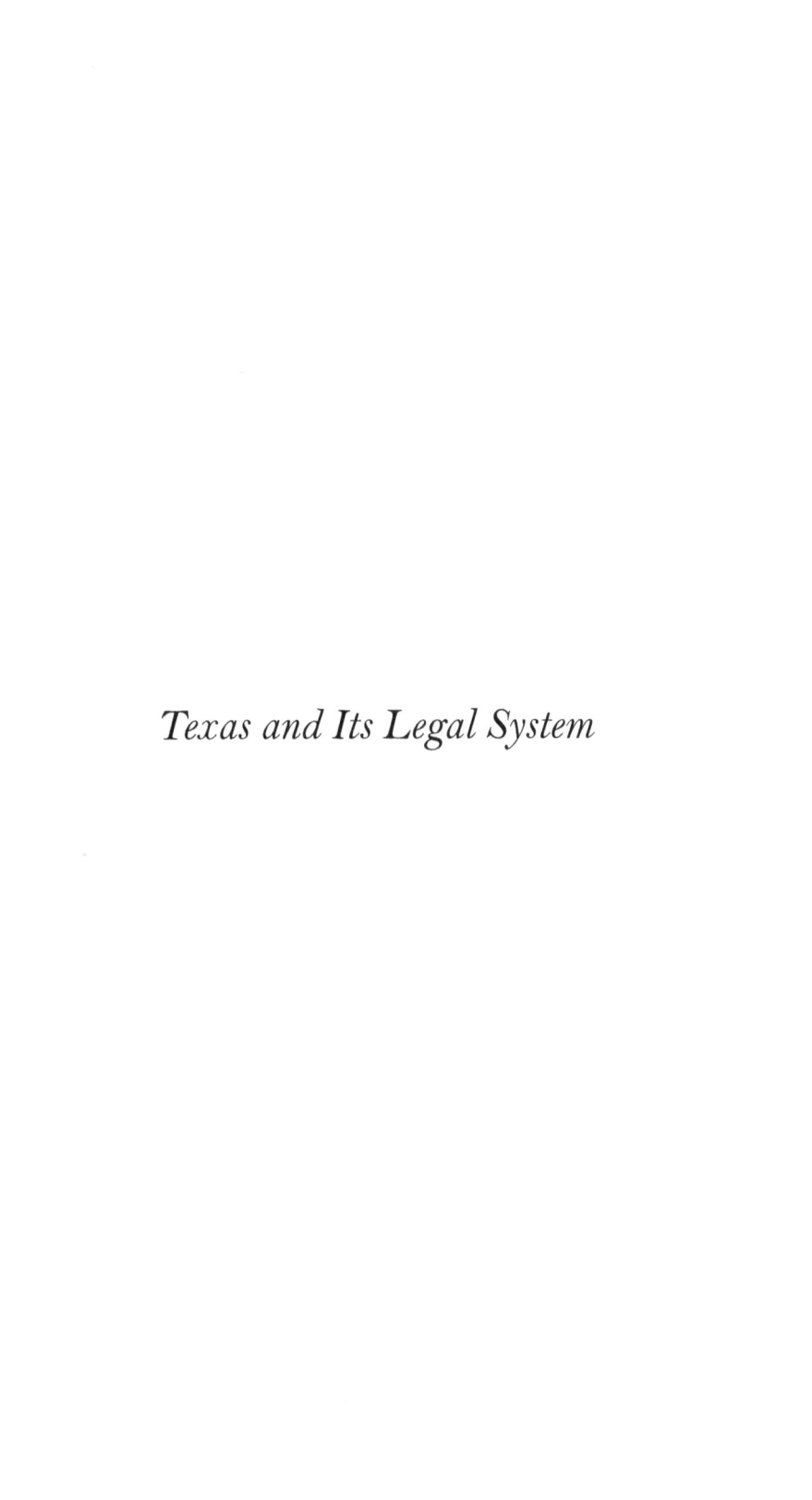

Texas and Its Legal System

Before leaving Eugene's house that morning Moliere went up the stairs to say good-bye and to offer more empty encouragement. She found the bedroom door ajar, Eugene stretched out on the bed, the bag with the smiling bear on it sucked against his mouth and nostrils. How stupid he looked.

Moliere moved too quickly to indulge her shock—to put it more precisely, her repulsion. She tore the bag apart and pulled it from Eugene's face. She tried to remember the CPR all the teachers in the district had been taught. She pinched Eugene's nose and fitted her mouth to his. The taste of his mouth was indescribable. She thought she would never get it out of her mouth, not as long she lived. She has not; about that she was right.

When Moliere found him Eugene had already been dead ten minutes. She knew he was dead even as she worked on him. But she would not concede defeat.

Moliere rhythmically compressed Eugene's chest in the way she believed the school had taught her. Each time she came up for a breath she yelled for Fanny and Tibor Rauscha. It felt like they took their time about it coming up the stairs.

How is it that I even know these people, she was thinking, how have I come to be here, why is it me trying to save this kid's life? It was as if they all fell out of the sky and landed on her.

Here's me, she was thinking, giving the kiss of life to a fat teenager who is already dead who smelled of death and soiled clothes even when he was alive.

It makes me nearly vomit knowing how turned on he would be. He probably knew I hated him. I hated what he did to the girl and for the uselessness of his life.

Where was his care for the girl? Who was desperate to save her? Let him be dead.

Coming into the room Fanny and Rauscha understood immediately. Rauscha swore. Fanny screamed. Moliere commanded someone to telephone the police.

Moliere knelt beside the bed, her breath gone, the strength in her hands gone. The foulness of Eugene's mouth made her dizzy and she thought she might be sick. It was the taste of someone beyond God's reach. This thought she never had before. At Forgiveness University they never taught that one.

It was midmorning on a Sunday. The roads were empty and not much was going on in Perros Salvajes—just churches and the sleeping in. The ambulance was there in four minutes. Police officer AJ Munoz was working a double shift that day and, in the way of things in a small place, he and his young partner took the call.

AJ left the paramedics to their job and herded everyone downstairs to get their accounts of what happened. He expected the usual Rashomon that characterized everything from fender benders to murders.

AJ told his partner—Tonya, the tall, dark kid who'd also been partnered with him the night Fanny invaded Moliere's house—he told her to take separate statements from Fanny and Tibor. AJ wanted everyone busy and out of sight while Eugene's body was removed from the house. He had the seen the effect on people when a body was zippered up into the shiny black bag and carted away. It was not nice. Worse from AJ's point of view, it made people hard to talk to.

AJ was kind to all of them but to Moliere especially. The first thing he said when she came down the marble staircase was, "Oh Christ, honey, not you." Not just because they were acquainted. Once he had the outline of the story in his head AJ knew Moliere would need the most care—odd, given that she was not the boy's mother. In his work AJ saw oddness all the time. He barely noticed it anymore.

AJ brought Moliere out to the sunny patio at the back of the house to hear her story. As they sat there talking it offended him that a pork roast was smoking on the grill. The smell was nauseating but it did not occur to him to remove it. It was charred and brown and ragged as an old football. Pigskin.

AJ saw that Moliere could barely make herself speak. She was caught in the sensation of removal that follows a great trauma. AJ understood exactly.

"I didn't know you knew this family, Katherine."

"Yes, you did."

"Did I?"

"They broke into my house three weeks ago. You took the call."

"Why were you here? Are you friends now?"

"It's a long and stupid story that I'm too upset to go into. I tried to help that kid and it didn't work."

"Eugene?" said AJ. He checked his spiral notepad.

"Yes."

"What'd you do that didn't work?"

"Brought him to church."

"Where'd you go wrong?"

"My idea was to have him meet the girl's father."

"Which girl?"

"Janet Staufer."

"Ah."

"Eugene needed forgiveness."

"Ah."

Moliere gave AJ the blow by blow, everything from the being kidnapped on Halloween night to finding Eugene suffocated. AJ listened with his whole body. He put his smart phone on the glass table between them. It was recording what she said. AJ would use a transcribing tool later.

"Janet's father told us both to go get lost," Moliere told him. "He upset Eugene. Today was Eugene's last chance."

"That is what he told you?"

"Who? Eugene?"

"Yeah."

"No, he didn't say that. But I know it now."

"Last chance for what do you think?"

"I don't know. To quiet his mind."

"Probably not. Kind of I remember him from when he was a child, that first time I met you. When the rape happened it all came back to me. I worried about my feelings regarding that child. I shouldn't tell you that."

"There was something broken about him."

"My wife always tells me you can't ever say you don't like a child. You should say he is not your favorite. It's a euphemism, you know?"

"Sure. What will happen to those two?" Moliere indicated Tibor Rauscha and Fanny with a gesture of her head. They were still somewhere else inside the house being debriefed by Tonya.

"How do you mean, Katherine?"

"Can they be arrested for child neglect, anything like that?"

"I don't see how. Not in this life."

Beyond the fact that Eugene died and how this came about there was not much to know from a policeman's point of view. But Moliere's clear contempt for Fanny and Rauscha interested AJ.

Like everyone else in Perros Salvajes AJ knew that Eugene raped Janet Staufer. As a member of the police force he knew details of the rape he wished he did not. This was true of lots of things he was part of as a cop; it was an aspect of the job. But this other thing—the behavior of Eugene's parents—interested him for private reasons.

After finding God two years before, after Franklin died, AJ worked at training himself not to investigate culpability beyond what should interest a police officer. Otherwise, he realized, there'd be no end to anything. People's defects apart from their behavior were in God's opinion none of AJ's business.

But what else was he supposed to think about in respect to the adults in this boy's life? If AJ did not investigate this then it would be the same as believing Eugene was born cursed. Which AJ did not believe about anyone. Because of his new faith.

"I don't want to have to look at those two when I leave the house," Moliere told him. "If I saw them I don't know what I might do."

"I'll fix it, Katherine."

AJ lowered his head and in an intimate voice spoke into the radio clipped to the pocket of his uniform blouse.

"Hold Mr. and Mrs. Rauscha just a little minute for me, Tony."

"Tonya." They both heard Fanny say "...the boy's natural mother."

AJ presumed that Tibor and Fanny heard his voice in whatever room they were settled in. If this had an effect on them AJ did not mind.

"You're a mess, honey," AJ told Moliere. "Go home. My partner will drive you." Moliere would not hear it.

AJ walked Moliere out the front door of the big house. It was one o'clock now and the day was clouding over. It did not look like rain though.

Eugene was not dead even 90 minutes. Hard to believe they could not call him back.

AJ and Moliere were in time to see the humorless ambulance rolling away from the house down the long driveway out to Nine Mezcaleros Road. The ambulance jounced indifferently over the two speed bumps. AJ thought about Eugene's body jolted in its shiny black bag.

One last kick in the pants, said AJ, praying. Poor bastard.

At home Moliere poured herself Scotch in the biggest tumbler she owned. She must have poured half a pint in there. Moliere liked Scotch a lot. It was a dependable friend, always suited to her mood. Seldom did she like it enough to drink in the daytime; like all committed drinkers Moliere made up rules about alcohol and generally observed them. If ever a day was an exception to the rules this day was it.

Had Fanny and Tibor had been ordinary people Moliere would have stayed at the house after the ambulance took Eugene away. She would have given them whatever comfort she had; that was what people did. Fanny and Tibor Rauscha were not people, ordinary or otherwise. Moliere would be damned before she did anything for them.

Fanny was sick with shock, of course, but she would get over it. She and Rauscha both would. In a couple of hours Moliere could imagine them eating the overcooked pork.

Moliere was leaving Perros Salvajes. It might take a year, it might take two years to find another teaching job and get out, but she was going. Monday morning—the next day—she would look at all her options.

With her big drink in her hand, full of ice and cold as a Coca-Cola, Moliere dialed her father in Las Cruces. Moliere and her father spoke at least once a week. Generally she tried to telephone on Sundays, not that her father had things to do nor anyplace to be at other times. But Léon was a teacher the same as his daughter and usually had the week's lesson plans to work on Sundays, so Moliere could count on him being home. She knew he would be at his kitchen table.

Léon picked up on the second ring and Moliere said, "Hi, Daddy."

"Good afternoon, Katherine. Sak pase?" He would have been expecting her call.

"Things are no good at all, Daddy. I was as at a house where a boy committed suicide this morning."

"Dear God, Katherine."

"Yeah, dear God. I just got home." Now she was sunk on the end of Franklin's red couch.

"What happened?"

"I tried to give him CPR. But he was already dead. The whole thing was horrible. I'm sorry to gift you with that but I had to tell somebody."

Talking about the morning brought back the taste of Eugene's mouth. Moliere drank to cover the taste.

"I'm glad you're calling me, darling. You sound shaken."

"I'm alright."

"You couldn't be alright."

"I'm cracking up."

"Was this a student of yours?"

"I barely knew him."

"So how did you happen to be with him?" After 40 years in New Mexico the Haitian inflections in her father's voice were dimmer than they once were but still definitely there. They were always most audible on the telephone.

"It's too complicated to explain. I only met his parents recently. To tell you the truth he was a nasty little boy, but the parents made him that way. He's dead and they have no idea it was them who killed him. It's all really cruel."

Léon was silent. He was searching for some comfort to give her, Moliere knew; that was what a father did, that was what people did.

"Get out of that house, Katherine. Don't spend the day alone. Go see friends."

"Right this minute I'd prefer to be alone."

"That would be the worst thing you could do."

"I can think of much worse. Don't worry. I'll go to bed early tonight. When I wake up it will be time to go to work. That's how I got through Franklin and this is not going to be anything like as bad as that."

"You don't have to prove to yourself what a tough guy you are."

"That's not it. I just want some peace. And quiet. Peace and quiet."

"You get too much quiet, Katherine. And please don't spend the rest of today drinking. There's no peace in that."

"Don't say that, Daddy. Of course I won't. You make me sound like someone with a problem."

"Even over the telephone I can hear the ice in your glass. Peace and quiet is not the same thing as drinking yourself into a coma."

"This is one of the few times I've ever felt in need of a drink. Instead of just wanting one."

"That's the worst reason to drink."

"Which is?"

"Needing. It will make you feel bad tomorrow. And I don't just mean the headache. Go running. That's your bliss you told me."

"I don't use that expression. You can always make me laugh."

"I'm not trying to make you laugh, Katherine."

"I've made up my mind to leave Perros Salvajes. I'll get another teaching job someplace else."

"Good. You've been nothing but marooned in that place, and not just since Franklin. I've always been asking myself, Why is it Texas for her? Come and see us next weekend, dear, and we'll talk about everything. Teresa would love to see you." Moliere barely knew Teresa. She was 14 years younger than her father and harassed by recurring kidney stones. As far as Moliere knew the pair of them hardly ever went out because of that. Marooned. That was probably the word Léon used to describe himself there in Las Cruces. But he still needed another two years till his pension from the Las Cruces school system. Then he would think about getting out with Teresa, if her health allowed.

"I don't want to think about going anywhere for a while, Daddy."

"You're right. It's a long way to come just to have dinner," Léon said. "Across the desert is a tedious trip. I don't know why people write poems about it."

"I can't think of any poems about the desert."

"I'm sure there are many."

Léon could probably write a poem about the desert.

"Why don't we come see you?" Léon said. "I don't think Teresa has ever been outside of New Mexico in her whole life."

What Moliere knew was that Léon hated Los Cruces more and more, with a new murder in the newspaper every week and persistent rumors of space aliens. The week before when they spoke Léon complained about the evangelicals who plagued his neighborhood, hanging on him at the supermarket like yapping dogs and going on about Jesus. It was not nice.

"Promise me you won't drink anymore today," he told his daughter now.

"Promise."

"On the level?"

"Always." Probably.

Before hanging up Moliere remembered to ask after Teresa's kidneys; this is what people do.

"Teresa is the same," said Léon.

After speaking to her father Moliere lay across Franklin's red couch to think things over.

"Talk to me, baby," she said out loud.

Moliere was not a tall woman and still was a bit too long for that couch. Just the same soon she napped so profoundly that when she woke she had no idea if she had been asleep a few minutes or several hours.

Moliere was a long time coming up out of sleep. She lay a while on her side and woke wondering why people use the word "sound" to describe a deep sleep.

Out the window the wet grey light was heavier now; Moliere noticed this. When the wind gusted the house shivered; for minutes after the house ticked until it settled. Moliere lay desolate on the couch, feeling herself to be without companions. If she was ever hired as the manager of hell she would build it to sustain for eternity exactly this Sunday solitude.

Impelled by anger Moliere pushed herself up from the red couch and went to the little office she had in the second bedroom of the house. Six weeks ago at AJ's suggestion she made a photocopy of Rauscha's file on her. She hid it in a plain envelope behind a cabinet; she thought this clever. Now she fished it out.

Moliere put the envelope into a larger one with a note to Tibor Rauscha.

You gave your energy to this instead of loving your son.

Moliere thought to add "One day you will answer to God for the choice you made" but then remembered she did not believe one word of that. It was only disgust talking and probably her encounter earlier that day with the Presbyterians. Instead she wrote

I'm keeping the originals.

Poem About the Desert
by Léon Moliere

Blighted as the moon is blighted
is the world round Los Cruces.
Vastness should be an
inspiration. It's not.

The widower is absorbed
now in his social studies.
His woman has aches
in her lower back.

We wonder why people
go to deserts and live.
Picture being Haitian
in New Mexico,

marooned.

"Somebody should have fixed that child," Judy DaCosta said to her daughter Fanny. She said this on the day Eugene died when Fanny telephoned with the news. For an instant Fanny thought her mother was referring to castration. Fanny was weighing the wisdom of that—as a hypothesis—when she realized her mother meant something more general—*fix* in the common sense of repair.

Whichever way she meant it Judy's comment was cold.

"Eugene was cursed to be unhappy, Mommy," Fanny replied.

"No one is born cursed, dear. It's a blasphemy against God to say so." It's hard to respond when someone calls you a blasphemer; arguing gets you nowhere. "We do God's will, whatever the hell it may be."

In Fanny's case what her mother said struck home. In just the few hours since Eugene died she would been wondering how much she owed God for not coming to the kid's rescue after she married Tibor. Not much, she wanted to believe, but it was hard to be sure.

"No one took care of that boy," her mother told Fanny, "not his father, not his mother, nor you neither it pains me to say. People with dogs do more for them than that child's people ever did."

Fanny said, "Tibor feels awful." Given enough time and virtuous behavior almost anything can be lived down, but maybe not this.

"I'm sure you're full of baloney on that score."

When her mother hung up Fanny sat staring at nothing for a long time with her phone in her hand. Her husband had gone to the hospital for the paperwork and she was all alone in the house. She could smell the pork loin still smoking out by the pool. God forgive her, it smelled delicious.

In her way Fanny was an admirable woman, but she was not nice. For a fact she knew this.

Ordinarily Carol napped most of Sunday afternoon. She napped most days but specifically she napped on Sundays. She went to an 8 AM service at her church, Desert Baptist, and afterward went to Java Caliente on Fuller Boulevard. Both rituals were central to her sabbath morning. She bought the fat Sunday edition of *The Dallas Morning News* and poked around in it while she ate the top off a muffin. Then she drove home and slept, most times on the blue suede couch in her living room. The routine—which is what she named it: "the routine"—helped Carol navigate Sunday, the darkest day in the week all because of its tranquility. (People who live alone hate Sunday the most. That is well known.)

No one ever interrupted the routine. When the phone rang at three o'clock Carol was surprised less that Fanny was calling—surprising enough—than that anyone should telephone at all.

Fanny told her Eugene was dead. Naturally it took a moment for this to work its way into Carol's head.

"He took his own life. His own life!" Fanny sounded like she was crying, heightening Carol's feeling that she was not fully woken up.

"Fanny," Carol said into the phone, "if this another one of your filthy jokes God will strike you dead." Carol knew already this was not a joke. She was playing for time.

"I'm not fooling, Carol. While I was downstairs with Tibor chatting with that woman I introduced you to he suffocated himself."

"What woman?"

"Halloween."

Carol realized she was on her feet. She was barely able to hold the telephone in her hand—from the shock, of course, but also from fright. They had killed Eugene. She and Tibor. They wanted him to be dead for years, and now he was. Now she was going to hell for it. Her hand trembled with cold.

"Tell me what happened. I'm trying to get hold of this."

Carol wanted to go back to sleep. She wanted one last moment in the old world before she left it, awful as it was. But her spirit was already transmigrating to a place of awesome fear. For what she did to Eugene God was going to send Carol to hell and burn her up over and over.

"It was all like I said, Carol." Fanny was still talking. "We were downstairs talking to my friend Katherine and then Eugene got bored with the conversation like he does and he went up to his room. It was not 20 minutes later, I swear to God, that Katherine went up to kiss him goodbye and found him on the bed. Eugene was *asphyxiated*, Carol. Katherine yelled for us to call an ambulance and we did. She gave him CPR. The EMS was there in only a few minutes. But it was too late."

"My poor boy."

In her life Carol never said anything remotely like "my poor boy" about Eugene. About Tibor or Georg, perhaps, though not necessarily and probably not with conviction if she did. But never had she said it about Eugene. To her own ears her words sounded fake.

Fanny was silent. Carol wondered if she sounded fake to Fanny too.

"Where is he?"

"Eugene?"

"Of course Eugene. Jesus, Fanny."

"At County Hospital. Tibor is there now."

"How is Tibor?"

"Fine."

"'Fine'?"

"He's upset but he's in command of himself. That's what I thought you were asking. Tibor said the cops would call and tell you, but I didn't want you to hear the news like that."

"Thank you, Fanny. I appreciate that kindness, at least."

"What do you want to do?"

"Do about what?"

It took Fanny a moment or so to answer.

"The arrangements. Putting Eugene to rest."

It was the time-worn phrase for burying somebody who was dead—"putting them to rest"—and still it struck Carol with fresh force. Rest. The son she never loved, whom she still did not love, God forgive her though God would not. Her son must have died exhausted. He wanted out.

What a life they gave him, she and Tibor. If Carol was going to be damned because of that then she had it coming.

Carol perched on the edge of the straight-backed chair at her desk. The window above the desk looked out on where the desert began. Already the mid-afternoon shadows were lengthening out there. It was the month of November.

"I don't know," Carol said. "I've never had to think about it."

"If you don't object the hospital will release Eugene to Tibor." Fanny was proposing something, Carol knew she was.

"Is that what Tibor wants?"

"I don't know if it is what he wants. I don't know what he's feeling. He's upset, sure he's upset, but I also think he's mad at Eugene."

"Mad?"

"Because Eugene did this to himself. It was nothing Tibor said, you know, but when he left for the hospital he was pissed off. Maybe that's only how Tibor is when he's grief struck. I don't know. This is a new situation for us."

"And thank God."

"I suppose."

When Carol started to speak she could not have said where she was going to finish when she came to the end.

"I'm Eugene's mother. I have the same rights Tibor does."

"It's your obligation."

"I'll claim Eugene's body."

"Just so you don't turn it into a fight."

"That I cannot promise."

"Because it's been a long day already."

"I don't stand up to Tibor very well, but on this I'll have to try."

"If you're wondering later this is not why I called. But I like your idea."

"Why do you think it's a good idea?"

"Because honest, Carol? Because I think you feel this worse than Tibor does. About everything, and I know you do. You're the more humane of you two. God help *me* if I die and I'm still married to Tibor."

"You're brutal, Fanny."

"This is a brutal day, Carol. Would else do you want to hear from me?"

"Call Tibor and tell him I'm coming—would you mind? I can be at the hospital in about half an hour."

"I'll text. Otherwise he'll want to talk about it."

Carol found her car keys and left quickly. She felt afraid to be alone in her house. If she stayed there in her house something was going to get her. She was sure of it.

Carol entered the marble—she thought it was marble—lobby of the hospital building. In an instant she collected the assorted emotions of the place—worry relief broken-heart humdrum adrenaline fatigue. All overlain by smells of the man-made things which make sterility.

Abruptly it occurred to Carol that she had no idea where Eugene might be. Nor what she was going to say when she saw Tibor.

Behind a high desk sat a thin and pink-faced old man. Carol asked him where she should go.

"Excuse me. My son has passed away and that's why I'm here."

For Carol the old man assumed his sad face. His yellow smiley face button did not change expression.

"I'm so sorry," he said. "You are the Mom—that's what you told me?"

"Yes, and, please, I don't want to chat. It's not you. With anybody."

"I understand. Of course, I do."

"Just tell me what to do."

The pink man got up from his swiveling chair—his show of kindness—and pointed out the elevator bank.

"Take any one of those to the basement," he said. "You'll see signs."

Naturally the place for wheeling bodies in and out of the hospital would be the lowest level of the hospital building. Conveniently near a loading dock. It needed to be away from where the living would have to look, which could only be discouraging.

Someone had made a decision to call this place of the dead "non-emergent services".

At the far end of the beige corridor Tibor Rauscha was squatting with his back supported against the wall. He was tapping at his phone.

Hearing the click click of Carol's heels on the linoleum Rauscha looked up. He radiated agitation—in such a situation who wouldn't? Carol was familiar with Rauscha's agitation. He was going to be more edgy than sad. She knew it was probably because someone told him to wait.

"Hello, Carol. Fanny called to tell me you were coming. Thank you so much, Fanny."

"Where is Eugene?"

"They've got him back behind those two doors somewhere," Rauscha said, jerking his thumb over his left shoulder. "They don't answer questions here. They treat something like this as a sort of crime, so right now they're in there talking to the two cops who answered the call this morning. I have just told you everything I know."

"Will they let us see him?"

Carol noted how Rauscha's face in the fluorescent light looked older than the picture of him she carried in her head. He was 38. His face was already acquiring the pudding quality of middle age. He was probably thinking the same of her.

"I said I told you everything I know, Carol. Why—you want to see him?"

"Yes, I think I do."

"Left it a little late, haven't you?"

"Shame me all you like. I deserve it."

"Hoping to make yourself feel better? Or to make yourself look better in front of the hospital people?"

"If we don't do this part of it right, Tibor, then we'll both feel we just disposed of him. That would compound my sin."

"You'd get over it."

"Probably you're right. But I want to do the right thing for him, for once."

"I fed him, I clothed him, I sheltered him, I paid for him to go to that goddam school the court sent him to. I paid the lawyer. You wanted no part. So I make the decisions now. *I* bury him."

"How?"

"Eugene only killed himself three hours ago, Carol. Forgive me if I haven't worked out the details of the whole thing." Carol flinched when Tibor said "killed himself".

Before Carol could collect herself a serene-looking woman—tall and solid, big chested in a way that brought to mind the phrase "foundation garments"—pushed through the heavy pair of doors defending non-emergent patient services. She looked from Tibor Rauscha to Carol, and then like the pink-faced old man upstairs composed her face in the expression of compassion. In her eyes she switched on kindness. She did these things in a sequence.

"Are you Eugene Rauscha's parents?"

"I am," Carol said.

"And you are?"

"I was his father."

"We're divorced," Carol explained. She took in the flat black color of the woman's hair, which had the lusterless color that comes out of a second-rate salon. She should let it go grey, Carol thought. It would look more becoming, and be less obvious.

"I understand," the woman said. "This is such a terrible thing, and I'm truly sorry." The woman did sound truly sorry. "I'm Mrs. Schäfer."

"Mrs. Schäfer," Tibor said, "Carol and I have never been in a situation like this. We don't know how this is done. What do we do once you release our son's body?"

"There's a routine to it, Mr. Rauscha, don't concern yourself about that. Let us know the name of the funeral home and we'll manage it with them."

"Are there papers for me to sign?"

"There are always papers to sign," said Mrs. Schäfer with a small smile meant to be philosophical. "Would you come with me?"

Mrs. Schäfer held aside one of the heavy doors. For a moment Carol feared she was being shown into a refrigerated basement. Dead bodies would be lying around on steel tables; imagining a scene like that would make any amateur flinch.

Worse, Carol admitted to herself that she had no wish to see Eugene—not just dead but at all. She still did not love him. She was only impelled to do the right thing. What that was and for whom she was doing it was hard to say. She shared Rauscha's scorn for herself.

It was not an autopsy room into which Mrs. Schäfer led Rauscha and Carol. It was an office space, quiet and carpeted. Officer Tonya walked out in the other direction and nodded shyly at Rauscha, a manila folder under her left arm. Tibor Rauscha nodded back.

"You know her?" Carol asked.

Mrs. Schäfer walked them back to the place where she worked—a small, ordinary office half on the edge of being caved in under file folders. There were photographs of happy children—hers, presumably—and a half-hearted philodendron serving as a book end up on a shelf. And AJ Munoz was there, sitting on the radiator with his arms folded and leaning away from the gun on his hip.

"This is Officer Munoz," said Mrs. Schäfer. "He was first on the scene this morning."

"We met," said Rauscha. Carol felt him restraining himself against impatience, summoning his politest manner. Rauscha only felt obliged to do this when he either wanted something or was not sure of his ground.

Officer Munoz nodded. "My condolences to you, Mrs.

Rauscha," he said. "And once again to you, Mr. Rauscha."

"In a situation like this one," said Mrs. Schäfer, "there is a police report to be filed. I know that's the absolute last thing you need today." For Carol, anyway, right that moment it was easier to answer someone else's questions than to think about her own.

"I need to ask you," said Mrs. Schäfer, "was your son ever depressed that you noticed?"

"All his life," Carol said.

"Lately especially?" Mrs. Schäfer looked right at Tibor Rauscha when she asked. They know we don't live in the same house, Carol thought. They know what we did. They know everything. Our sins have found us out.

"No," Rauscha answered, "not especially lately. Not that I ever noticed." He answered, Carol noticed, without a trace of defensiveness. Tibor Rauscha was a temporary gentleman.

"Would you agree, Mrs. Rauscha?" asked Officer Munoz.

"I'm no longer, Mrs. Rauscha."

"My apologies. How should I address you?"

"Miss Peña."

"So noted." Officer Munoz wrote that down on a small spiralbound pad like Carol imagined a reporter would carry around. Otherwise he appeared not to take any notes at all.

"But the answer to your question is no. Eugene lives with his father. I saw him briefly on Halloween when Fanny brought him by. That was just for a few minutes. He seemed the same as always." And that was a sorry thing to say.

"She brought him to your house for trick-or-treat?"

"No, just to see me."

"How did the visit go?"

"It was tense."

"Why do you think it was tense?"

"Fanny surprised me. She was hoping Eugene could stay overnight. But I could not."

"You had plans?"

"Yes." Carol could not help looking closely at Officer Munoz's face. He looked like someone who'd been up all night. The whites of his eyes were a tired shade of red. Not pink but close.

"And you were out of town recently, Mr. Rauscha?"

"Yes, I had work to do in Dallas and was away for several days. How did you know I was travelling? Does it matter?"

"I don't think so, no. But Miss Moliere mentioned it to me when I took her statement this morning. Doesn't make a difference." Carol thought, He's warning us not to lie.

"I'm trying to understand what might have pushed your son to do this terrible thing to himself," said Officer Munoz, "when, as you tell it, he has been mostly on an even keel."

"He has never been on an even keel," Carol replied. "I think he got tired. The life he was given exhausted him."

Carol spoke quickly before her ex-husband could interrupt.

"Tibor and I are not affectionate people," said Carol. "I should be honest. We didn't start out that way but it's where we ended up. We were never kind to Eugene. The last couple of years have been really bad for him, between our divorce and what happened with that girl, who I'm sure you know all about."

"Yes."

"I think Eugene looked ahead at what life was offering him and saw only more of the same. He must have felt like his only choice was to say no."

Spilling all this did not make Carol feel better. She was shocked by the truth of the things she was saying.

"Did he ever say something like that to you? Like his only choice was saying no?"

"I never asked."

"Does that sound plausible, Mr. Rauscha? What Miss Peña was just telling us?"

"Yes."

Tibor was hating all this speculation, Carol knew, all this having to reflect. This was not the post-mortem he was expecting. They had both tried not to think about Eugene in detail and now they were being officially compelled to do so.

The tired-looking cop and Mrs. Schäfer must have assumed that, like regular people, like regular parents, Carol and Tibor Rauscha endlessly turned these questions over in their minds, lost sleep over them. Little could they guess; little did they imagine.

"My son Eugene was born to be unhappy," Tibor Rauscha said. "It was something God put in his character, I think, like a test nobody could ever pass. This is a sick thing to say, but I'll say it because what does it matter now. It's that I'm surprised Eugene had enough commitment in him to keep that bag wrapped around his face."

The brutality of it shocked them all silent. Rauscha did not look bothered. Probably congratulating himself for candor, Carol thought.

"That's all from me," Officer Munoz said. "Thank you.

Again, my sympathies."

The officer began packing up, including the smartphone on which Carol realized he had been recording their conversation. She thought, He is supposed to ask if he can record us. But she was not sure of her legal ground. She admitted to herself that she did not care. She did not deserve justice.

"Where should I release the body?" asked Mrs. Schäfer.

"I will get you a name," said Rauscha. He spoke firmly, intending to forestall a counter claim from Carol. Carol said nothing. Now that he had taken control of the situation she realized she was glad to be relieved of obligation, and she knew it.

Carol did not like herself in the least.

Carol and Rauscha were shaking hands with Mrs. Schäfer and Officer Munoz when the phone rang. Mrs. Schäfer said all right and thank you to whoever was on the other end of the line.

"Would you like to see him now?" she said to both Rauscha and Carol.

"Eugene?" asked Carol.

"Yes. I can lead you over. You're not obligated to."

"I would prefer not," Tibor Rauscha said. "I need to get home and see about my wife." Smooth, Carol thought. What's my excuse?

"Understood."

"I'll get the details of the funeral home to you this evening." Rauscha was already through the door and walking off.

"Tomorrow morning is soon enough," Mrs. Schäfer called after him. "What about you, Miss Peña?"

Carol could hear Mrs. Schäfer's wrist watch ticking. It was almost six o'clock now. The view out the window looked at the parking lot—Carol could see her gold Accord out there, the one Rauscha leased to her for nothing. Up the scrubby hillside was Fuller Boulevard, quiet as an empty church on a late Sunday afternoon. The sky in the west was an electric indigo. The sun was just gone down.

"No," Carol said. "No. Thank you, Mrs. Schäfer."

Afterglow, thought Carol. That's the word I want.

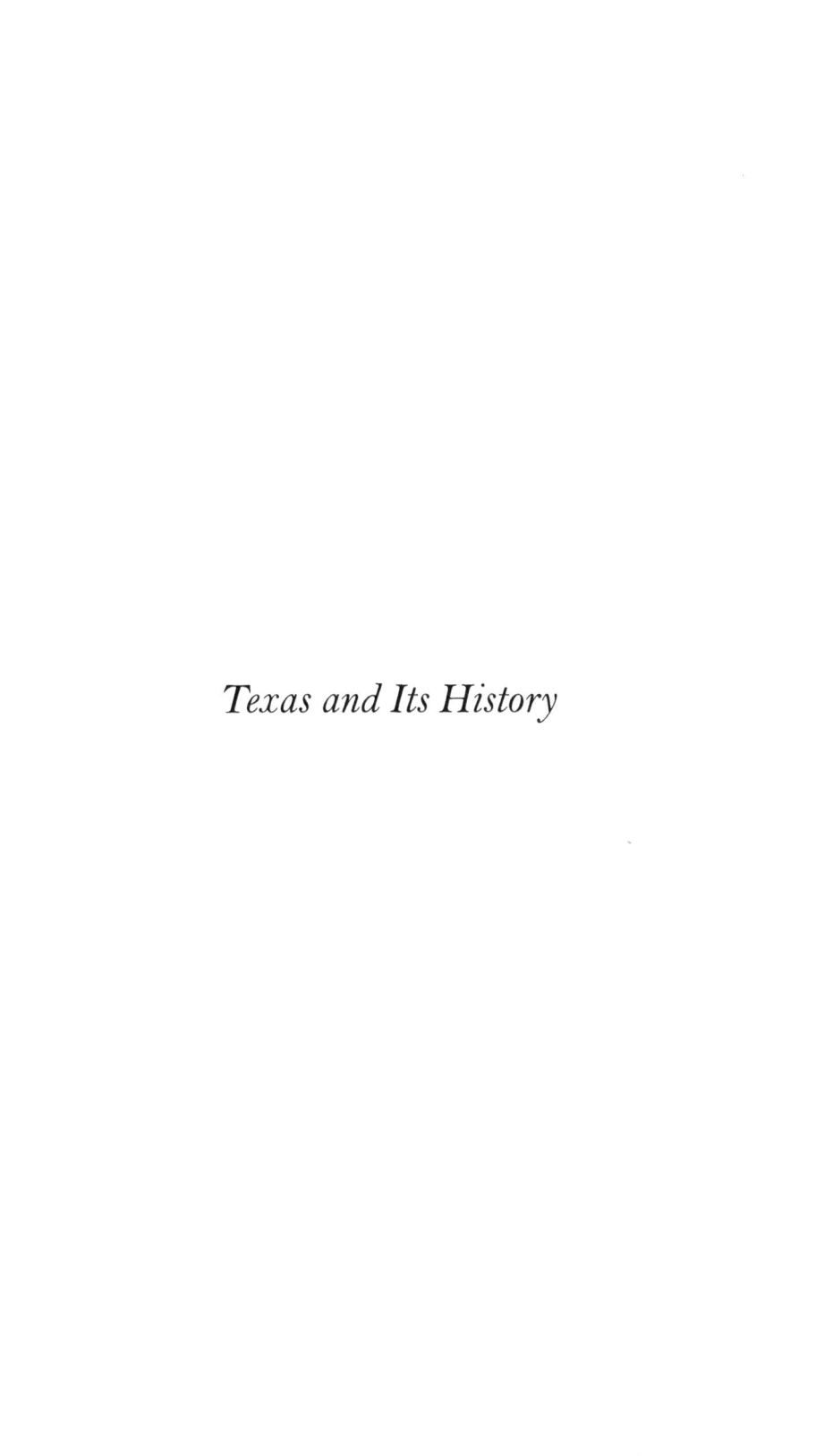

Texas and Its History

Fanny talked hardly at all for almost five months after Eugene's suicide—an extraordinary thing for her. She was tired of herself and Tibor Rauscha both. Just thinking about the effort of speaking wore her out.

Rauscha did not have any trouble acknowledging that this was a relief as far as he was concerned. It would have been hard to be all alone in the house, but conversation he did not need.

Fanny was surprised to find she missed Eugene in the big house. The kid's presence used to redirect the tension between herself and Tibor. Now there was nothing but one another's company.

"Every time I pass that room I feel a little sick in my stomach," said Fanny to Rauscha more than once that winter. If he was tired of hearing her say it she did not care.

Christmastime they went to Cuernavaca. The place they stayed was swank, a gringo Shangri-La. They were sullen with each other the whole time. Every night of their stay

Fanny was a little drunk on wine. It made a change, anyway. When Eugene was alive they never went anywhere. They could not imagine doing it.

Once they got home things escalated. One night Fanny cut Rauscha across the face with a box opener she was using to open a package. He had grabbed her by the shoulder to make a point and Fanny did not like it.

Rauscha fell to the floor of the kitchen, more shocked than hurt. It was not a bad cut she would given him, close to a swing and a miss. But she got his cheek a clean slice, and a cut to the face can really bleed.

Fanny stood over her husband as one might stand over a slain enemy.

"I guess you ain't pretty no more," she said. Both laughed out loud in hysteria. ("Hysteria" in its clinical sense.)

Rauscha grabbed Fanny and pulled her down. His blood dripped on her face as he flipped her over and lay on top of her. He's put on weight, she thought.

Rauscha wrestled the box cutter from Fanny and held the blade up to her face.

"I'm going to cut off your nose. I want that nose."

"So you're always saying." Fanny struggled to breathe under the weight of him.

"I'm going to put your nose in a box," said Rauscha. "Then I can look at it whenever I want."

The morning after that time with the boxcutter Fanny woke at six, as she did most days. Tibor Rauscha's blood was all over her pillow. He was rolled over and facing away from her. She knew he was awake. They were naked, from habit. Fanny got up and found her clothes puddled on the floor where she left them the night before.

Rauscha grunted good morning. He dragged himself to the bathroom while she dressed.

"You got me a good one," he called to Fanny. "Holy shit. I'm ruined."

"You once told me you like it rough," Fanny said from the bedroom. It was something like a conversation. They hated each other now.

Even before Mexico Fanny took it for granted that she was leaving Rauscha; after Eugene died it was all over but the leaving. That would take five more months. By the time spring came, though, and what with everything, Fanny still lived with Rauscha in the big house on Nine Mezcaleros Road.

The other thing happening that winter was that Fanny's mother, Judy DaCosta, came to visit for Fanny's birthday and did not leave. There was an outbreak of dengue fever in West Texas, of all things, and Fanny wanted her mother close.

Fanny's mother disliked Tibor Rauscha with an intensity that mother-in-law jokes did not begin to cover. She all but hissed like a cat when he came near. Rauscha knew this. He was made restless by Mrs. DaCosta's views about him. At the beginning, when Fanny and he were engaged, Rauscha tried being nice to Mrs. DaCosta. It did him no good.

The first time they shared a meal together in the big house on Nine Mezcaleros Road Rauscha said to Fanny afterward in bed, "She barely acknowledged me." Fanny had never seen him with hurt feelings before.

"She can't place you," Fanny said. "You're not Black, you're not White. My mother's kind of old-fashioned binary."

"I'm Chicano," Rauscha said. That was one of the occasional times Rauscha tried being wry; wry was a bad mode for him. One way he and Fanny's mother were alike was that they lacked a sense of humor.

To begin with, Mrs. DaCosta was a religious woman of the unforgiving type. Mrs. DaCosta did not forgive people who divorced, men who divorced especially. She presumed her own virtue. She did not make a lot of noise about this but she did presume it.

For another thing, Fanny's mother believed they would all be judged in the next life for failing their obligation to Eugene.

Jesus Christ, Fanny reflected.

Judy DaCosta grew up on Tulsa's north side. There were not many White people in her orbit. Most of the time Judy was invisible to White people except occasionally if something happened. She came to prefer this.

Judy was married at 19 in 1987. At the time she worked in the Tulsa public library restacking books while she took classes at the U of T. That was where she met Juan DaCastro, a sergeant at Tinker Air Force base. Juan was four years older than Judy. There were bigger differences than that. He was from New York and of Dominican extraction. His skin was dark as Judy's but he had white friends from the Air Force. Another difference was he had a sense of humor.

Fanny's parents moved to West Texas after Juan's twenty years were up and he was eligible for a pension. Juan came for the big money as a roughneck in the oil fields. He did alright. But it was brutal work. It aged him.

When Fanny was a baby girl she and her father had a routine they performed for Judy. They did it once spontaneously and Judy laughed, so they kept at it. With time the repetition became annoying.

"Who's the most beautiful girl in the whole world?" Fabio would ask, picking up beautiful Fanny and spinning her in the air.

"Mommy!"

"Only when she loves me, Fanny."

"Mommy loves you *all* the time!"

"But it's a hard-won love, Fanny. Every day you gotta earn it again." That was the punch line. Fanny and her father worked for their laugh. Most of the time they got the feeling Judy appreciated the effort, at least.

The problematic content of this memory made Fanny resolve to be nicer to whatever man she chose than her mother had been to her father. Fanny was not being traditional. It was only that, otherwise, why bother?

After Eugene's death Fanny's policy on being nice broke because her marriage broke.

Fanny missed her father when she thought of him sometimes. All her life Fanny never liked the company of women unmixed with men. Now she was glad of her mother and Hilda in the big house with her all the time.

The first of February, dead center of winter in West Texas. The week before a cold wind blew a dust storm off the desert for three days. Dust in the sky hid the sun. Grit got in everywhere; it wore on everyone's nerves. The wind alone worked on AJ's mind. It unsettled his spirit. Wind, if he were asked, was AJ's chief complaint about the part of Texas where he lived.

And then the wind stopped. The dust fell out of the sky. Calm fell over the world. The sun reappeared and the air warmed up. For the first time in what felt like a long while AJ quieted on his inside.

Riding down Nine Mezcaleros Road it was easy to slip into an idea of spring. AJ was paying a visit to the Rauscha house for the first time since that day the boy died. That was now about 90 days in the past.

For once AJ was working a day shift. He was alone. He had arranged these circumstances to allow him opportunity to check in on the Rauscha household.

Toward the end of the year before, presented to the force like they were a kind of Christmas gift, Chief McOlmec invested in five electric cars. McOlmec's intention was to save some money and earn friendly media attention for the department's concern for what it called "sustainability". AJ thought the cars little better than the scooters guys working for the parks department drove; how he would pursue a fleeing criminal in one of those electric cars was impossible to imagine. Two officers fit so snugly in the front seat of the electric cars that their shoulders touched. AJ disliked the coziness.

At the gate of the big house AJ unfolded himself from behind the wheel of the little car. His knees hurt doing it. He braced against the door frame to push himself up on his feet. AJ was getting old before he was ready. This ticked him off.

Beside the iron gate AJ pressed the plastic buzzer and waited for some response. The last time AJ was here he and Tonya waited what seemed an age for this gate to open. He remembered Tonya leaning on the buzzer, trying to convince whoever was up at the house that she was serious about wanting in. The siren on the ambulance was closing on them all the time. Normally Tonya was stooped both because she was shy about her height and because she was new at her job. But borne by adrenaline she was proposing to climb the fence. Then the gate swung open. It might have taken all of three minutes. They sent the ambulance in ahead of them. At that time the new police cars had not been deployed.

Now an electrical female voice said over the speaker, "May I help you?"

AJ looked up at the glassy blue eye of the security camera and assumed incorrectly that he was speaking with Fanny. Putting on his policeman's smile he faced up at the blue eye and said, "Good morning. I'm Officer Munoz. I hope you remember me."

"I'm sorry but I don't. I don't believe we ever met." Even mediated by electricity this female voice had a modulated pace, a calm, a restraint which Fanny's did not ever.

"Then I apologize for bothering you." AJ laughed as if the joke were on him. "I was hoping to speak with either Mr. Rauscha or his wife. Both if that is possible. Are they at home?"

"They're travelling today."

"I'm here as part of our community-policing outreach." AJ made that up on the spot. Chief McOlmec did not subscribe to the community-policing philosophy, which he disliked for the autonomy it gave his cops. "On the day their son passed away I was the responding officer," AJ said.

"They are getting along alright." This private conversation was being broadcast to the neighborhood. To AJ this was the opposite of a secure technology.

"Are they in need of any aid?" he said to the watching blue eye of the camera. AJ heard himself speaking in the formal diction he put on every day with his uniform. Perhaps that was why the voice was a moment answering.

"Allow me just a minute to figure out how to open the gate," said the voice at last.

"If I recall it was a green button next to where you're probably standing."

"I see it. Come on ahead."

The gate swung wide for AJ, scraping a little on its hinge. The little cop car did poorly on the three speedbumps up to the house. AJ's bones rattled under his skin each time.

Fanny's mother waited for AJ on the four-step portico of the big house. He guessed right away who she was. He liked her looks.

Judy DaCosta was more slender than her daughter but of shorter than average height in the same as Fanny was. She had the same strong features and same dark skin. Unlike her daughter Mrs. DaCosta wore her hair clipped close to her head. Whatever the intent her short hair flattered her profile.

Handsome, AJ nearly said aloud.

Mrs. DaCosta came down the steps to meet him. AJ remarked this because when he was in uniform Black members of the public usually indicated some wariness. They thought anything could happen with a cop—jail, gunplay, anything. In this, AJ believed, Black members of the public were prudent.

"I'm Judy DaCosta," said Fanny's mother. "Sorry nobody's home but me. Even the housekeeper's gone out. There's just the cleaning crew of señoritas swarming inside the place right now." Mrs. DaCosta wore a subtly checked dress AJ knew was called a "nap dress". (He knew this from Mrs. AJ's catalogues.) It was becoming to her.

"I'm sorry to miss them," AJ said.

"The señoritas? I can bring you to them if you like." Once out of his car AJ was only just above eye level with Mrs. DaCosta. He was of average height.

"No, your daughter and son-in-law. Since that day that I was called here I've thought about them a lot." Truthfully it was Rauscha who preoccupied AJ, and not Fanny much at all.

"Come sit down," said Mrs. DaCosta.

She led him to the marble bench that went around the Trevi Fountain.

"Oof," said Mrs. DaCosta as she sat down. "My knees have been talking to me lately. I'm too young to have that complaint."

"It's nothing to do with age," said AJ. He knew this from experience. Also he wanted Fanny's mother on his side. "It's the way we abuse them," he said, not knowing what he meant.

They sat in the cool aura of spray thrown off by the fountain, and this was agreeable. At midday it was warm for the time of year. Whatever winter Texas used to have doesn't come around anymore, AJ reflected. He was carrying too much weight and on a hot day he felt it.

"Are you Mrs. Rauscha's mother?"

"She's still Fanny DaCosta. She's back to using her family name. But yes, I'm her mother."

"The resemblance is unmissable." AJ thought Mrs. DaCosta looked to be in her late forties, like he was. She could have been older.

AJ realized his eyes were roving over Mrs. DaCosta's face like a lover's. That would do him no good in this conversation.

"I always thought she had more of her father in her," Mrs. DaCosta replied, "but thank you. I came for Fanny's birthday last month and I can't seem to go home." She was being pleasant to him, which is another way of being prudent.

"That must be nice for your daughter."

"I'm sure."

"The day her son died…"

"Eugene was not her son." Mrs. DaCosta smiled. She was only underscoring a point and meant no harm—the same as she had, maybe, when she reminded AJ that Fanny had taken back her maiden name.

"Your daughter was so shaken that day. I felt for her."

"Crying and so forth?"

"Not crying. Shaken. She was beyond tears."

"And Tibor was how?"

"He was solemn. Really solemn. I'm not even sure solemn is the word I want."

"Uninvolved? Detached? Cold? Disinterested? Are any of those words a better fit?"

"So your feelings about him are mixed?"

"You're very funny. I'm only being a mother-in-law, Mr. Munoz. Should I say Officer Munoz?"

"I honestly don't care. Call me AJ."

"What I like or do not like doesn't matter. Fanny's who I care about."

"Is it OK here?"

In his professional life AJ often had conversations like this one, conversations in which the other party was fighting with themselves not to say something they would later decide was indiscreet. AJ learned to be patient and just let the indiscretion come. If people wanted to talk you just had to wait for them. There was no trick to it.

"My suspicion is Fanny's looking for the exits." Here it comes, or so AJ hoped. "Keep that one to yourself."

"Why would you say that?"

"When Fanny first moved in," Mrs. DaCosta said, looking around the big house and its full acre, "when Fanny first moved in here I hated being in this house. It was so cold."

AJ inclined his head toward Mrs. DaCosta.

"Are you using metaphor?"

"No. It's genuinely cold inside. All that marble. Even with all the money in the world like Tibor's got who wants a house like this?"

"It's not a question I've had to think about."

"It's a young man's idea of a fabulous house. Tibor does not know how to live happily with his money. He doesn't know what to want. And still he's a proud son of a gun."

"I suppose."

"The house would work better as a mausoleum."

"Another question I have not had to think about."

"And the way Tibor treated his son bothered me."

"How did he treat Eugene?"

"Like a mistake." Now we're getting to it, AJ thought. He said nothing, letting Mrs. DaCosta feel the weight of the quiet. From out on Nine Mezcaleros Road he could hear the traffic mutter. The muttering helped his cause by underlining the silence.

"I was too afraid of being a meddling mother-in-law and said hardly anything about it to Fanny. Now it's on my conscience."

"When you did speak what did she say?" AJ could not bring himself to say "Fanny". Was that a given name? he wondered. Was it short for something? AJ was a Catholic and they named their kids after saints. There was no St. Fanny in his tradition.

"She did not find it in herself to do anything about it. Now I think it troubles her. Please keep this to yourself. I'm asking you."

"Of course."

"I notice you don't write anything down."

"I'm not collecting evidence at a crime scene, Mrs. DaCosta. This is just conversation."

"Well, it's a crime not to love a child. *Dislike*, I can fully understand that. A great number of children I've disliked."

"I won't fight you there."

"Do you have children, Officer Munoz?"

"In fact my wife and I have not had that blessing." In fact this was a sadness to Mrs. AJ, but he said nothing about it to Fanny's mother. He did not feel the impulse.

"Well, let me tell you from experience then. Not to love is a crime."

"Not one that will get you arrested usually. Hearts break every day."

"They never thought there'd be consequences. Who anticipates suicide?" AJ had an answer for that but this was not the time.

"Don't think Tibor wasn't upset that day," said Fanny' mother. "He was."

"I don't care. But since you brought it up, why did you come back to it?"

"Fanny told me he was shocked silly. And she can read Tibor. Now he seems to have put it away someplace. I don't want Fanny putting it away someplace. Not if she's going to learn anything from the experience and become a better person for it."

AJ did not know it then but Fanny inherited her habit of directness from her mother the same as she did her good skin. What AJ did know was that Mrs. DaCosta had a rigid tenderness for her daughter that he liked.

"How long will you be staying here?"

"Maybe I'll move in for keeps. Tibor would love that. Most of my work's here in Perros Salvajes anyway. It might make sense to stay. I'm getting tired of life on my own."

"What sort of work do you do?"

"I'm a personal shopper."

"I never met one of those."

"I make a specialty of well-off minority ladies."

"You're busy with that?"

"The complexion of this county is changing. Ever notice?"

"I'm a policeman. They pay me to notice everything."

"Twenty years ago when my husband and I moved to Hay Agua I thought for a while I was all wrong about Texas and Black people. But not for long though."

"I'd like to know what you mean. For the perspective."

"For the first time in our lives—my life, I'll speak for myself—for the first time I could go more than two miles from my house and not feel people were reacting to my dark face. If you get what I mean it was revealing."

"I can guess. But I never had exactly that same experience you're describing."

"No."

"My parents were proud Mexican people and they did not think I was brown enough. They used to tease me about it. Hurt me, though."

"We all suffer the effects of experience."

On the same reflex the two of them stood up.

"Anyway," said Mrs. DaCosta, "it only turned out we all collected in Hay Agua. But now it's changing. I wonder if everything's changing."

"Put me down for an optimist." AJ smiled.

"Experience has not given me that luxury." AJ felt surprised by her condescension. He bristled a little.

"Fanny might live to have that luxury—who knows? Better than this luxury." Mrs. DaCosta nodded toward the big house behind her.

"I'm sorry if your daughter is unhappy. If you think of anything I can do for her—or for you—here's my card. I don't give those out to just anybody."

"What does 'AJ' stand for?"

"Avenging Justice." AJ liked that joke and he appreciated it when people set him up. A small joke was a good note to end on.

Avenging Justice folded himself into the little police car. He worried that he looked funny doing it in front of Mrs. DaCosta. He did not want to appear less capable. And by that he meant less manly.

The car went off down the drive, purring electrically, almost silent except for hitting the three speed bumps. AJ came away from the big house without the answer he wanted. He still could not frame the question properly.

It was about this same time when Fanny persuaded Rauscha that they ought to hire someone to live fulltime in the big house, someone who could cook.

"You're away so much now," Fanny argued. Before this Rauscha never wanted a live-in anybody in their house. This exasperated Fanny.

"It's only because you can't invest yourself in the part of a wealthy man," she would say. This was Fanny's strong belief.

"I don't want strangers."

"You're a misanthrope."

"That's not in question. Jeez, Fanny." They had this exchange often enough that to their own ears they must have sounded rehearsed. Everything was tired between them.

That spring after Eugene killed himself Fanny got her way about having someone come live with them in the house. More and more Fanny was aware that Rauscha was afraid of crossing her.

Hilda Guitteras moved to Nine Mezcaleros Road in March. Most of her first week there it rained all over southwest Texas. In consequence of the bad weather Hilda became an intimate of the house fast.

Hilda was tall and 30 pounds heavier than she needed to be; Hilda was 43. She happened to be native to Perros Salvajes but was living in Santa Fe at the time she saw Fanny's ad on Craigslist. Hilda's children were grown and gone (like Hilda's husband) and she thought she might like to come home.

Raising her children Hilda was always working two jobs (putting her in that unhappy place where she made just too much to receive public assistance. She had the sort of life one grinds out rather than "lives" in the sense that advertisers use that term.). While residing in Santa Fe she supported her family working in diners and a tourist "café" near the Canyon Road. She learned how to cook the simple food Tibor Rauscha loved to eat—cheese omelets and meat loaf—"nutrition to make us feel good about ourselves and no baloney." (That was the kind of joke that Hilda made. Fried ring baloney was among her specialties and became one of Rauscha's favorites. Fanny wondered if Hilda was trying to murder him, cooking that way. She waited to see.)

Hilda said affirmative things all the time; in fact, she used words like "affirmative". Because of life Hilda had a lot of half-digested ideas about positive thinking. Rauscha found her bromides tiresome but for the sake of the omelets he trained himself to put up with them.

A bonus was that Hilda kept the house in order between visits from Marianna and her cleaning crew. No one asked her to do this. But as Fanny heard her telling Marianna one day, "No me gusta estar ocioso. Me pongo nervioso. I don't like sitting on my ass, you know what I mean?"

Marianna did not want competition; Fanny could tell. Marianna's reaction to Hilda was to be more abusive to las camareras.

Fanny and Rauscha did not tell Hilda that the room where she slept used to belong to Eugene.

In the months after Eugene died Tibor Rauscha could not have said if his sleep pattern was better or worse than it had always been. All his life Rauscha slept poorly; in his heart there was a kind of fighting that would not let him sleep. Not that he would know the reference but he would certainly recognize the feeling.

Just the same, that first winter Rauscha stayed on the road as much as he could because he passed the nights better in hotels.

It was more than just hotel beds that kept Rauscha away from home. For one thing, the all-girl kibbutz his house had become—Fanny, her mother, Hilda—got on his nerves. For another thing, Rauscha could not stomach the presumptuousness of strangers when he was at home in Perros Salvajes. Strangers afflicted him with condolence. Rauscha hated people's interest in him, specifically their belief that he would be glad to know they cared about him. Which he was not.

After Eugene died the managers at Rauscha's Honda dealership in Perros Salvajes all sent Fanny flowers with a note. As if Fanny were Eugene's mother. They were cozying up, Rauscha knew, cozying up. In every gesture of compassion he understood the element of calculation, the element of something expected in return one day. To this Rauscha was accustomed. What got his back up was the thought of any hint of sincerity.

For another thing, the smell of lilies gave him headaches. Fanny gave all the flowers to Mariana to take home.

And worse than flowers were the local religious entrepreneurs reminding him of God's comforts. They sent him cards with watercolors and florid sentiments on the inside referencing a bible verse. For weeks these cards came to the house on Nine Mezcaleros Road. Rauscha had his own arrangements with God, and he was every bit as serious about them as any of those Bible beaters. The only difference between them and Tibor Rauscha was that *their* lives were a 24/7 tax exemption. Tibor Rauscha had to pay his own way.

Rauscha was indignant—that was the word, he decided, *indignant*. He was afraid to leave the house for fear of meeting someone offering comfort.

And then there was Andy DiNapoli. That winter Andy's aspirations to Congress fell all to pieces. Andy did it to himself. He wanted Tibor Rauscha to stand by him.

After Eugene died Andy telephoned to offer condolences. Rauscha saw the number come up on his phone. He let it go to voicemail. He never called back. Then in the spring Andy experienced misfortune himself. He related his own emotional state to what he presumed Rauscha's to be.

At Christmas Andy's wife—Mrs. Andy—told him she was leaving him for a Wisconsin man. Andy did not take this well, not surprisingly.

"Come to find out," Andy told Rauscha in the first of the long eMails that became an affliction that winter, "she met the fellow at an ALEC conference two years ago. Two years! The one and only time I brought her to one of those things and see what it got me. I feel taken in, Tibor, honestly I do." Rauscha wished Andy would bring his troubles elsewhere. He wished everyone would bring their troubles elsewhere.

Andy took to eMail like a crazy person.

"Winter and spring," Andy wrote, "I'm away on the people's business in Austin and Ophie is spending whole days in our bed with this man. I think she relished telling me. From what she also says, Tibor, the guy's got money (which why am I not surprised?). I suppose he has the kind of life where he can take the time off if he wants. I asked Ophie, Tell me, is it love? She says to me, 'It's not love, Andy. It's fire. It just burns.' You can imagine what I'm thinking, Tibor. She's 47-years-old."

Ophie?

Imagining the extinguishment of Andy's erotic life and the flaming commencement of Ophie's disturbed Rauscha. It got to him. Rauscha wanted to shoo it from his mid. Because he envied Ophie her feeling of fire.

Worse for Andy was that once the school year ended his kids were moving to be with the Wisconsin man who set their mother alight.

The eldest daughter, Reagan, the only one willing to talk to Andy, said to him, "None of us like Texas, Daddy.

Wisconsin is like as far from Texas as we can get and still be in America."

"Say nothing till you've seen Wisconsin," Andy warned.

Reagan urged Andy to be led by discretion. Andy was too far gone for discretion. He wasted no time embarrassing himself.

In Texas Andy built his political career by moving on from the Baptists and portraying himself as a model Presbyterian. But at the time of her affair Mrs. Andy was still a paid-up Catholic. So Andy wrote a letter on State of Texas stationery on the subject of her adultery to the Diocese of Galveston & Houston. The most terrible part about his wife's sin, he explained to the Catholics, terrible not for Andy but for Reagan and her two younger sisters, was that Mrs. Andy told the girls that whatever she wanted to call what she was doing with the Wisconsin man was good in God's eyes.

"Should she ever present herself for Communion in any Wisconsin parish," Andy wrote, "she must be refused. I wish you to relay this to the Wisconsin bishops, your colleagues. The scandal to the church would be too enormous. I raise this subject gravely. It gives me no pleasure to do so."

Clearly it gave Andy a great deal of pleasure to do so, pleasure of the self-poisoning kind. Everyone knew this because Andy released his letter to the world with a covering press release through his office. It was as if he was announcing a civil suit on behalf of his state-senate district.

Andy's constituents were divided between mockery and an impulse to look away.

"Washington is finished for me," Andy told Rauscha in one of his eMails. "I don't kid myself. I still got the lock on my senate seat. This much I know." Rauscha regretted the check he wrote to Andy's congressional PAC. But Andy might yet be useful, so OK, he would eat the donation if he had to.

Unless he happened to mention Lobos Aullando and its water issues Rauscha never replied to Andy's lovelorn eMails. Replying only encouraged Andy to write back. Rauscha did not want that.

In April Rauscha went to Galveston to visit Lobos Aullando for the first time since the previous October. Construction on all of it was stopped until Rauscha knew for absolute certain that the county would turn the water on.

Rauscha was feeling declining urgency about the project anyway. The only reason he went there in March was because he knew Andy DiNapoli would be away in Austin on the people's business and would be unable to join him.

The walkaround was just Rauscha, his project manager and the contractor. Even for March it was a cold day. All that morning it poured rain intermittently. If the day were ten degrees colder it would have snowed in Galveston. As it was the rain hit the three men like glass beads into their faces. It was hard believing water was even an issue for these people.

"There's no denying the place looks sad," said the contractor, Rudy something. He was a red-faced man in a too-blue suit. He wore burgundy boots—one of those cowboy dandies Rauscha found tiresome. And yet Rudy something was somehow what people called real Texas.

"The framing on the houses is going to rot standing in the open air like this," Rudy something told Rauscha. "At least let me wrap them in tarps."

But Tibor Rauscha said no. The project was not getting another dime out of him until somebody committed on the water.

Rauscha's one-year option on the development right expired in June. If he let the deadline pass he owed nobody anything. As he had made clear to Andy, if the water did not flow he would let the date come and go. Now, walking a site that looked more like an archeological dig than someplace with a future, Rauscha decided on the spot to let the option expire anyhow, water or not.

That evening Rauscha fixed up his mind about this as he was returned to the airport. He ignored his exceptionally chatty driver, some guy Andy recommended, in order to think.

After checking in for his flight Rauscha walked the full length of the departure terminal waiting for his puddle jumper to Dallas/Ft. Worth. He could not decide if he was hungry enough to want any of the things sold in airports. His clothes were annoyingly wet from the weather but inside his own head Rauscha was warm. Inside his own head a new vision was blooming, a fully made idea expanding like a red giant to enfold everything else.

If I walk away from Lobos Aullando, Ruscha was thinking, I clarify my life back to what it was before everything happened. I get rid of Andy DiNapoli. To do that I would willingly pay money. But I won't need to pay money. Letting the option drop I save money. The place can go to rot and I'll never need to visit Galveston again. Blessing upon blessing. A theory of everything.

Rauscha loved the feeling of being clever. It seemed to him he had not felt clever for a long time.

Then his bubble popped.

"I thought I recognized you," a man's voice said behind him.

Rauscha turned around to see a White man, taller than himself but bent a little and balding. That girl's father. Staufer.

"I knew you from the back," said the father.

"Yes?"

"I just landed from Dallas. For months I've wanted to tell you how sorry I was when I heard about your son."

"Thank you." Rauscha saw in Staufer's eyes an understanding that he would not make this whatever it was easy.

"It just gets sadder and sadder, doesn't it?"

"What does?"

"This life."

"Were you fond of Eugene?"

"I tried to remind myself that he was a child, but I just couldn't do it. To do what he did—all the things he did—he must have lived in such pain. But I let anger eat me up. I ought to have found another way. I'm sorry now."

"I don't know why you're telling me this," Rauscha said. Which was true. Rauscha could not imagine why this man was talking to him. Don't tell me your problems, he thought. That was his life's motto.

"You might not know it, Mr. Rauscha, but on the day he died your son approached me as I was leaving church with my daughter." It was clearly costing the guy something to get this out. Advantage Tibor Rauscha.

"It happens that I do know it." Rauscha did not know.

"He was with some friend of your family," Staufer said, "and she spoke for him. Your son wanted my forgiveness. I couldn't give it."

"Your conscience bothers you?" Rauscha felt he had some leverage but he could not name it yet.

"My conscience doesn't worry me." The man's voice took on a noticeable edge, but he mastered it. "My anger at what your son did to my daughter ate me up the last few years. I wish now that for one morning I'd been able to put it aside. That's all I'm trying to say."

"Too bad Eugene didn't find you in a better mood that day."

"What?"

"I still say it sounds like conscience."

"No. Recognition."

"Conscience." Rauscha was pleased to see that his blow had landed.

Staufer sighed hard and, thank God, left. He walked off in the direction of the taxi cabs. Probably already telling himself that he tried his best, Rauscha thought. "Well you didn't," he said, not realizing that he said these words out loud until he became aware of a toddler standing next to him. She was staring.

"You'll trip on those laces," Rauscha told her. "Get someone to tie your shoes." The child looked frightened.

The pleasure Rauscha had been feeling in his new idea about Lobos Aullando was gone. Pleasure, Rauscha realized, pleasure, any idea of pleasure, was gone forever. By the time he landed in El Paso that night he was reconciled to this realization.

So be it.

Texas Redeemed

Easter morning Carol Peña slept late. Her clock radio, ordinarily so dependable she never gave it a thought, failed to go off. She never did figure out what went wrong with it.

Whatever it was, an hour past her getting-up time Carol lay atop the bedclothes in her simple cotton nightgown, the adhesive surfacing sleep that comes after daylight still on her. Her brain knew she should wake but could not move her.

Carol dreamt herself as a girl in blue shorts going with her father to the beach in Galveston. They stood on the shore at low tide and watched quiet waves. Then she was dreaming of arriving late for church with her father and finding the sanctuary half empty. Up on the altar was a preacher she did not know looking like he was not sure what to do. Then she was grocery shopping on Fuller Boulevard. Almost all the stores were closed, their windows boarded or empty, the doors all locked. The stores that were open were ones she did not know.

Beyond all this was nothing. She could not see the nothing but knew it was there. The sensation of the nothing was vivid.

In this borderland Carol saw an angel kneeling at her bedside. In a puddle of light the angel knelt wearing the white linen angels are known to wear. It knelt with its face buried in whatever it had for hands.

Somehow Carol knew the angel meant her no harm. To get its attention she shook the angel at its shoulder, gently. It turned its face up to her, and when it did Carol knew that the angel's heart was sick because its eyes were gone. That is how you tell.

Carol was not dreaming.

On Nine Mezcaleros Road it was Easter too. In that house they ate lamb on the holy day. Fanny's mother used to say that Tibor Rauscha had more than he could say grace over, yet there we were, saying grace over the lamb. The prayer was led by Mrs. DaCosta.

Mrs. DaCosta was still in residence. She did not speak to Tibor Rauscha unless circumstances compelled it, which as far as she was concerned was never. Her tongue was frozen in contempt; Mrs. DaCosta was a comparatively quiet woman anyway.

Fanny could not be bothered building bridges anymore. Those two had no prospect of ever getting on. Why invest energy?

Hilda grilled the lamb beside the patio, next to the pool. She made a lemongrass paste for it. Tibor Rauscha found it delicious.

Hilda ate her own dinner on the patio, where the air still smelled good to her of grilled meat. The pool pump puttered. In the observably sinking sun at the far edge of the desert Hilda lost herself in thoughts of old New Mexico and her life there.

When the house phone rang Hilda snapped out of her reverie and brought the phone into the house.

"It's Miss Peña for you," Hilda said, handing the telephone to Rauscha. The way she said it sounded sort of theatrical. Fanny and Judy both looked up.

"How nice," Rauscha said, taking the phone from Hilda.

Leaving the room Rauscha noticed that the three women fell into conversation immediately.

No one imagines I have feelings, Rauscha reflected.

"Carol, what a pleasure." Right away she was telling about the angel.

"Tibor, without words it spoke to me. It communicated in a high voice—a high-pitched sound that was not language but that I understood. I got every single word."

"You sound like you're on speaker, Carol. Was the voice anything like that?"

"Laugh if you like, Tibor. I met an angel this morning."

"That's great."

"I met an *angel*. It's a fact the same as this telephone in my hand is a fact."

"It's dinnertime here, Carol. What do you want?"

"The angel wants us to rebury Eugene."

"Oh?"

"It said we made a mistake in the location."

"So why didn't the angel come to my house? I chose the cemetery. I paid the funeral home."

Carol sighed. "I don't know," she said.

"Are you drinking, Carol?"

Carol took a long breath audible on the telephone.

"Yes," she said. "I had one drink in order to be able to call you. But I was not drinking at seven-thirty this morning when it happened."

"When what happened?"

"The angel."

By this time Rauscha had walked the length of his house and out into the small "garden" of sad scrub on the south side. He could see Nine Mezcaleros Road one acre over to his left. Shadows in the desert to his right. The daylight was all but gone from the western horizon but there was a bench out there so he sat down. It was spring and the days were getting longer.

"Are you still on?" Rauscha said.

"I hear a breeze across the mouthpiece," Carol said. "You've gone outside the house."

"Yes."

"I'm supposed to give you every opportunity to agree to what I'm asked to propose. Please just listen, Tibor."

"You're insane, Carol. You don't hear the things you say."

"The angel told me that in the next world Eugene grieves for us. Eugene wants us to forgive ourselves."

"He really gave his message to the angel?"

"Yes."

"It must have been Uriel. That's the repentance angel."

"Don't fight me all the time, Tibor. Please. Especially not now."

"Just pointing out."

"The angel *related* this, Tibor."

"Christ Almighty."

"Eugene wants to come home. For our sake. He wants to rest in the ground below his old bedroom window."

"The angel wants Eugene to be buried here at the house?"

"Out by the fountain."

"Sure. Why not?"

"You're mocking me, Tibor. I expect that."

"Anything else before we're done here?"

"Our words don't matter anymore, Tibor. Our words are forfeit because we did not love Eugene."

"Oh, Jesus."

"This would be our recompense."

"Where are you getting these words? Tell the angel if it comes back that this is not what I want."

"It *is* what you want. Eugene knows it is."

"Que?"

"Eugene wants us to repair the damage we did to ourselves. Not to him, to us. He knows that as long as we keep him out there in the cemetery we'll only keep our bleeding wounds open. We'll go on being haunted."

"I have well water."

"What?"

"He was embalmed."

"He's in a metal box, Tibor. With snaps on it."

"The county won't allow it."

"I researched that question this afternoon. We can request a waiver."

"'We'? It's my house, Carol."

"I'll take charge of it, Tibor. The same way I didn't take charge when Eugene died."

"You should make some friends, Carol. You've become a fragile woman over the last several years."

Carol told Rauscha nothing more. After a moment's consideration she hung up. She conveyed all she was asked to relate.

Now it was up to Rauscha.

Texas At Its Physical Limit

Late on a Wednesday Katherine Moliere was alone in the teachers' room at Emma Tenayuca School. Before going home she had two hours' of papers to grade. School was the most home she had in those days. To Moliere home was not much of an idea anymore.

For company Moliere had the occasional passage of someone in the hallway in squeaking rubber shoes. From further away came the b-flat tone of the custodian buffing the floor tile of the corridor, a conversation somewhere nearby. The reassuring sounds of school after hours.

Moliere's phone rang in her backpack. To her subsequent regret she dug for the phone and answered.

"Hello, Katherine. This is Fanny."

Moliere should have hung up then. But from reflex she said, "You changed your number."

"I did it for New Year's. The old number sure was not bringing me any luck. Getting a new one was sort of symbolic for me."

Moliere did not reply. Fanny continued. Fanny always continued.

"We're burying Eugene again and I was hoping you'd come. There. I said it right out loud. Probably there'll be lunch after."

All the past five months Moliere banished Fanny and Rauscha from her mind. After Franklin died the psychologist she saw taught her some tricks for doing that with pernicious thoughts, as which Fanny and Rauscha qualified. Sixty seconds hearing Fanny's voice and all that good work was undone. Especially once Fanny started telling the part about the angel.

"I'm hanging up now," said Moliere.

"Tibor *believes* in angels," Fanny was saying as though she had not heard a reply; with her bad hearing maybe she had not. "He believes in them though he'll never admit it publicly. Half the time it's just a whimsy with him. The other half he really thinks angels are around in the atmosphere. Like those warblers you see zipping around. Carol was smart when she introduced the angel into their conversations."

"No."

"There was a convergence."

"No."

"Right about the time she called Tibor was going through one of his religious cycles. Probably thinking about Easter coming and whatnot, that's what got him started. Now he spends a lot of time in his chapel."

"He's got things to answer for."

"Listening for angels, I suppose. We all do, Katherine."

"Not like him."

"Apparently Eugene forgives him for everything. Eugene's got a different vantage point now."

"You should be ashamed."

For some moments Fanny said nothing. Moliere noticed this silence. She heard how loud a Fanny silence could be.

"I'm encouraging you to be less cynical, Katherine," Fanny said at last. "For your own sake."

"You're failing."

Again Moliere heard the unfamiliar sound of Fanny not-speaking.

"I *am* ashamed," Fanny said after a bit and more quietly. "I don't know how to get good with God, Katherine. It's got me talking to myself."

"That must be something."

"Tibor hopes Eugene will get born again sometime. He hopes that him having been born in Perros Salvajes will turn out to have been one of God's misfires and can be corrected down the road. *My* thinking, if you're asking, is that this reburial is a second chance at being a family."

"And this time Eugene will be less trouble to you if he's in the ground all the time."

"Whew. I don't remember you being this unkind, Katherine. You got me in the heart with that one." It sounded like Fanny's voice broke but the effect could have been put on.

"Your heart is where I aimed," Moliere told Fanny.

"Look, Katherine, I only wanted to let you know. You cared a lot about Eugene." And at that the taste of the boy's mouth on the day he died came back sharply to Moliere. She thought she might vomit in the sink across the room, the taste was that vile.

"I don't believe you."

"Believe me," Fanny said, and proceeded to misinterpret what Moliere meant. "Before he left for Wyoming yesterday Tibor got on the phone with our lawyer and told him to figure out all the permits and whatnot."

"You can't bury Eugene in your front yard because you're hoping for forgiveness."

"In Texas it turns out you can."

"It's too late for all of you."

"When you replay this conversation in your head, Katherine, I want you to know that I've been in earnest. Will you do that?"

"Goodbye."

"If you change your mind about coming you've got my number."

"I'm deleting it." And she did.

Moliere could speculate that Eugene had a possibility of being redeemed. There was no such possibility for the people who made him the way he was.

Once when love was young Moliere drove with Franklin to the wedding of his sister Molly. Molly lived in El Paso.

Moliere and Franklin had been a couple for about two years. Later in the same summer that Molly was married they got engaged themselves. Driving to El Paso that morning they were dressed up, Franklin handsome in his one good suit he hardly ever had reason to wear, Moliere almost glamourous in a dress the color of crème de menthe that showed all her strong shoulder bones and the beige and the freckles of her skin. Franklin had the deepest erotic attachment to her skin. He loved the din of its DNA, loved the freckles, loved, therefore, the dress.

On the radio that morning was an item about a narcotics arrest the night before in Los Revers, the county next to Perros Salvajes.

"When I was new on the job I did two of those smash-the-doors-in deals," Franklin said. "Scary as hell. You never know what's waiting for you. People yelling, babies crying. The babies crying make you feel evil."

"At times," Moliere told Franklin, "at times I wish you wouldn't tell me that side of your job." Little did she know. "One time I was worried about you so hard I threw up." She promised herself never to tell him that one but then it came right out.

"All in a day's work, m 'am," Franklin answered.

"Thank you for your service."

Moliere knew all along that Franklin was proud of showing physical courage. It was boyish of him and only added to her fondness for him. Franklin used to tell her being a cop spoiled him for the ordinary work other people did. The two of them would have been grand together.

After Franklin died Moliere realized she never really understood why Franklin became a cop. He used to talk about the pension after 20 years, the way they all did. And once she met an uncle of his who'd been a Texas Ranger, and he made it sound rollicking. Franklin would never have used a word like "rollicking" though.

"Where else could you find so much human nature?" Franklin said. Maybe what he said was all there was to it.

"Drugs are awful for what they eventually end up doing to people," Franklin said to the radio.

A different morning Franklin came home and told Moliere about a call he answered with AJ Munoz the night before. Along the stretch of interstate that clipped the top part of Perros Salvajes county two truckers saw a teenage boy walking—or, better said, tottering—on the shoulder of the highway and then pitching abruptly into the brush. The truckers talked it over for less than 20 seconds before they pulled over and trotted back to see what they could do for the kid, which was nothing. They wrestled with him and got him to sit up. In that position he heaved convulsively and then went over sideways, dead. They phoned 911. Franklin and AJ were another seven minutes coming and the two men had to wait with the kid's dead body.

"Sixteen-years-old," Franklin told Moliere. "Why was a 16-year-old out walking on the interstate at three in the morning?"

"I don't know. Start with crap parents?"

"In a dozen ways start with crap parents. Every time start with the crap parents."

Some of the cruelties Franklin saw on his job were sad to tragic but all the same part of life and nothing to get philosophical about. Others made him angry because they did not *need* to be. The teenager's death was in this second category.

Franklin told Moliere, "Before that night I never saw anyone be dead."

"What'd you do?"

"Do about what?"

"The boy who died."

"Called the ambulance," Franklin said. "There was nothing else to do. In that situation we're not much more useful than you civilians. What's needed is not us, you know? But I have to tell you it was strange taking down the story from those two truckers with the kid lying dead at my feet more or less. AJ was very good with them."

This conversation took place about a year before Franklin was murdered, about two and a half years before Eugene Rauscha killed himself.

In the middle of the night the teenage body was collected. Franklin and AG escorted the ambulance to Perros

Salvajes County Hospital. The routine called for the two policemen to stick around until the parents arrived and gave an account. The kid had his high-school ID in his wallet. AJ got the job of phoning his home to wake up his folks.

"They were awful," Franklin said.

"I cannot imagine."

"Not for the reasons you think you cannot imagine. *They* were awful. The parents were."

"What were they?"

"Ignorant."

"I mean their background. Rich people? Poor people?" Moliere was framing the picture for herself, imposing context.

"Dark people? Light people?" Franklin teased. "They were no one you could plant a prejudice on, Katherine."

"Don't say prejudice. That's mean. Say social insight."

"I think the husband told us he was a contractor."

"What kind?"

"Probably whatever you've got. It didn't matter to me one way or another. I'm not sentimental about the virtues of working people."

"Me neither. I teach their kids, remember?"

"It was going to take a few days for the toxicology report but walking into the hospital they knew. They *knew*. Their kid was 16 and looked 40."

"So what happened to him? Had he snuck out of the house?"

"Told his father he was going to a friend's."

"The classic deception."

"Sure, but it's three in the morning and his parents don't

even go out looking for him? Phone him up? Fuck. My father would have beaten me for doing that, and he was a nice guy."

"My father has often said nothing good happens after two a.m."

"These parents were not people who had insights. AJ had to wake them up."

In those days Chief McOlmec had a policy officially called Human Kindness. The chief's idea was that, selectively, his officers would attend tragic-story funerals in which the department had played a part. "It's just human kindness," said McOlmec, thus the name. In time the practice was stopped for lack of interest (and, maybe surprisingly, too few real tragedies in Perros Salvajes County to qualify) but not before the teenager's funeral. Franklin, who at that time was still in the position of starter cop, got the job of going.

"Poor stupid bastard," AJ reflected. AJ meant the boy who died. He was being sincere. But he was still not taking a morning off to go to the funeral.

Franklin put on his dress blue uniform, white gloves and all, and drove out to the cemetery in Tierra de Trueque where the boy was being buried. It was late spring. At ten a.m. the air was already fried. At the graveyard Franklin parked his berry-red Corolla among the dozen or so pickups that parked along the cemetery's circular road. There was a single silver Infinity Franklin later realized had been rented special for the day by the boy's parents.

At the graveside Franklin attracted interested looks in his deep blue uniform and campaign hat with its Montana crease. No one from the police department had told the family he was coming. Franklin nodded good morning to several people, every one of whom looked away, probably guilty of something.

The dead boy's red-headed father caught Franklin's eye and glared. Later Franklin concluded that the man associated him in some way with the death of his son, or so Franklin said to Moliere when he told this story.

Like the stranger he was, Franklin positioned himself to one side of the mourners. The brim of his Smokey Bear hat was tugged to his eyebrows. He was near a small collection of people smoking as they waited for things to begin. Franklin was the only one who did not look dressed for a barbecue. Under his jacket his dress blouse was soaked in perspiration.

The dead boy was hiding in a shiny wood box. The box lay next to the empty grave. Piled up beside the box was a mound of light-colored dirt.

The boy's parents stood across the narrow hole from the pile of dirt. They wore matching West Texas A&M shirts in maroon and white. To a policeman's eye the shirts looked shiny new. The father, Franklin noticed, was a short-statured man, over-muscled in a way he probably hoped would inches to his height, the way some men will.

A squat little girl in shorts stood next to the mother—the boy's younger sister, Franklin deduced.

A woman in black slacks and a sleeveless black blouse began to speak. The woman was skeletally thin and hard in in her face.

"Well, Shane," the woman said, talking to the shiny box, "you've gotten yourself into your last fix." The people there chuckled knowingly. "Good Lord, Shane, in your 16 years you found enough trouble for three boys. Skipping school, brawling when you did turn up. Cussing all the time, taking a poke at your football coach. And whoever heard of a boy your age with a restraining order against him? What was that girl's name?"

"Angelique," someone prompted. People laughed at memories of Shane and Angelique.

"You might say you took boyhood into uncharted territory, Shane." This was a good joke and now people laughed more freely; it was going to be that sort of preaching. Franklin noticed how Shane's mother squeezed her husband's arm. He wondered how often in her life she had ever been the center of attention.

"Shane, you're in the Lord's hands now," the thin woman said. "Heaven help you each."

When the laughter quieted the woman added more quietly, "Into His hands we commend your spirit, as the Bible tells us to do. I don't believe we need worry too much about your spirit in the next world, Share. God is merciful."

Somebody said, "Amen."

Here Franklin realized the woman was preaching extemporaneously. Remembering that the boy lying in the box came of these people Franklin wondered if, had Shane not been dead, he would have found the preacher hilarious.

"My eyes," she said, "this morning my eyes and the Lord's eyes, even Shane's eyes, are on our two friends, Gretchen and Reinhold. Both of you know how this company of friends feels for you this morning. You do know, kids, don't you?"

"We do. Amen," said Shane's mother. She flicked a glance at her husband. She looked like a woman who had learned to watch for sudden moves.

"You've had your tough times," the woman continued, beautifully holding for a beat before adding, "most of them to do with Shane. Don't grieve now for what your boy did not become. Forgive him what he did become. Today let him go to God's house."

And again everyone said amen.

Franklin was so many steps away from the circle of mourners that he looked like an eavesdropper. These people have no center, he was thinking. No rituals. They are weightless with a made-up-on-the-spot idea of God. They have no systems of belief.

Now the red-headed father stepped forward and placed a bag of marijuana on his son's coffin. It was a small bag, strictly a ceremonial gesture.

"Some bud for my bud," said the father. "Join the angels, boy. That's what you always wanted. Now's your big chance."

The father looked through the double row of family and friends directly at Franklin, the cop who invaded the family circle. The father was defiant as any bad boy ever was. Franklin felt hot and awfully tired.

The thin woman closed not with a prayer but with an invitation to gather at a nearby park for barbecue. After that the crowd did not stay ten minutes. They went off to the funeral picnic and left Shane in his box beside the hole.

Cemetery workers came forward and slipped canvass straps under the bier on which Shane's coffin rested. They lifted. The box was lowered into the hole. A compact tractor moved into place. It pushed the pile of dirt over Shane and buried him. Inevitably the bag of weed disappeared into someone's pocket.

"Is there a problem?" the father asked Franklin after accepting the last condolence and starting for the silver Infinity. His wife waited a few steps away to see what this exchange would become.

Franklin, hating Chief McOlmec with all his heart, replied, "No problem, sir. I only came to express my sympathies to you and your wife. For you this is a sad day."

Just slightly the father dropped his guard.

"Guess he's out of it now," the father said, titling his head toward the space where Shane had been. "He's a lucky one," said the father, indicating with a tip of his head the vacancy above ground where his son had been.

"Thanks for coming out," he said to Franklin, and went off.

Apart from the hole-fillers Franklin was the last person at the graveside. The little bulldozer was pushing dirt in on top of the box in dry scoops that were quickly filling up the grave.

"No wonder you got high all the time," Franklin said to the dirt.

Three years later Moliere remembered this story when Fanny predicted she would repent her decision not to attend Eugene's second burial. Which she has not.

To his wife Fanny (and to DeLorean Mueller, his lawyer) Tibor Rauscha delegated the job of obtaining the variance required by Perros Salvajes County to bury Eugene out in front of the big house. That was accomplished at the beginning of June. The next job—digging Eugene's new grave—was a collaboration of Fanny and Carol.

The logical place to put Eugene was in an ungardened space to the left of Trevi Fountain as one went up the drive to the house. The grave would be hidden from visitors until they pulled up; then they would be staring right at it. The grave would forever be visible out of all the front windows of the house.

On a broiling Saturday morning Fanny and Carol met at the Café Caliente to talk it all over. Carol had a new sketchpad she purchased the day before in an art shop. As the two women talked of what Eugene's grave might look like she made drawings. Fanny said she was surprised to find Carol had a knack.

"I always loved art," Carol replied.

They started with something that looked like an 18th Century family vault—a blunt rectangular box above ground. Fanny demurred.

"Now that I'm seeing it out loud," she said, "it looks too much like a grave."

"What else you would want for his crypt?" Carol asked, and earnestly.

"Don't say the word 'crypt'. It makes my skin just prickle." Fanny folded her arms against the real chill she felt.

"El secreto," Carol teased. In this conversation Carol was feeling a little like girlfriends. She believed she was beginning to understand Fanny a little.

Huddled over the sketchpad they sat shoulder to shoulder. Fanny wore her braids down that day but they were shorter by six inches from what Carol remembered. Here and there the braids were punctuated with silvered sequins. Carol's hair was straight and newly copper colored. A portly man standing near the pastries appraised them. Not the pastries.

"Try for something uplifting," Fanny said.

"Like what did you have in mind?"

"Something quiet. Quiet and uplifting."

"Like in marble?" Carol flipped a page of her pad. Her charcoal pencil was poised.

"There's too much marble in that house already. How long does wood last? Good wood, nothing cheap. Marble to me says dead."

"Probably not very. In ten years we'd be rebuilding the thing."

"Tibor won't pay twice, I can tell you that. He can be sometimes miserly."

They went around like this for a bit. At last Carol suggested a flat stone for a marker. It would be about five feet long—not quite as long as Eugene when he died—and flush with the earth. She sketched quickly, captured by the idea.

"If we set it back toward the brush," she said as she worked, "a little farther from the fountain than we've been talking, then the landscaping becomes the center of attention. Instead of the not-a-crypt."

What materialized from Carol's pencil was a sketch that made Fanny think of a magical door into the earth. Through which they might all go visit the dead Eugene. Fanny physically shook the picture of that from her mind.

"You cold?" Carol asked.

On the second draft of the drawing Carol alluded to a crucifix at the top of the slab with Eugene's birth and death dates below it. "He was christened," Carol explained. At Fanny's suggestion Carol indicated a border of shrubbery around the stone slab. The magic door.

"I like the idea of landscaping," Carol said. "Unobtrusive but, you know, there."

Fanny agreed.

"People should see it," she said. It was her acknowledgement.

The next week they went together to consult a stone cutter who had a shop just outside the main gate of the Perros Salvajes county cemetery. The friendly man there asked to see Carol's drawings.

"I can see you worked really hard on these," he said. His admiration was sincere.

"Can we gild the crucifix?" Carol asked.

"We do it all the time," said the man.

Carol also proposed scratching an image of Eugene's face into the slab, bottom right.

The first time Fanny saw the sketch Carol made of the face was at the stonecutter's. Carol had copied the image from a photograph of Eugene she had by her front door that showed him at about age eight instead of 15. Even so it reminded Fanny specifically of how Eugene looked the morning he died, flat on his back and dead already.

"No."

"Tibor wouldn't go for it?"

"Hell with Tibor. Look at the way you made his eyes look. He's got zombie eyes. It would creep me out, Carol, Eugene looking that way at me all the time. Even when I was in the house I'd know he was staring out there. It would be worse knowing there was no one he was staring *at*."

Carol conceded but was plainly disappointed. The stonecutter watched all this and said nothing.

With the man's help Carol and Fanny settled on polished Texas llanite for the stone.

"Llanite's soft," he explained, "in two different senses. It's easy to work and it's a *warm* stone. Because it's a rhyolite." Rauscha would later tell Fanny that the look of llanite reminded him of olive loaf, which he detested. It made him nauseous to look at llanite and olive loaf both.

About the shrubbery Fanny telephoned Rita O'Gara, the same landscaper who replaced Rauscha's maples every time one died. Fanny did some research and decided they should want China rose for the border around Eugene's grave.

"Cultivating that particular shrub on the edge of the desert is going to be a headache," O'Gara said. "I'm only telling you that to be up front."

"That is a problem for another day," Fanny told her. The near-term job was digging a hole.

In late June on another sweltering morning a single backhoe bumbled down Nine Mezcaleros Road with its red caution lights flashing.

There was some trouble negotiating the turn in through the gate. The narrow drive with its guard of stunted maples presented another challenge. At the top of the drive the backhoe man broke two toes from Oceanus' left foot. It was a clean break, though. Fanny put the toes in the pocket of her blouse and later that day reset them with an epoxy resin. Tibor Rauscha never said a word about it so he must not have noticed.

Rauscha was away for two days in South Dakota and so missed the digging of Eugene's hole. This was probably intended. He said he was meeting with a South Dakota banker. He wanted to protect his wealth from estate taxes, he told Fanny. South Dakota was the place to do it.

"What do you care about estate taxes? You'll be dead with Eugene."

"At least I'll die without that grievance," Rauscha replied. "There's also an income-tax play." He left for the airport in a funny mood and was more quiet than usual.

Carol was there the morning they dug the hole. When she arrived the driver of the backhoe was already getting to work. All by himself he marked out the dimensions of Eugene's grave with serious red ribbon.

The precision of the backhoe man's skill with his bucket was remarkable. Each time he dropped it the bucket bit deep. It deposited each load of earth in precisely the same spot, a growing dome of dirt that was being saved for the berm that would be built around the grave and planted with China rose.

In the quiet of midmorning the noise of the backhoe at work was loud enough to carry out to Nine Mezcaleros Road. Janet Staufer heard it and was curious about the new sound, or so they later assumed. She came through on the path that connected her house to the big one, a path she had not used for two years. She was standing fascinated at the top of the path as she watched the backhoe at work.

Carol noticed Janet first. She nudged Fanny.

"Oh Lord," said Fanny. This was more than an expression.

The backhoe driver waved to Janet. She made a waving gesture back. The man carried on. After a short time more he got down from the machine. From the toolbox under his seat he retrieved a tape measure. Playing the tape out six feet he dropped it into the hole to see how far he had got.

"More!" Janet shouted from where she stood at the top of the trail. The man smiled when she said this. She sounded happy so, alright, more.

"Two feet more to go," he called to Janet where she stood.

Carol and Fanny let Janet watch until the work was done. Then Fanny telephoned Janet's brother Timmo to come bring her home.

All candor, Fanny told Timmo what happened.

"Normally she won't ever speak," Timmo reflected when he came to see the hole too.

The next afternoon a different angel appeared to Carol. This angel crowned the grave's design.

The angel appeared to Carol at the far western reach of Fuller Boulevard where the big retail stores and the supermarkets dissolved into low-scale rental housing. In this borderland was a place that sold statuary for gardens—cherubs and Madonnas and so on. The angel was up against the fence and visible to Carol as she drove past.

Carol's angel was down on both knees, face buried in its hands. Its posture so closely resembled that of the angel who visited Carol on Easter morning that she said to Fanny it made her heart feel full.

When she brought Fanny to the garden shop a day later Fanny said the angel statue appeared to be grieving.

"I have knowledge of this," Carol said. "To me it was like a second apparition, as if it were reaching out for my attention. It was just like my annunciation."

"Why good fortune?" Fanny asked, all ears. "Isn't that the opposite of what the angel said Eugene wanted?" she asked. "Look at its wings. They're folded down like a dog's ears when it's been bad."

"I don't think that."

"If you're asking me that's antithetical."

"It's unloved," Carol replied, adding more quietly, "the way Eugene was. No one has wanted it."

"That ought to tell you something," Fanny said.

In the end, literally in the end, one day before Eugene was restored in front of the big house, Fanny took delivery of the concrete angel. When the men asked where to put the angel it was left to Fanny to decide its placement. Carol and she had not discussed this. The thing was not four feet tall but it weighed 175 pounds. It was unlikely that it would ever be moved again.

Fanny had the two men from the garden shop place the angel slightly to the side of the hole they would dug, alongside where Eugene's head would lay. It was within the low berm that had been built up around the grave and which had already planted with the China rose. Fanny hoped more than ever that the shrub would succeed and grow tall.

Eugene slept in a huge cemetery, probably a mile square, called Resto del Cielo, 18 miles in the direction of El Paso. Tibor Rauscha saw it from the interstate whenever he drove between Perros Salvajes and the airport. Even in the dark at night going home Rauscha was aware of Eugene sleeping in his grave. He had not thought of this when the funeral guy suggested it as the place to lay his son.

Now his son would change his resting place. Now Eugene would sleep right under his father's bedroom window. It was hard seeing how that was better.

The same funeral home that planted Eugene in Resto del Cielo handled his exhumation eight months later. It was a blazing, soundless Saturday morning.

No one was there but the funeral director and the two guys hired to helped him dig Eugene out of the ground. They used a (different, smaller) backhoe to unearth Eugene and a portable hydraulic hoist to pull him up. The funeral director, removing his suit jacket, operated the hoist. He was a magician with it, gentle as could be. Once Eugene was fully above ground, depending from the hoist by chains, they checked the snaps on the box, just to be sure. Then the funeral director swung it with precision toward the open doors of the hearse; he was an artist. The other two men guided Eugene within.

They were late to Nine Mezcaleros Road because of the intersection on Fuller Boulevard, where the traffic light was still not fixed; in traffic terms it was a free-fire zone and even a hearse was given no quarter.

An hour later at the big house the funeral-home team slid Eugene back out into the daylight. They put his casket on a gurney suggestive of the one that took him away on the day he died. At the cemetery the men had not wiped the box clean of clumps of claypan from the grave. Some of it fell away when the guys hired by the funeral home set Eugene on the ground.

Eugene counted the mourners. Fanny in a knee-length navy skirt and one of her hats. His father tieless in a polo shirt and royal-blue jacket; Tibor Rauscha half looked like a yachtsman. His once-pretty mother Carol, sad as anything. Fanny's mother Judy beside Carole looking less sad than purely solemn.

AJ Munoz, the policeman who came to the house the day Eugene died, was there. He was in a jacket and tie, not his policeman's uniform. Mariana was there too, probably currying favor with Fanny. Hilda stood beside Mariana.

There was not much to it. None of them had any feeling for ceremony and they had not given a thought to what they would do at the graveside once Eugene was home. The guys from the funeral home, wet with heavy perspiration in their dark suits, looked from face to face for some signal of what was wanted. When no signal came they organized the hoist for the second time that morning and once again lowered Eugene into the ground.

As Eugene was going in Mariana took her beads from the pocket of her skirt and started a rosary in Spanish. AJ Munoz said the responses. Whatever any of them believed, including Eugene at that point, the prayers leant the moment the missing sacral touch.

When the rosary was said they all stood silent. Eugene was in the ground again. They all breathed out. At least that was over.

Officer AJ Munoz shook hands with everyone and he left. He had come to the reburial in his own car, a bronze-colored Civic six years old. The others went into the house and ate cold chicken and macaroni that Hilda made.

Eugene was left out in front of the house with the funeral-home guys. They earned extra money that day shoveling fresh earth into the hole. The dirt was much darker than what you typically find in West Texas; it had more clay in it. It had been mixed by Rita O'Gara with a hope that it would hold water a little better. The dirt was trucked in by a sixth person, the wife of the funeral director, who'd been waiting a quarter mile up Nine Mezcaleros Road for the call from her husband.

After an hour Eugene's mother and Mariana drove away without coming to see him. No one came the next day either,

Sunday. In the morning Eugene thought he could hear the bells of the Presbyterian church ring. All day his father and Fanny stayed indoors.

On Monday morning Rita O'Gara came by. On top of the grave she added more earth. She was worried in her head about subsidence. She seeded the new soil with buffalo grass. She staked the perimeter of the grave and softly watered the ground, soaking it thoroughly and deep. Then she put her tools away and tidied. Eugene listened to her footsteps go.

Eugene slept beneath the picturesquely grieving angel that his mother purchased. From then on he dreamed no more.

Texas At Its Logical End

The school year in Perros Salvajes ended in the first week of June. That same week Moliere got a call from a middle school in central Louisiana—the Elizabeth Magnus Cohen School in Métayage. They would be pleased to welcome her to the staff when the semester began again in late August.

Now it was July and Moliere had still not sold her house.

House or no house Moliere was going to Louisiana.

Moliere began a general clean out of accumulated goods. She made a list of things she needed. A new bag was one of those things. She wanted the bag for her collection of teacher sweaters. In a month she was moving to Louisiana and the bag she had had not been used since the camping trip with Franklin. It had a busted zipper.

Moliere drove to the big-box stores on Fuller Boulevard to shop. On her way back home she was going to the thrift store run by God's Grace Mission, the Unique Boutique. In the backseat of her Civic she had a box of Franklin's country-music CDs. All of them he owned in his teenage years.

Before he died he had loved them sentimentally.

"Even when they're boasting," Moliere once said to him, "the men in those songs all sing about what losers they are."

"Not all of them," Franklin said. Franklin's musical taste was the only weak thing in his character.

Moliere looked forward to parting from the cowboys. It would be a relief to be rid of those little plastic discs with big-hatted cowboys on their jewel cases. She would give them away easily; that part of Franklin had no valence.

First Moliere drove to the Kohls that anchored the prosperous middle stretch of Fuller Boulevard. There was a burst water main that day and Fuller Boulevard was close to being a Venetian canal. It took her 25 minutes to figure out a way into the shopping mall.

In the Kohls Moliere browsed the many duffels. Glen Campbell was on the PA singing *By the Time I Get to Phoenix*. Glen was not so subtly asking Moliere for one last chance before she gave him away. Almost at her elbow as the song played out was Janet Staufer and her father. Moliere noticed Janet first because she was swaying to Glen Campbell and humming.

In that instant Moliere met the eyes of Janet Staufer's father. The taste of Eugene came into her mouth.

"Hello," the two of them said at once; in a musical play they might be about to burst into a duet. Tonally they were at a loss, so there was irony. Janet had no interest either way.

"Good seeing you again." Just saying it Moliere felt stupid. Lie after lie.

"How are you?" Mr. Staufer asked. "And how is the

Rauscha family?"

"I don't know. I've spoken to the mother once in the last six months. Really I barely know them." It was the whole story in a nutshell.

Mr. Staufer tipped his head skeptically.

"Their son approached me," said Moliere. "I'm a teacher."

"He was at your school?"

"No. I've been sorry about that morning ever since."

"We're both sorry. I should have acknowledged what you were trying to do."

"I understood." In fact, she did.

"My daughter was beginning to get her confidence back." Mr Staufer spoke more freely now that Janet had moved farther off down the aisle—uninterested or anxious, Moliere could not know. "Seeing that boy again seemed to send her right back down the drain. For a long time after what happened she would not leave the house. Things are basic with her, you know? She can't explain all that happens to herself. Neither can I."

For the man to admit this took courage. At Moliere's Forgiveness University courage was an honors course.

"I didn't handle it right," Moliere told him.

"I ran into his father once at the airport a few months ago. I tried speaking to him but he would not... He wouldn't hear me."

"The father's an idiot."

"I know that. But it has nothing to do with what my response to you or that boy should have been."

"Mr. Staufer..."

"Rolf."

"Rolf, Eugene was doomed by those people. Even after what he did they should have... Meeting you that one morning didn't push him over the edge. Please don't think it did." Moliere nearly added "you give yourself too much credit" but she called this back. Even though she could have given a symposium in narcissism at Forgiveness U. Moliere was the sort of person intrigued by paradox.

Behind Mr. Staufer his daughter was swaying to the song Kohls had programmed next, *Amarillo By Morning.* There are so many songs about cowboys leaving town.

"Janet likes this kind of music," Moliere said.

"She likes all the kinds." Looking at his daughter Mr. Staufer smiled.

Just then Franklin spoke to Moliere in a pretended cowpoke voice. "Give her the CDs, Katherine." She heard him so clearly that at first she thought it was Mr. Staufer putting on the West Texas drawl that Franklin liked to affect when he was playing around.

Moliere really knew it was Franklin.

"May I give Janet a present?" she said. "I mean right now. It's in my car."

"Let the song play out. We both like this one. Do you remember it?"

"I had a friend who liked it."

The cowboy arrived in Amarillo and then the three of them left the artificial chill of the big store. Outside they entered the profound heat of West Texas in July. Crossing the swoony parking lot Janet kept to her father's right side. She was keeping him between herself and Moliere and Moliere's blue car.

Opening the car door Moliere leaned in across the back seat. Straightening up she offered Janet the carton of compact discs. Janet did not take them.

"It would have overjoyed my friend to know you had these," Moliere told Janet. She handed the box to Mr. Staufer and smiled at Janet. From the look on the other woman's face Moliere could not know how Janet felt, disinterested or anxious.

"I'm not always sure Janet understands about presents," said Mr. Staufer. "But thank you."

That same evening Moliere was packing her books in boxes and thinking about whether she had really heard Franklin speak. Could a voice from heaven be relayed through the Kohl's public-address system? In theory why not?

Then, with her mystic instinct for the fraught moment, Fanny rang Moliere's doorbell.

Moliere was annoyed to find Fanny waiting on the so-called porch. But that's not to say her feelings rose to the level of surprise, and certainly not to the higher plains of anger; they did not. By this time Moliere was exhausted by Fanny. The place of anger in Moliere's heart was unoccupied.

"Whatever it is, Fanny, I have nothing for you."

"Well hello to you too, Katherine." Fanny looked shy, like an adolescent boy come to ask for a date. Moliere thought she was most likely trying this on to test its effect. Fanny had cut her braids severely since they last saw each last in November, the day Eugene died. It showed the beginnings of grey in her hair. At the same time it made her look like a teenager. Moliere took it in but did not properly process the paradox.

"Please, Fanny, whatever it is I'm busy now."

"I merely want your house."

This was the kind of thing Fanny said, a statement rooted in the air like a Banyan tree. It was intended to put a person off their guard. The calculation was transparent and because it was transparent tiresome.

But exactly this turned out to be the unexpected thing that Moliere had not known she needed. Happens all the time.

"I'll pay you cash," Fanny said as if Moliere had inquired about terms. But Moliere was already beginning to think of something else.

"Hello? Speak to me Katherine. You look stupefied. I'm sincere about this."

Fanny was the one who looked stupefied. All her braids were gone and this had the effect of widening her eyes. Even if Fanny made her nuts Moliere had to concede her eyes were gorgeous. Fanny remained not just striking but undeniably pretty.

"What are you talking about?"

"I thought you might have had a stroke," Fanny said, "from the surprise. Within reason I'm ready to give you your price."

"Before I go back inside is there anything else?"

"I'm not someone who goes around giving advice, Katherine, but you shouldn't be afraid all the time to say yes to things. And I'll just speak for myself, but I am in the market for a house I can put my mother in. Having her around all the time for Tibor is not working. It's been like one of those movies."

"Fanny, stop being like this. Hear yourself talk."

"I'm not following."

"You pretend you don't."

"The broker you listed with—what's his first name? Dieter?—he told me you're moving to Louisiana in a month and you still haven't sold this house. He alluded to some trouble you're having."

"He should not have done that. Now he's my ex-broker."

"Well, that's your call. But I would say, and again, speaking for myself, don't be this way about it. Dieter's only trying to sell your house, which is what you asked him to do. And personally to me it would be like rounding a circle."

"What are you talking about? You'll have to forgive my ears."

"Is that a joke about my bad hearing? Because if so that is not nice." Fanny's short hair made her hearing aid more visible than it used to be. But Moliere was not being mean. And when she gave Fanny nothing in reply Fanny said, "To have my mother living in your place. That's what I'm saying about the circle."

Somehow Fanny seemed to downshift in size, to make herself smaller. Moliere could not stop noticing the threads of grey in Fanny's cropped top. Moliere doubted even Fanny's grey hair.

"Forgive me, Katherine," Fanny said in a small voice Moliere knew was meant to signal contrition. "I know how you and I keep getting off on the wrong feet. From that first night I came to your house I never meant to give you the runaround. Do you remember that night?"

"If I ever forget there's a police report that helps keep it fresh in my memory."

"All of the other nonsense only came to me later."

"What came to you later?" Moliere told herself not to ask questions, which only prolonged things.

"The business with Eugene last Halloween. That triggered you, didn't it? I want you to know, Katherine, for the record it was like someone else was driving my car that night. I was so locked in, you know? Believe me when I say I'm sorry, plus about those two goons. But I'm glad for the experience, in a way. It taught me a lot."

Fanny had no trouble holding Moliere's gaze when she said all this, which should tell you something. Fanny had nerve, give her that.

"And then," Fanny said, "that morning when you tried to help Eugene. I have to say now I didn't know *what* you were up to."

"I was not up to anything. That child was drowning. He was begging for help and you all ignored him. That he even had me was only because of you—*and* the two goons."

"Silver lining, anyhow. It's not that I'm a cynic, Katherine, but until I met you I couldn't imagine anyone acting from unmixed motives. That's a compliment in case you cannot recognize one."

Fanny was correct in the first case. There are no unmixed motives. But saying so to Fanny would have resembled the offer of comfort. Moliere was not going to offer comfort to Fanny or even its resemblance. That was what people did, but when that reflex fired in Moliere nothing happened. This misfiring—click click, like the broken igniter on her kitchen stove—released the grip of grief on her in an instant.

Grief shaped like a house.

For the first time since Franklin died the house—with its thin sheetrocking that had a smell, with the way it creaked whenever the wind blew hard, not just stressing the framing but jiggling the hardware of the kitchen cabinets, with its scenes of Franklin everywhere, with its so-called porch—the house released Moliere then. It asked to go to Fanny.

Moliere felt sly.

Moliere realized Fanny was still speaking, running on like someone talking in her sleep.

"It's no one's fault, not really," Fanny was saying. "I've been thinking about it a lot."

"I'll sell you the house, Fanny."

"Really? I didn't think you would."

"What price did Dieter quote you? We've had several."

"Three-eighty."

"For you it's four. If you pay cash."

"That's sharp practice, Katherine, especially when I consider our history. But here's you in the driver's seat. Are we paying Dieter his commission?"

Dieter got the deal done immediately. Neither Fanny nor Moliere attended the closing three weeks later. Dieter was approved to sign as witness on behalf of both parties to the transaction. Moliere got her price and Fanny got the house. But Fanny's mother Judy never got to meet Moliere, and that was the only shame.

Judy hated that house as much Moliere used to hate it. Two years later she moved back to Hay Agua.

Ever since Christmas in Mexico Tibor Rauscha could not tolerate the touch of Fanny, his wife. Naturally it did not get any better after she cut his face open or all the rest of the things that happened.

This was fine by Fanny. Nights when her husband slept home she began a habit of sleeping on the brown leather couch in her office. At first she made excuses for why she slept on that couch and did not join her husband in bed. After a time she did not bother about the excuses.

Even nights when she was alone in the house Fanny preferred the couch over the bed. The long couch half embraced her; the bed had associations.

And still Fanny went on living in the big house on Nine Mezcaleros Road.

In late July Fanny moved her mother into the house previously owned by Katherine Moliere. Judy did not care for the house but she was beginning to let herself like Perros Salvajes. Now that she was closer to El Paso than she would be in Hay Agua her personal-shopping business was flourishing. She was making good money. Two of her clients—interestingly enough they were both widows of men who made their dough in home building —became something like friends.

But in Moliere's old house Judy was not at home. She complained to Fanny almost immediately that the house ticked like an ambivalent watch.

"Click click," she said. "All night long click click. Sometimes I lie there worrying the place is going to fall to sticks. If I wasn't awake already it would keep me up nights. And I walk into cold patches, the way you do in a lake. There's a pressure against me when I walk through them. They're never in the same place, so do not tell me the house has a draft. You don't think the house is haunted by the spirit of the man who died, do you?"

"That's not a funny joke, Mommy," said Fanny.

"Don't think I was joking. I see shadows, Fanny, honest I do."

On the subsequent Saturday when they were out buying cotton blankets Judy remarked not altogether out of the blue, "Why don't you leave him?" (Judy owned some of her daughter's abruptness without Fanny's aspect of calculation.) "Neither of you gets anything out of it," Judy said. "At least it's clear to me you don't."

"Divorce means we failed," Fanny said. "I'm ashamed to be a failure in public. Starting with the conventional reasons."

"You're a selectively conventional girl, Fanny," her mother observed.

"I'm not exotic."

"But all I am saying is leave the man. About divorce do what you want. It wouldn't be the worst thing I ever heard."

But it was not her mother's opinion that finished it with Tibor Rauscha for Fanny.

What finished it for Fanny was an almost chilly evening later that month—Bastille Day, as it happened, though in West Texas that fact was neither here nor there. Earlier that evening Fanny had oiled her hair and thought it would be pleasant to bring her skull outside to let it breathe some air that was not conditioned.

Fanny sat herself on the hard bench around the Trevi Fountain. It was of no significance that 30 feet to her right Eugene slept in the ground behind the China rose. One month after the reburial Fanny was already accustomed to him there. She did not give Eugene a thought.

Behind Fanny the big house loomed outsized and pointless. In the less than three years she lived in the big house it had been neither threatening nor welcoming to Fanny. It was just a structure, like so much of what one finds in life. Seven bedrooms and only Hilda sleeping in one of them regularly. There were two kitchens for people who did not cook, counting the one beside the pool. A chapel where no one prayed. A game room—billiard table, ping-pong, foosball—for people who did not pursue pleasure of that nature.

For an unmarked length of time Fanny sat on the bench enjoying the chill and the air moving over her skin. After a while of this Fanny found herself thinking of a drink, a large glass of bourbon, not some ladylike glass of wine. Fanny seldom drank to excess, except lately, but even a small drink gave her a little detachment. Fanny believed detachment was her essential requirement, get it how she could.

Fanny was on the instant of standing when she heard the crunch of her husband's footstep on the pebbled path coming around from the back of the big house.

She got to her feet.

"You don't hear the crickets tonight," said Tibor Rauscha. He sounded reflective.

"Crickets mind the chill?"

"They must. I don't hear them."

"I was just going in," Fanny told him, and walked past.

"It stinks the way we live," said Rauscha.

"Is that so?" Fanny was being rhetorical. She presumed her husband understood this.

"I'm sorry it's like this way, Fanny." He appeared to be all sincerity.

Fanny looked him back. She could tell he was going somewhere with this.

"I used to ache all over when I saw you. From the first time I did."

"You thought I came to shake you down."

"I had mixed feelings." Her husband's small joke bothered Fanny because it came close to making her laugh.

"Your nose was what did it to me." He reached out with his finger and tried to touch Fanny's nose. Once it would have been an affectionate move. Now Fanny snapped her head away as if dodging a horsefly.

"Again about my nose."

"I wanted to possess it. Possess you, Fanny. If I had the nose I had you, and the other way around too."

"You'd have me by the nose. I don't find that touching."

Fanny walked on but her husband lunged, grabbing her left arm so tightly it hurt. Bad luck for Tibor Rauscha that his wife was right-handed. Fanny pivoted and hit him with the hard of her hand across his face. Her husband's own nose began to bleed elaborately because Fanny broke it.

"Don't be interfering with me, Tibor."

Fanny knew she had better leave the big house before she rearranged a third piece of Tibor Rauscha's face. Another six months and he would not look the same at all.

It was conceivable, Fanny thought, that leaving the next morning Tibor Rauscha did not remember anything about the night before; he was like a man subject to blackouts if a thing got to him, which would almost make it a kind of personal discipline. Fanny had to concede that this would be in character. In any event her husband said nothing about his blackeyes and swollen nose when he came downstairs to get his coffee from Hilda. Hilda naturally asked what the hell happened.

"Goddam walls," Rauscha told her.

"You in any pain?"

Leaving for the airport that morning Rauscha said goodbye to Fanny formally, almost cordially, like a houseguest, absurdly lacking in awkwardness. They did not kiss nor embrace because they had not done that for a long time.

Fanny wondered what story her husband would work up to explain his eyes to the people he was seeing that week in St. Louis, or if he would even bother about that.

At this time Moliere was living on the second floor of la Estrella motor lodge on Highway 19. The place was built to look like somebody's idea of a hacienda. It was constructed of a substance meant to suggest adobe or another kind of natural material.

Moliere was at la Estrella since selling her house to Fanny and Fanny's mother in late July. Her new school helped find an apartment to rent in Métayage and she signed the lease. But the place they found had a tenant in it who would not vacate until August 15th. That was a week before school started in Louisiana.

Moliere might have used the time to travel but she had no interest in travel. There were no places she had any interest in seeing, city or wilderness. Why would she go—just to gawk? It was nothing to do with money either. That summer Moliere thought more about money than she ever had in her life.

Among the practical steps Moliere and Franklin took when they became engaged was getting life insurance. They took that step because their mortgage bank pressed them to do it and not out of a mutual recognition of mortality's likelihood. When Franklin was murdered Moliere received a payout of $525,000. That and the nearly $250,000 she cleared from the sale of her house to Fanny must have made Moliere among the wealthiest elementary-school teachers under 40 in the state of Texas.

All this money made Moliere uncomfortable. This was mostly owed to its source, of course. But it was also partly owed to Moliere's unfamiliarity with affluence on any level. Her idea was to live with her money for a while and see how she felt about it. Then she would make decisions.

In the time that she was living at la Estrella Moliere spent one long weekend in Las Cruces with her father Léon and her sister Patricia. Léon's gumbo of an imagined Louisiana—a creole of Cajuns and crawfish stew and gangster politicians—reminded Moliere of what was wonderful about him. That is to say, he made the world in his head and then lived there.

"Give me a couple of years," Léon said, "and maybe Teresa and I will join you there. Lespwa fè viv."

Patrice's husband Duval left the Air Force the previous winter to reimagine himself as a day trader. He wanted his sister-in-law Katherine to be his client. Duval was put out about it when Moliere said no thank you. He was still in a pout when she returned to Texas and would not say goodbye.

Moliere spent the two weeks at la Estrella working on lesson plans for eighth-grade math. She looked forward to teaching bivariate data, for example, a subject whose relevance to everyday life most kids were quick to grasp. But making simultaneous linear equations come to life would require more of Moliere's imagination. She never asked students to take her word for it when they asked the relevance of math to their lives. Had she done so nothing would stick in their heads.

Apart from her farewell to New Mexico Moliere was leading a more solitary life than even she was used to, and it was alright.

Most mornings Moliere rose early to run before the West Texas heat became too intense to sustain human life. After working on her lesson plans for the coming year she read in the afternoon by la Estrella's modest pool. She spent so much on shampoo to wash the chlorine out of her hair that she gave up on the goop she always used on it. She grew to like the sprung silhouette around her skull. Franklin was right.

After the first week Moliere stopped keeping a bottle of Scotch in her room; it was becoming too much of a friend. If she wanted a drink she went out someplace from which she could walk back. It was akin to self-rule.

At night she was comforted by the sound of vehicles hitting a foot-deep pothole out on Highway 19. She felt close to the drivers when that happened, and that was company.

Half a dozen times Moliere went for dinner or a sandwich with teachers she knew from Emma Tenayuca School. Twice she saw Allen Luu. Allen was organizing a sendoff for Moliere at the house he shared with his fiancé Julie. But then Julie told Allen the wedding was off and so was she. Also off, therefore, was the farewell party for Moliere.

"I'm so sorry," Moliere told Allen when he telephoned. Really she was not; Moliere never liked Julie and believed Allen caught a break when she left him. "Why don't you come over to la Estrella and share a bottle of wine with me? We can sit by the pool like movie stars."

"For reasons that might not be obvious I'm trying not to drink much at the moment," Allen said. Moliere hated when people told her they were not drinking. It made her feel accused of something. "Why don't we go across the road from you to la Barbacoa? I like their fish tacos. But it has to be a rule that we don't discuss Julie."

Moliere agreed to this condition and two nights later they were sitting at the bar in la Barbacoa. And immediately Allen was talking about Julie and drinking margaritas besides.

"It was not something she wanted to do," Allen was saying.

"What wasn't? Be married, split up or break your heart?"

"Break my heart. The first two I think she was OK with."

"Unforgivable." This was an appropriately loyal thing for Moliere to say and came out of her mouth inevitably. She was on her second drink and still no dinner.

"It's not unforgivable. She wasn't mean about it. It simply hurts. I've got nothing to be angry about." In fact, Allen was wearing a UT El Paso Miners tee-shirt that Julie must have thought he would like. It had Paydirt Pete on it.

"I don't believe you. You're wearing her shirt."

"It's mine. She gave it to me."

"You've got no vitality currently, Allen. I can read it off you."

"'Long Live the College of Mines'?" He was looking down at his tee-shirt.

"You're evading."

"I need a joke."

"Did she give you a good reason?"

"She told me she realized after two years that what she would really needed the whole time was not a big romance, just someone to hold her. More or less that is a direct quote."

"On the level?"

"Yep."

"Two years' worth of being held? That is some clinch."

"I give good clinch."

"The whole time you didn't sense anything coming, you know, from her emotional life?"

"Nope."

"It's better you found out before the wedding."

"That's what my other friends tell me."

"Are you in touch with her? Because don't be." Moliere was compulsively eating salsa chips from the dish there on the bar. She really needed tacos. A third margarita and she would fall on the floor.

"Not in a regular way," Allen told her. "A couple of texts about practical matters. A lot of her things are still in the house. And both our names are on the lease. It's like practice for a divorce."

"Just don't agree to a meet-up." Moliere was surprised to find herself handing out advice. She would not have called herself wise in the ways of romance, before or after Franklin.

"Labor Day she's coming with her brother to move things out. It's the first time I'll be meeting him."

"What do I care about the brother?"

"Context." They were both getting drunk.

"Why don't you go be elsewhere when they show up? Otherwise they'll probably ask you to help carry things. And knowing you, you will." Moliere hoped Allen did not think she was flirting because she was not. She was affectionate from drink, that was all.

"Don't make me sound like a chump, Katherine. I don't need that."

"Chump you're not."

"I miss seeing her—OK? I miss the feeling in my chest when I looked at her." Allen knew she was not flirting. "Even with her stuff still everywhere the house feels empty to me."

Moliere was distracted by her need for dinner. From hunger and tequila she was at that place in the progress of tipsiness where one observes oneself speaking, where words seem to come out of the mouth as solid objects.

"For me it was the opposite," Moliere said.

"What was?"

"With Franklin. I was aware of his stuff in my way everywhere. I felt crowded in a way I didn't when he was still there."

"By him?"

"He was elbowing me. Not to get my attention, just elbowing me absentmindedly. I could hear him talking but it was like overhearing. He was not talking to *me*, you know? I was losing my mind. Let people help you is all I'm telling you, Franklin."

"Allen."

"Allen."

"Did you get beyond that?"

"Beyond what?" Moliere was losing sight of whatever point she was making.

"The fear that you were losing your mind. It would help me to know. Unless of course you didn't get beyond it, which wouldn't help me at all."

"I'm still hearing his voice sometimes though not lately. So no is the answer. He'll probably come back."

"I don't think it will be like that for me. Our situations are different."

"You're right. Compassion is pointless. Comparison."

"I like your hair that way," Allen told her. "If I may say so."

"When Franklin died it blocked out the sun."

"I know it did. I remember."

"I was sick with it. I was so angry at myself I was sick with it."

"Angry for what? You didn't pull the trigger." Moliere flinched at that image.

"Because on the last day of his life I was awful to him. That night when Franklin went to work I was not speaking to him. He was speaking to me but I was not speaking to him. It was over something stupid, something racial."

Moliere had never said this to anyone but her therapist. Now she thought about it she was not surprised that it came out with Allen. She saw how he looked over her face, puzzling, trying to make a guess.

"Don't cry, Katherine."

"Naw, let me cry. I never cried about this. Lucky you to be here at the exact moment when I decide to let go."

"It's OK. Cry."

"I'm better now. I get around in the world. We were supposed to talk about you tonight."

Allen stood up from his bar stool and took Moliere in his arms. She cried and made a patch of Julie's shirt wet. She loved Allen then because he did not try to stop her tears. Usually men did. Tears, she suspected, made men feel guilty for something. They hated that.

Abruptly Moliere was aware that everyone in la Barbacoa was trying not to stare at the two of them. Observing the woman in tears the people there would have guessed that this suspiciously tall Asian man was breaking her heart. Naturally they would have cast him in the role of the brute and taken her side. It was cultural.

But Julie was right, Allen gave good clinch. Julie missed a good one in Allen. She should have cut him out for stars.

"Find a therapist in Louisiana, Katherine," Allen said.

"You bet I will, Allen. You can put all your money on me."

By the time her husband came home to Perros Salvajes from St. Louis Fanny was gone. She never returned to live in the big house. Instead she moved from the brown couch in her office to her mother's empty house in Hay Agua.

Fanny and Tibor Rauscha still needed to speak several times each day about the business of RauschaTech, of course. But her husband behaved as if the move out to her mother's house was no more worthy of remark than her move to the couch in the first place. He never mentioned it.

In Hay Agua Fanny went to her mother's hairdresser. She asked to have her hair cut down to her scalp the way her mother wore it. Close to the skull suited Fanny. It was certainly easier to take care of and she did not mind the way it showed all the knobs and creases of the bone beneath the skin; she felt this gave her head character. But she looked older, too, that way.

The years creep up on me, Fanny thought when she looked in the mirror. The years and the whatnot.

Carol Peña got the phone number for Judy DaCosta's house in Hay Agua from Hilda. She telephoned Fanny out there on a Thursday afternoon.

Whatever sorority Fanny may have felt in the spring for Carol when they were unearthing Eugene—and that was not much—had been purely situational on Fanny's part. "How did you know I was here?" she asked Carol.

"Your assistant told me you went. She was funny about not giving me the number. She seems nice."

"I told her not to give it out. I guess she generalized."

"She's protective of your location."

"I'm only staying here for a while," Fanny told Carol. She was sure that was not true. "Now that my mother's living full time in Perros Salvajes she wants to sell this place. She's not comfortable leaving it unoccupied, not with all that's happening in the world."

"You're not coming back to Tibor?"

"I didn't come here to make plans." Fanny liked how that sounded. Something shrugged off her shoulders when she said it.

"If you don't come back let me know," although why Fanny should do this Carol did not say. "I'm selling my house too," she added. "That's part of the reason I'm calling you up. But please don't tell Tibor."

"Why are you selling the house?"

"Can you keep a secret, Fanny?"

"No."

"I never know when you're joking."

"I'm answering you honestly. I always forget what I promise. Keeping secrets is at the top of the list. I can't tell you how many people I've disappointed. I'm only replying to your question."

"My question was pro forma."

"To most people."

"Maybe it doesn't matter. It's only that in a few weeks I'm leaving Perros Salvajes. Because guess what, Fanny. I got a job in El Paso. But try not to spill the beans to Tibor. Not yet don't tell him."

"Now I'm surprised." Most of all Fanny was surprised to find herself jealous of Carol's fresh start, if it was that. "What kind of job?"

"It happened like it was ordained for me."

"Tell me there's no angel this time."

"I know you're teasing, Fanny."

"To tell you the truth I'm not."

"A few weeks ago my father flew in from Mexico and I dove down to El Paso to see him. He got a new girlfriend he wanted me to meet so I said OK and went there."

"How old is he that your father's got a new girlfriend?"

"Sixty-six. Women like him."

"That's nice."

"The road to the airport takes me past the turnoff for Rogelio Sanchez. Out of the blue, you know, I start thinking about Georg sitting there in his cell. In actual fact I don't know if they have cells in a prison or if it's something like a school dormitory. But the image of Georg sitting all by himself was strong in me. I could have drawn a picture of him I saw it so clear."

"Carol, you provide too much context. That is always what you do. Just tell me about the job and that's all." Fanny had been glad for the interruption when the phone rang but now she was remembering the thing she found wearying about Carol. It was Carol's naked need for a friend. It would put anyone off.

"It all pools together, Fanny," Carol said. "That's the point I'm trying to make. Anyhow, just listen. In the way things happen the very next Sunday I am in church waiting for service to begin. I'm browsing the newsletter, you know, idly. There's a notice in it that they're looking for an administrator in the prison ministry at Rogelio Sanchez. And that's what I mean by it was ordained."

"Because it happened in a church."

"Yes."

"Fair enough. When do you start?"

"Three weeks. Their funding is partly tied to the school year. I don't know why, not at this point."

"Have you done any ministering? How did you sell that?"

"I won't be doing any ministering, not at first. You study years for that. I'll be managing the office. I'm not even sure I'll have contact with prisoners, although I suppose I should tell Georg I'm there. Not that he'll want to see me, the way he is. It's sad."

"You told the prison minister though? You'd have to."

"When I called them up to tell them about myself I thought I should come clean and explain how I was married to Georg once. For them that seemed to be like a kind of job recommendation for me, which after when I thought about it was not really much of a surprise. I could certainly talk from experience about the hope of redemption. Anyway I don't think they were swamped with applications. So now I need to sell my house."

"That'll take you longer than three weeks." Fanny was well aware that the speed of her own deal for Katherine Moliere's house had been a fluke.

"I'm aware of this. That's why I need you to keep it on the down-low."

"'The down-low'?"

"You know the saying I mean. I have a stupid fear of Tibor messing this up for me."

"I'll keep it on the down-low for as long as I can remember not to mention it," Fanny said. "Now I *am* teasing you. But I'm also telling you sincerely."

"According to our divorce I'm supposed to stay within 25 miles of your house."

"*My* house?"

"Yeah. You didn't know?"

"That seems really draconian. If I were you at the time I would not have agreed." In her imagination Fanny was already trying on images of how she would conduct herself in a divorce proceeding. She had no reason to be bitter about anything that had happened in the marriage but she was not going to be taken advantage of either. If it came to that she would try and remember to keep it simple. And pointed.

Christ, life made her so tired.

"The restriction was because of Eugene. Now that condition doesn't obtain, as my lawyer likes to say. Before we ask Tibor to revisit the agreement he tells me we should get everything arranged. That's the reason why I'm hoping we sell the house quick."

"I know a guy." Fanny was thinking of Dieter. Dieter knew how to get things done. "I'm not someone who goes around giving advice, Carol, but if you can't sell the house quick won't Tibor have you over a barrel then? If he says no to you what happens?"

"I'm banking on how much he'd like me further away. Only pure meanness would make him say no. That's my theory."

Fanny thought about that a moment. She told Carol, "Pure meanness I would not say was Tibor. He overthinks. You should be alright."

"Do you mind me telling all this to you, Fanny? It's your money too, and it's your household."

Fanny had not considered this. From recent habit she was so focused on any strategy that kept her distant from Tibor Rauscha she forgot to remember that she was still married to him.

"Tibor's financial arrangement with you is nothing to do with me anymore, Carol. I don't want anything from him, not even goodbye if it ever comes to that."

"You can say that, Fanny. You're in a better position than me."

Fanny knew there had to be a least a little barb on this statement. But she did not think she heard it.

"I recognize that," she told Carol. "I'm only relieved there's no angel." This was a preemptive jab. Disguised as joking.

After that phone call Fanny almost never thought about Carol again except in passing.

Before Fanny could forget herself and spill Carol's secret Carol herself telephoned her ex-husband, Tibor Rauscha, and told him almost all about her plan to move to El Paso. She explained that she was going to sell her house and work in the prison. It did not pay much and, she said, Rauscha should please keep sending the alimony.

Carol's lawyer, Heidi Schmidt, urgently advised her to pursue her argument by telephone.

"Whatever you do," Schmidt told Carol, "don't go to the house. If you do that things can only go south." With which had he known Rauscha would have agreed.

Schmidt even wrote Carol a sort of script, including indicated pauses where Rauscha might be likely to ask questions; the way it all played out, though, in the end he did not ask a single one. Having a script helped Carol corral her impulse to tell her former husband everything. (She would have been surprised to learn that Tibor Rauscha acknowledged the restraint this required, especially after Carol put Georg among her mentions.)

Rauscha made Carol get to the end of her script. Another way to put it is that he heard her out. In the end he consented to dropping the clause in their divorce decree requiring her residence in Perros Salvajes. Carol gambled correctly that Rauscha did not mind having her further away. To him this was worth money.

"I'm only glad there's no angel," he said.

"Fanny told me the same thing."

"You talked to Fanny about this?"

"I tested my news out on Fanny first, just so now you know. Before you make more remarks, Tibor."

"I'm only interested."

Rauscha was acquainted with the sound of hurt in Carol's voice. He wanted no more of her hurt feelings. He wanted more than anything to head them off.

"Tomorrow morning I need to speak to DeLorean anyway," he told Carol, which was untrue but face-saving. "Don't worry. I'll say to him make the change."

Tibor Rauscha felt the greatest fatigue wrap around him the moment those words left his mouth. Since summer began he noticed all the time how he got tired in his response to things.

Fanny believed Rauscha was indifferent to her leaving. Fanny was wrong. On the contrary, in the big house he was too much with himself, even with having Hilda walking around. Rauscha was feeling like he had run out of room to run.

Most of the time now Rauscha was at home. He did not need to travel as much as he had been doing even two months before. The server-farm business was saturated and RauschaTech had no need of more capacity. It was a subscription-based business and still generating revenue. But having nothing to grow was boring.

Rauscha wanted to believe he had a next act. But not for anything could he guess what that might be. Carol had a next act. Somewhere right that minute Fanny was plotting *her* next act; Rauscha was sure of it. And come to find out, Andy DiNapoli now had a next act too.

The previous winter when his wife Ophelia left him (and the whole state of Texas) for Wisconsin Andy had made a spectacle of himself; everyone said he was ridiculous. Then on a late evening in mid-May the Texas state senate was debating abortion again. The bill aimed to redefine consent. Andy stood up in the chamber to propose a rider that would automatically relieve an aggrieved spouse of either sex (to be fair) of the obligation to pay alimony if adultery could be proven. His amendment, Andy declared, was "lifted from the seabed of my own hard experience"—notwithstanding that Ophie had not asked for alimony, as she crossly explained in an eMail to *The Galveston County Daily News* the day after Andy's motion. About that part no one cared.

Andy's amendment immediately created a side but ultimately passing controversy regarding its relevance to the abortion bill. (Which is how Ophie got wind of it, since from force of habit she continued keeping tabs on Texas from Racine.) Andy himself—personally—was taken up even if his amendment was not. His profile elevated. He was invited to join a bipartisan caucus of family-values legislatures in Austin.

Then the world took still another turn.

Three months after Andy's political resurrection the chairwoman of the Texas public-utility commission, Gretel Ernst, was shot and, shockingly, *killed* by her brother-in-law, Jochen Leicht. (There was bad blood between the two that went back years. In the high emotion of a family wedding it just vented. Why Jochen brought a gun to the wedding was a question no one thought to ask.)

In Austin it was presumed that Ernst's successor was Emory Lückenzahn, who sat on the nominations committee in the state senate. But in the same week that Ernst was murdered photographs surfaced on Facebook showing Lückenzahn, his face ablaze with drink. By itself that might not have killed his appointment to the PUC except that in the picture he was wearing rocketship pajamas and had his arm around a woman in lingerie who was not Mrs. Lückenzahn. The photographs contradicted Lückenzahn's longstanding expression of concern for wholesome values.

The governor was a friend of wholesome values and he turned to Andy. Flat on his face in February, Andy was now likely to be named the new PUC chairman. The day before the news was to be announced Andy called Tibor Rauscha from Austin to tell him.

"Probably you already twigged to it, didn't you, Tibor?" said Andy. "You keep tabs on everything in the state, I know you. For the moment let's dispense with me and turn the spotlight on you. How are you holding up?"

Rauscha said he was holding up fine.

"The other day one of your water-resources fellas telephoned me. Are you still interested in desalination?"

"No."

"Me neither, so I was surprised. Anyway, your guy mentioned just in passing that your current wife has relocated."

"Who was it said that?" Inside Rauscha's head he was firing people furiously.

"Never mind. You won't beat it out of me."

"That's nice, Andy. Real nice."

"When wives leave a man it's hard. But now looking back I see how it got me unstuck morally, even emotionally—psychologically. When God cancels one flight, Tibor, He schedules another."

"So far my flight's not being called. If I was a more serious drinker I'd be in the airport bar." Rauscha wanted no consolation from Andy DiNapoli. Six months ago he would have needled Andy for his Christian Zen. But not now. Andy was up in the world. Tibor Rauscha was down. Andy had something going for him. This grated.

"Listen harder to your soul talking, Tibor," Andy was saying.

"Pardon me?"

"Quiet down on your insides. People will always tell you the key to life is to keep moving forward. But it's not. The key to life is simply sticking around until the situation changes."

This was a preposterous thing to hear from the future PUC chairman. Rauscha was alert to several ways of interpreting it. For one, Andy might be gloating. More likely he was hedging his bets, since Tibor Rauscha might yet be of use to him; Andy's heart was still aimed at Washington, Rauscha was certain of that. Andy was foolish but he had a wide streak of shrewd; Rauscha observed that in him.

It was also possible that Andy was concerned for Rauscha. Of all the interpretations this one annoyed Rauscha most. He was glad now that he agreed to go on paying alimony to Carol. Somehow that was a thumb in Andy's eye, though he could not have said how.

The call from Carol came on a Sunday, historically never a good day for Tibor Rauscha. The call from Andy came on the subsequent Tuesday evening. After that one Rauscha went out back of his big house to his pool, which he never did much.

At the shallow end of the pool Rauscha undressed himself. He piled his clothes atop the cold gas grill.

Tibor Rauscha stepped naked into the water. Rauscha waded nearly noiselessly toward the deep middle of his pool until the water was up to his neck. He stood still as he could and the water hardly moved. At night out on the edge of the desert the air got cold fast, even in July. The frigid water was a shock to Rauscha's skin. A welcome shock.

Standing in the water Rauscha placed his hands lightly on the surface and watched them float. He watched his hands drift on some secret current. Rauscha speculated that hands must be mostly air or else why would they do that? He tried to remember why people weighed less in water. Or was it only that they believed it?

Whatever the case Rauscha stood neck-deep in the cold water with his knees flexed. This took weight off them. Lately his knees had been talking to him; Fanny's mother used that expression. His knees talked to him of premonitions.

The enclosing night sky was a comfort.

Rauscha bounced on his toes. In the icy water he could not feel his feet. His eyes settled on a kind of hard-plastic sarcophagus on the opposite side of the pool's flagstone perimeter. It had not been opened for three years or more. Rauscha knew it was full of pool toys. A combination lock hung on it. Rauscha did not remember putting the lock there but it had to have been him. How the hell would he ever get it off should he ever want to? Telephone somebody, he assumed.

In the box must have been the orange life vest that belonged to Eugene. Rauscha once hired a high-school kid to teach Eugene to swim. The kid would clip Eugene into the orange vest and try coaxing him into the water.

"Don't be afraid," the kid would tell Eugene. "The vest will make you float. It's fun." The kid tried to make his voice impersonate fun.

"I'm not afraid," Eugene replied. "I don't like the way my skin hurts when it gets all wet." No wonder his son hardly ever bathed, Rauscha reflected. He paid the teenage kid for six "lessons" before all three of them had enough and stopped pretending.

In his mind Rauscha knew he should miss Eugene. That he didn't was not the same as saying he was in rebellion against nature or anything sensational. It was only a fact.

The night Carol told Rauscha she was pregnant with Eugene she said, "You'll make such a wonderful Dad." Rauscha had to look at Carol twice to make certain she was not being sarcastic. Had Carol been carrying a girl he might not have minded as much. Girls, Rauscha considered, women in general, were not as obvious as their opposites. If Eugene had been a girl Tibor Rauscha might still be married to Carol. Their child would still be alive. He thought that.

Rauscha spread out his arms and patted the surface of the water with the palms of his hands. Every path you choose ends in a different place, he told himself. People who believe in fate are no better than children.

Tightening his body against the cold Rauscha sucked air deep into his lungs and ducked. For as long as he could hold out he crouched on the bottom of the pool, hardening his body against the cold and taking his lungs right to bursting. He broke the water gasping.

Two things that social worker wanted to know when Eugene raped that girl: Did he have friends and was he ever violent? No to both.

"Eugene couldn't stir himself to be violent," Tibor Rauscha told the woman. "Or to have friends."

"And what about yourself, Mr. Rauscha?" asked the social worker—Ms. Gertz—who was a plus-sized woman with a distractingly low hairline. She was tall though.

"In my life I never hit anyone. That's not my M.O." Rauscha said nothing about friends.

"There are other ways of being violent," the woman said.

"I'm aware of that ma'am. I'm not a sociopath."

"Silence can be violent," said the woman.

"I can see you've already made up your mind about me. You've cracked the case of Eugene."

Rauscha saw he had hurt Ms. Gertz's feelings; she was so sure she was doing well. More to the point, if she considered him uncooperative she could make his life harder. To head that off Rauscha invited her to start coming to the house for her "therapy" sessions with Eugene.

Things were no different at the house. Eugene would not come farther than the top of the steps to speak with Ms. Gertz. He sat up there the same way he sat on the steps into the pool when the swimming instructor came; he never dove in. Perhaps talking to Ms. Gertz also made his skin hurt; that was certainly the effect she had on Rauscha.

Most times Eugene would pass their hour together in silence; in anyone else it would have been impressive to sustain silence with another person for that long. With Eugene it was just his habit.

Mrs. Gertz did her best. She let the silence hang in the air and wait for Eugene to fill it, the way cops do. Nothing. She handed up a couch pillow for him to hug. A few times she brought her dog with her. The dog used to shoot right past Tibor Rauscha and up the stairs to Eugene. That dog knew her job.

And still Eugene said, "If Dad's here I don't want to talk." So Rauscha was sent away to another corner of the house. Fine by him.

After a while Ms. Gertz said her back could not take sitting on those stairs anymore. She recommended a different guy who, unlike herself, was certified as a shrink. Eugene was going to him on Wednesdays in a cab from school when he killed himself, so the second guy must not have been very good.

Tibor Rauscha bent his neck back and watched the night receive the moon. He looked up at the stars coming out above Texas; he had heard someone say once that the stars were indifferent. He wondered if Eugene was up there, watching. Maybe after dying people see right through this life.

Then Rauscha remembered that Eugene was not in the sky but over the roof on the other side of the house, in the ground. Nine months after dying he must have been all bones by then.

The icy water of the pool got into Tibor Rauscha's own bones. It froze him through.

Which parts of his failures needed forgiveness? he asked himself. Which were just mistakes? If he was going to be rigorous about it then the difference mattered.

People cannot live like that, on edge.

Rauscha stood freezing in the water wondering if Carol was right, if Eugene forgave the pair of them for whatever it was. Rauscha did not want a general absolution. There was no education in that. Carol was maladapted to this life.

That dog Mrs. Gertz used to bring loved Eugene because Eugene fed her the biscuits. Ms. Gertz passed the biscuits up to Eugene and he passed them to the dog. That is all it was.

Maybe Rauscha should have bought the kid a dog.

Andy DiNapoli did not know it yet but he could leave Rauscha whenever he chose; he would realize it soon. Carol could leave. And any day now Fanny could leave, really leave. Tibor Rauscha could not leave. For one thing no one would ever buy his big house because no one wanted a house with a suicide's body buried in the front yard; you didn't even need to be superstitious to think that. If reburying Eugene was a trick played on him by Fanny and Carol then it was a work of genius.

Rauscha splashed his way out of the pool. Once his naked body was fully exposed to the desert night the cold hit him even worse. Shaking violently he hugged himself hard and stood dripping and shaking. Having stripped out of his clothes on impulse he had no towel to wrap around his body.

Tibor Rauscha was not a person attuned to ironic Moments. But standing there, seriously cold, he remembered saying once to Fanny that he felt naked and alone. And now he was not feeling metaphorical. In the desert nighttime he was naked and alone and shivering.

Just then Hilda appeared.

"You never swim," she said sort of accusingly.

"Skinny dipping," Rauscha told her. "I wasn't expecting you to come outside. Pardon my nakedness, Hilda." That might have been the oddest sentence Tibor Rauscha ever spoke. "Pardon my nakedness." In a different context it might have sounded zany.

"Need anything? You want your clothes?"

"I didn't think you'd come outside. Excuse me."

"It's OK with me." Hilda appeared to Rauscha genuinely disinterested in his nakedness. In her life maybe she had seen enough naked men to last her.

"I'll be dry in a moment. Shut us down for the night, would you?"

As Hilda went away Tibor Rauscha saw her glance at his genital, shriveled to walnut size against the cold. This became one more thing to him.

An hour before daybreak Moliere woke, or thought she woke. She was surprised to find herself in bed with Franklin. Was Franklin not dead? Was he not dead a long time?

Franklin lay on his right side, huddled into himself. He slept that way. How had he found her at la Estrella? How did he know? Moliere wondered about it and looked forward to asking, one of the many questions she had stored up. Casual wonders happen so often; Moliere asked herself why. That was another one to ask.

Impelled by an urgency that did not name itself Moliere fought to surface from sleep. Concerned not to wake Franklin she pulled down the motel sheets with stealth. That was the word her brain served up: stealth.

It was hard to say for certain but in the east the sky might have been brightening. In the twilight Moliere felt her way by her fingertips to the window. She sensed, she smelled the secret aniline that makes skies blue. But first the morning was going to bring rain. Standing there in the dark Moliere could smell it coming.

Down in the street two men came running. They wore workingmen's heavy clothes, blue or green; what with the light the way it was Moliere could not say. They were led by five powerful dogs on five long leashes. The dogs pulled desperately against the leashes, wild to run. The men came after them, clumsy in big shoes. It came to Moliere that each dog was a different breed.

Watching the dogs and the men Moliere knew she was seeing something marvelous, something hidden ordinarily. Standing at the window she spoke aloud in the empty room.

"When you wake," she said in the room, "remember that you saw this."

Moliere spoke the words aloud but only just above a whisper. But not for fear of waking Franklin; she knew he was not really there.

Moliere was impatient for sunrise. That was the urgency that stirred her from bed. It was August now and every day the sun rose observably later; dawn that morning would not come until after six. Summer was ending again.

The time in West Texas was 5.23 a.m.

Moliere's ears told her the moment she left Perros Salvajes County. The broken asphalt of the road ended and the sound of the drumming ended. The highway hummed her to the east.

All morning rain poured down. Until Moliere reached Van Horn it hardly let up at all. Once it stopped a grey sky settled over the country for the balance of the day. The sky had a blank look. She saw miles and miles of Texas.

There were signs on the interstate pointing her to Dallas and Shreveport but they were still hundreds of miles away.

Moliere had budgeted a leisurely two days for the drive to Métayage. Louisiana was going to be another place altogether from Texas and she wanted her first look at it to be long and considered. Moliere's plan for that first day was to make it as far as Fort Stockton. Before resting for the night she would visit Franklin's grave in Green River and tell him all about how she was leaving.

Moliere had not been to the grave since the day they put Franklin in it. She did not inherit her parents' traditions of visiting cemeteries. Had someone asked why Moliere could not have answered. Except to say that the idea repelled her in its pointlessness. Her dead were not in the ground.

The original of Green River Cemetery was 130 years old. It was in the center of the city, which presumably grew up around it and which must have been a convenience when the place was growing. Eventually the place filled up.

In the 1980s new land was acquired on what was then the edge of Green River. Now the town had grown up around that place too. On three sides a modest commercial strip—Bessie Colemen Road—embraced the cemetery. Its fourth side was a cluster of new houses brightly painted. In their happy colors the houses showed their backs to the graveyard.

Moliere remembered Franklin's sister Molly saying the two cemeteries were laid out according to some Christian feng shui popular among German immigrants at the time. The bodies were put into the earth feet east, heads west. At the time Molly explained it to her Moliere's attention was clouded and so she could not recall the point of this arrangement. But she remembered being told. And she remembered that Franklin was no exception to the burial protocol.

Visitors passed into the cemetery perpendicular to the graveyard axis. The gates of the place were a filigree of cast-iron curlicue. It was glorious compared to the seven-foot high cyclone fence circling the rest of the place. Any of Moliere's middle-schoolers could have climbed that fence with ease. (Middle-schoolers might have been put off by the idea of breaking into a cemetery because they do believe the dead are in the ground.)

Built into the west pillar of the great gates was an electronic directory. The setup resembled an ATM in the wall of a bank branch. Moliere typed Franklin's name, the first time she had done that in nearly two years. His plot number came up on the screen of the machine. She left the car's engine running and its door open and the whole time the car dinged at her. Come back come back come back come back.

The grass planted on Franklin's grave had established itself. In August the grass was fried, of course, but come the fall it would green again; Moliere knew that much about grass. Between Franklin's birth and death dates on the headstone the gold shield on the tiny peaked hat had lost a bit of its gilding; weathered out, Moliere supposed. In time all the gold leaf and probably the little hat would all be gone. Then it would be hard for anyone looking at the gravestone to understand what the scraping between the dates was intended to mean, assuming anyone looked.

A panel truck stopped for a red light outside the cemetery gate. Cowboy music leaked from the driver's open window. It was only a radio playing that music.

A thousand feet up in the sky the sun broke through the cloud. Flashes of light hopped and faded, hopped and faded, over Franklin's grave and over all the graves. "Jesus lights" Franklin had called this phenomenon. As an emblem of grace given away free it was so obvious that Moliere snorted.

Franklin snorted too. Moliere heard him. The naturalness in her voice when she spoke should not have been a surprise. She *noted* the naturalness.

"Stop playing, Franklin. If there's something to say come on and say it."

Nothing. Of course nothing.

"Talk to me, baby."

Nothing.

"I hear your voice. Say I'm not crazy." Moliere listened. "I'm not even sure I remember the sound of you right," she said to the air. "Anymore."

Nothing. But nothing.

Under the bright sun Moliere felt lightheaded. She was hungry and could have done with a candy bar or something like that. Bracing herself against Franklin's headstone she settled down behind it in the small shade it gave. Moliere was leaving. Only not yet.

After all the rain in the morning the ground was soggy where she sat. She did not mind. She listened to the noise of life coming from the avenue. She was glad for life. She began to feel it might be good to nod and sleep where she was for a little while, if sleep would come.

Now she turned her face up to the sun, which was nearly overhead. Now she closed her eyes. Behind the pink reverse side of her eyelids floated blue handwriting and a big dog's head and bare tree branches and the crescent of a thumbnail. There was a taste of pineapple in her mouth. It was alright.

www.ingramcontent.com/pod-product-compliance
Lightning Source LLC
Chambersburg PA
CBHW060412030726
47495CB00003B/546
9780578275550